Winner Takes it all

By Laura Rossi

GW00374491

Book 3 in the Counterpoints series

Editing by Gem Louise Evans

Cover by Talia's Book Covers

To my readers, you are sensational

And for Jules Bianchi (1989-2015)

This is a work of fiction. Names, characters, businesses, places, events and incidents are either the products of the author's imagination or used in a fictitious manner. Any resemblance to actual persons, living or dead, or actual events is purely coincidental.

Prologue

Berlin 1992

Water, water everywhere, Christopher thought, his big green eyes wide in surprise.

It was the first time, he couldn't hear the sound of the cars passing by, the engines' roars muffled by the heavy rain. It had started raining in the morning and it hadn't stopped ever since.

He walked to the front of the boxes, stuck a hand out and stared as the water slammed on his small palm, hard and fast.

The tarmac was wet through, puddles were forming on the box lane but still no announcement had been made from the race marshals. The race was still on, the drivers were still pushing hard, driving through the rainstorm.

They are blind-driving, Christopher realized as a green car drove through the box lane and stopped in front of his team of mechanics. Very quickly the car was eased back inside the box. The driver was retiring the car.

He watched the man climb out, shaking his head, his helmet completely fogged up, his tracksuit soaked.

They are driving and they cannot see.

Two cars sped by then and Christopher followed their slipstream, as they went through the straight and into the curb side by side, water splashing everywhere, fighting for their place in the race – neither of them stepping down but pushing hard to beat the other.

He knew what it was like to drive and not see a single thing. Christopher had had his helmet covered in water, his tracksuit soaked to the point his arms had felt heavy. It was one of those things his father had told him to get used to.

"Racing means taking risks. It means making the difference. What makes you faster, stronger than another driver isn't just the car. It's your head. You shouldn't care if it's sunny or raining. Not even if it's snowing. You change the asset of the car, you choose different tires, but racing is racing ever the same. You fight till the very end, no retreat" James had told him on more than one occasion, when he had taken Christopher on his go kart. *"You know this track by heart. I want you to drive with low visibility. You won't be able to see the*

whole curb, but you will be able to sense it. You know the track, you know your car. Focus on the tarmac and feel your limits, push when you feel safer, brake when you are unsure"

Christopher remembered that first lap, the memory was embedded in his mind.

He had cried under that helmet, he had cried under the rain that first time but he hadn't stopped driving. He had taken it slow at times- when he could see absolutely nothing- but he had kept going, hearing James shouting, as he sped by.

"Don't be scared" he had shouted and waived at him, lap after lap. *"Don't be scared"*

"I don't understand. Why are they not suspending the race for adverse weather conditions?" Christopher turned to the sound of his mother's voice and stared at her worried face, as she spoke with the team manager in the boxes.

The race marshals were discussing it and a decision would be made soon, the team manager reassured Carmen.

It was only a matter of minutes before two cars drove back in the box lane, abandoning the race. Only fifteen cars were still out, fighting in the darkness, as the rain slowed down and almost stopped, only to fall down hard again a moment later.

Christopher took a few steps back and looked up to the screen. His mother's thin, soft hands were on his cheeks instantly.

Carmen smiled a little, looking down at him and then her eyes were back on the screen.

The framing stayed on the black and white car leading the race, until it changed brusquely and the camera rested on a set of broken red barriers.

There had been an accident.

The camera zoomed in and showed a car, smashed against the inside of a curb, its front part completely bent inside out and broken.

The impact had been so ferocious and violent, that it was impossible to even read the number that had once been painted on the front.

The camera moved around the car, through the heavy rain and Christopher stared blankly at the screen, as race marshals started running fast towards it.

There was no one near the accident scene and the driver was still trapped, inside the car.

"Oh my God" Carmen's hand slipped off Christopher's cheek, as she let out a terrifying scream and covered her mouth in despair.

The camera focused on the driver's helmet, as it dangled to the side, the driver's body lifeless, his arms sprawled out of the car. The helmet was black and red.

It was James.

He wasn't moving. He wasn't responding to the paramedics and the front of his tracksuit was covered in blood.

As they eased him out of the car, Carmen's screams in the background, Christopher stared eyes wide at the people surrounding his father. One of the paramedics shook his head, desperately looking for his pulse. Another one raised his arms up to his face.

Don't be scared, Christopher thought, grabbing his mother's skirt. *Don't be scared.*

Chapter 1

The hospital waiting room was packed.

Isabella looked around feeling nauseous, desperate for some sort of distraction, as a strong smell of disinfectant plunged into her nose.

She got up and paced the room, back and forth, up and down, for what felt like an hour.

She learned every little detail of the flooring, every little inch of the white paint on the walls. Worried faces came and went, stretchers were carried through double doors in the E.R.

Still no news of Christopher.

Isabella let out a deep breath – she hadn't even realized she had been holding- and checked her watch, then her phone. She looked outside the window and then her eyes were back on the emergency and accidents door every time it opened, hoping for even the slightest bit of information. Hoping to be taken out of her misery.

It was a constant coming and going of doctors and nurses. Everyone around her spoke German and each time someone in scrubs entered the room, her heart would miss a beat.

She would extend her hearing, hoping to grasp at least Christopher's name.

That would have meant something, at least that someone had news. Nothing.

I spoke to him, he is alive, Isabella reminded herself- in a desperate attempt to calm her nerves.

She pushed her hair back, placing it behind her ears- closing her eyes as she did- reliving the moment Christopher had been pulled up on the ambulance, her lips pressed on his hand.

Was he moving his arms, his legs?

She touched her forehead and closed her eyes shut, trying to recall if Christopher had moved at all on the stretcher. She just couldn't remember.

Why can't I remember if he was moving?

Both hands covered her face then and she let them be her hiding place for a few instants, as tears silently ran down her cheeks.

I am going to throw up, she thought feeling her stomach clench.

The long wait was eating her up from the inside, slowly and relentlessly.

Where is Hillary? Isabella wondered.

Her manager had texted her a while ago. Hillary was in one of the MB cars on her way to the hospital, together with Mr. Johnson – the MB chief executive wanted to see for himself how Christopher was doing.

As she slumped on one of the plastic chairs again, wiping her rigged cheeks with the back of her hand, Isabella watched images of the accident go by on the small flat TV in the waiting room.

Christopher's picture appeared on the top right side of the screen and the lump in Isabella's throat seemed to grow wider.

More footage showed Christopher on the stretcher, paramedics easing him on the ambulance and this young woman leaning down to kiss his hand.

Me, Isabella looked down at her hands and shook off the thought.

What does it matter?

It didn't. Absolutely nothing mattered more than seeing Christopher, seeing that he was fine.

Why didn't I kiss him more? Why didn't I fight my way into that ambulance?

At some point, the news report had shown images of journalists standing outside the hospital. The news of him being there had spread quickly.

Why is it taking so long? What are they doing to him?

Isabella let out another deep breath.

She had tried- god only knew how many times she had tried- to ask the receptionist for any sort of information, but she had been told to take a seat, over and over again, and wait for the doctor to come.

How can I sit still? HOW?

Isabella looked up at the screen again and watched the results of the race go by.

The race had been suspended due to adverse weather conditions. According to the chart, Chiellini drivers won first and second place, while Performance racing driver Thomas classified third.

Noah had been in seventh position, when race marshals had decided to end the race.

"Hey, how is he?" Hillary dashed towards Isabella, as she stormed into the waiting room. Aaron Johnson followed, his face glum and pale. He stood beside them in silence, letting his phone ring, his attention on Isabella for news.

She stood up and shook her head, not trusting herself to speak for a moment. She managed a smile, feeling Hillary's hands take hold of hers.

"Doctors haven't come out yet. I have no news. They told me to wait here..." her voice came out broken.

It was normal, standard procedure- Hillary reassured her. Doctors were probably running all the tests. They would let them know of Christopher's conditions, as soon as all the results were back from the lab.

"But did he say something to you? Was he... talking? Moving?" Hillary said the words quickly, like it was some sort of a crime to even doubt that Christopher was okay.

He was okay, he had to be okay.

This was Christopher they were talking about. He was born with a wheel glued to his hands, he was a pro.

It wasn't his first crash and it wouldn't be his last.

Racing was like fighting, the same rules applied- Hillary knew that. If falling correctly was just as important as hitting during combat, crashing safely was as vital as driving fast in car racing. And Christopher knew exactly how to crash and walk away unscathed.

All three of them took a seat then and Isabella simply nodded.

Hillary is probably right, Isabella thought.

She knew how things worked. Doctors only came out when they were absolutely sure about their diagnosis.

The door of the emergency room flapped open once again and in walked a woman with ginger hair, tied up in a ponytail and green scrubs. She walked up to the receptionist and started talking, without making any eye contact with people in the waiting room.

"Alfred is still flying to Paris for a business trip, I don't think he even saw the accident. I texted him" Hillary checked her phone, giving in to the constant beeping sound in her pocket. "Christopher's mother is at the airport in Madrid, trying to get here"

Oh my god Carmen, Isabella thought and a shiver ran down her spine.

She pictured Christopher's mother waiting on a standby list, desperate to get to Berlin to see her son, her only son, the angst torturing her slowly.

"Excuse me" the woman in scrubs addressed them.

Isabella stood up from her chair instantly "Are you Miss Bresciani, Mr. Taylor's girlfriend?"

Isabella swallowed hard and looked sideways, while Mr. Johnson and Hillary exchanged glances, and then back at the doctor.

"Yes" she said. "That's me"

It was the first time that anyone had called her that and it took Isabella half a second to gulp it down.

Christopher Taylor's girlfriend, it replayed in her head while her cheeks turned bright red.

It sounded amazing.

Cover is off, she thought, her face softening, as she met Hillary's dark brown eyes.

If rushing to see Christopher after the accident- running side by side with him to the ambulance- hadn't given her away already, this was it. This moment here. The ultimate proof.

"You can see him now" said the doctor in English and signaled to follow her through the doors. "But please, not all at once"

Hillary and Mr. Johnson nodded. "Of course" her boss said, her face unreadable.

Isabella nodded again- her mouth dry- and walked next to what she discovered by the name tag was an orthopedist.

"How is he?" Isabella found the courage to ask, once inside the long white corridor.

"He's okay" she smiled reassuringly "He has pain all over his chest but we ran tests. His CAT scan was negative, no broken bones, no internal bleeding, despite the speed and the strong impact with the barriers"

"Can he… move?" she asked, her voice shaky.

"Yes. He's fine" the doctor nodded and watched Isabella let out a deep breath.

She needed to see him, touch him, hear him speak. Her hands began to shake, as they approached his room.

"Can he leave the hospital now?"

"Not yet. We are keeping him twenty-four hours, as a precaution. He did hit his head a little, so it's best if he rests some more" the doctor said. "This way"

They walked through another door and Isabella's eyes lit up instantly.

Christopher was sitting up, no needles in his arms this time, free and untied to the bed.

A big bruise under his eye, almost covered his entire left cheek. His upper lip was scratched and his hair was spiky and messy.

And he was just perfect, Isabella reckoned.

My Christopher.

He smiled wide when he saw Isabella walk in the room.

"Ciao, signorina" he said and took her in his arms, welcoming the warm feeling of her lips on his.

She kissed him gently, her hand reached up for his cheek carefully, too scared of causing him any more pain.

Was he in pain?

She searched his face a moment and drank in the sight of him.

He looked fine, he was really going to be okay.

His deep green eyes were staring at her intensely, taking away all the angst and worry that had been devouring her moments before.

He took her by the shoulders and kissed her again, passionately this time, while his hands moved up to cup her face.

I am here, I am okay, it was like he was trying to say to her.

Isabella's body began to shake under his touch.

The blood was back in her veins.

She could breathe in, really breathe in now and not gasp like she had been doing over the last hour, like there was no air in her lungs. He was safe.

And he is moving.

"Hi" she finally said and looked into his eyes once again "Doctor said you are good" she went on after a few instants, realizing the doctor had moved to the corner of the room to speak to one of the nurses.

Walking in, she hadn't even noticed other people in the room, her eyes had been all for Christopher.

"It takes more than that to get rid of me, luv" he grinned.

"Doctor also said I am your girlfriend" Isabella smiled, with her eyes, her lips, her voice.

"I know how much you like 'secret lover' but I didn't think it was appropriate" he took her hand and let her sit on the bed next to him.

Ha, well so much for the 'secret' lover, Isabella thought recalling Hillary and Mr. Johnson's faces back in the waiting room.

She reached for his face and stroked his cheek, enjoying the roughness of his scruff and then brushed gently against the small but deep scratch near his mouth.

"I'm sorry, I keep touching you. I guess I just want to know that you are okay" Isabella smiled a little.

"Don't stop touching, please" he smirked and reached for her hand.

"Does it hurt?" she asked.

"Nah" he shook his head slowly. "It will scar though…" he mumbled.

"It's just a scar" Isabella lifted her shoulders only to let them drop again, carelessly.

She searched his face again. He wasn't smiling- his lips sealed in a straight line- and Isabella examined up close the black bruise under his eye.

Quick, make him laugh. Make him feel better.

"The girls are going to go crazy once they see the scar. Christopher Taylor, the ultimate bad boy"

He chuckled and held on tight to Isabella's hand, the one she had placed on his cheek. Then he leaned in and turned to kiss the inside of it, his lips moving slowly in her palm, sending sparks all over her hand and up her arm.

"And what does my girl have to say about it?" he said in between kisses.

"Your 'girl' is crazy about you already" she looked into his eyes and went on "It will heal, the important thing is that YOU will heal"

"I can't believe I crashed" he said and took in a deep breath.

As his chest moved to make room for air, Isabella saw his face cringe in pain.

"Chris…" her hand slipped down to grab his just then, as Isabella turned towards the doctor, ready to call out for help.

"I am okay" he squeezed her hand tight and managed a smile. "I just hit my ribcage. I can't believe I made that stupid mistake"

"It wasn't your fault. The tarmac was very slippery. They had to stop the race for a while after you crashed" Isabella began to shake her head but Christopher didn't let her finish.

"Tarmac is always slippery, Isabella. If it isn't rain, it's because of the oil or marbles here and there. I should know that. I should be ready for that" he went on, talking more to himself than to her. "I can't believe I'm here and not on that podium"

I can't believe I lost control of the car because of the words of a fucking stranger, Christopher tensed.

But it wasn't just because of that. He hadn't crashed just because someone had told him he was worth more dead than alive. Christopher knew that. It was the tension inside him, the things he had been putting off for so long that had come back to bite him. What had his father taught him all those years?

"You get in that car with nothing on your mind besides driving and winning, you hear me? Everything else stays outside. Otherwise you'll mess it up. The car has to have your undivided attention"

That was the reason behind the crash. He had been distracted by so many things – that man, the book about him and his father coming out, the tension between him and Noah.

"It doesn't matter now" Isabella said and Christopher's stern eyes were on her in an instant.

"I would have won the race today, I know I would have"

"Shhh, It's done. It doesn't matter now. What matters is that you are okay" her lips trembled a little, as she said the words, but Isabella kept her voice steady.

"You know how many times I drove into that curb, Isabella? A hundred maybe. I know how it needs to be done" he shook his head "I know exactly where the car needs to be, to make a clean exit. I knew I shouldn't have been on that trajectory but I somehow let the car drive into it. My God, the car. I completely destroyed the car and…"

"Stop talking" Isabella squeezed his hand and moved closer to kiss him again.

She was inches away from his face when she said "None of it matters"

"Yes, it does. I had the race in my hands. I felt like I could do it. I could have reached the boxes to change those bloody tires and still lead the race. If I hadn't lost my concentration in that damn curb" his empty hand curled into a fist, taking the white sheets on the bed with it. Isabella's eyes went to the crimpled linen, as Christopher went on. "Do you know what it feels like to be so close to something and then losing it a second later?"

Yes, she thought looking up at him, unable to shake off the image of Christopher's limp body in the car.

"I thought I had lost you" she began, her voice almost broke. "I almost lost you"

"You didn't lose me" Christopher's voice softened, as he ran a hand through her hair, while a tear ran down Isabella's cheek.

He wiped it away with his thumb and his face seemed to brighten up a little.

"I know. Just like you didn't lose Berlin. You didn't, Christopher. You lost this year's race but Berlin will be still here, for you next year. You can't do anything to change all that now" Isabella shook her head, trying to calm Christopher's nerves "It's done. But you are still here to try again next year. That's what matters. Not the race. Nothing else. Just that you are here" she smiled and his hands played a little with her soft, brown curls.

"Thank you for being here with me" he said.

"Nothing could have kept me away from you" Isabella smiled and bit her lip.

Before Christopher could say anything back, the doctor approached the bed, shuffling a stack of papers in her hands.

"No trauma and no broken bones doesn't mean you can walk out of here and take it from where you left things, Mr. Taylor" she explained, after having read his blood test and CAT scan results to them.

"Can I leave now? Can I go back to the boxes now? The race is still on and I think my team needs the support…" he said, his voice expectant.

Isabella opened her mouth but before she could say anything- before she could inform Christopher that there was no race to go back to- the doctor cut in.

"I am sorry, but we are keeping you here for twenty-four hours, as a precaution" the doctor explained, her face apologetic. "From tomorrow when you leave the hospital until Thursday, I want you to rest. No training, no physical activity. You have to take it slow. Thursday, you will visit your doctor in London and he will decide if you are fit to get back on your training schedule and ultimately take part in the next race"

The woman answered some of Christopher's questions with patience and consideration and then left the room, inviting Isabella to stay as much as she wanted.

Once the doctor was out of sight, Isabella moved to the side and laid down on the bed right next to Christopher, pulling her legs up on the sheets. Gently, she curled up beside him, leaning her head on his shoulder, closing her eyes for a moment, grateful to be by his side, grateful Christopher was fine.

She silently thanked life for everything she was feeling and for everything she hadn't lost.

The worry, the sadness, the angst had all brought her where she was now, to the point she could no longer hold her feelings back for Christopher.

Above all, she was grateful her eyes had been opened wide.

"For a moment, when I saw you weren't moving" she began to say and couldn't help but notice Christopher take in a breath just then. "I thought I had lost my chance, my chance to tell you everything I wanted to tell you. I thought I'd lost my chance to be by your side like I wanted to. I was so scared"

Why did I have to almost lose him to understand? Isabella felt her eyes watery again, as she thought of all the times she had held back, too afraid to live her emotions, too scared of being let down.

"I am here, Isabella" he said and raised his arm, to hold her tight against him.

As he moved, Isabella noticed his face tense, his eyes shut tight in pain.

"Don't move" she tilted her head up to look at him but Christopher didn't stop.

Taking in a deep breath, he wrapped his arm around her shoulders and pulled her down on his chest, his grip strong and determined.

"I am okay" Christopher reassured her and the wince molded into a soft smile. "You know what I was thinking when they lifted me out of that car?"

Isabella shook her head slowly and waited for him to carry on with his thought.

"All I could think of was you. That I never told you just how crazy I am about you" he paused and touched her cheek. "I am crazy about you. Whatever you are doing to me, don't stop signorina" he smiled to the side and closed the distance, his mouth desperate to touch hers.

Isabella welcomed the kiss- his lips burning like fire against hers-losing herself in his arms. She savored the taste of his words and the warmth of his strong body, so close to hers.

"I am crazy about you, too" Isabella said after a moment and bit her lip, as she smiled.

Christopher's eyes brightened instantly then and his grip tightened around Isabella's waist.

"That lip is mine to bite" Christopher claimed and he moved down, to grasp her lip between his teeth, making Isabella gasp for air, as her whole body seemed to burn like fire.

Yes, it is, Isabella thought looking straight into his deep green eyes, enjoying the feeling of her lip pulsing with life, where Christopher had just bitten her.

"You know, I think we need to cool it down here. Hillary and Mr. Johnson will be here as soon as the race is over" Christopher smiled, their noses brushing, as he slowly returned back to reality.

About that…

"They are outside, in the waiting room already" Isabella said and then added "Race marshals had to stop the race, Christopher. It was too dangerous to drive. The rain wouldn't stop. Chiellini won, Noah had issues with his car and classified seventh"

Christopher looked down at his hand, as it curled into a fist. He looked up again a moment later, gathering his thoughts. His stare seemed to reach behind Isabella's back, like he was looking at something behind her.

"Well, at least the team gained some points for the championship" Christopher said a moment later, his voice a little flat. "Maybe it's better if you sit on the chair, take some distance. Or Hillary and Mr. Johnson will figure it out" Christopher said, referring to how close they were sitting. "Us I mean"

They looked so intimate just then, lying on the bed, touching and holding hands, Isabella only a whisper away from Christopher.

"It's a little late for that" Isabella looked down, her head tilted to the side, as a small, awkward smile spread across her face. "I walked side by side with you to the ambulance in front of basically every journalist on track. I kissed your hand and followed you here. The doctor called me your girlfriend, right in their faces. I think they pretty much know for sure right now" Isabella said and stayed exactly where she was. "About us, I mean"

Christopher searched her face, a look of amusement written all over his.

"And how come Isabella Bresciani is not freaking out about this?" he teased.

"Because the issue has been outweighed by *this*" Isabella pointed at him, lying in bed.

He smiled to the side and bent down to kiss her, his arms tightening around her body.

Then the room went quiet for a moment, as Christopher tried to organize his thoughts and take in the reality of things. His mind was back on the race, back on that track. He kept having flashes, like his brain refused to let go.

The race was over, he was out and Noah had barely made it in the points' range.

If only the race marshals had stopped the race before I crashed, the thought crossed his mind but he shrugged it off immediately after.

It was not a good idea to overthink things, to wonder what it could have been if. 'Ifs' were a dangerous thing, Christopher knew it all too well. His whole life had been about 'ifs', about his father, about his upbringing and what it would have been like if James had been by his side.

No 'ifs'. I am here and she is here, Christopher looked down at Isabella again and kissed the tip of her freckled nose.

"I need your help with something" he told her, as they held on tight to each other in silence.

"Anything you want" her eyes lit up.

"I need to borrow your phone"

"Sure" Isabella reached for it in the back pocket of her pants.

"I have to call my mother" Christopher said, his voice serious.

"Oh" Isabella nodded "I know for sure Hillary called her already, to let her know you were okay. Your mother is on a waiting list at the airport in Madrid, trying to get here"

"Okay" he said, "But it's my voice she needs to hear"

Isabella nodded again. She understood, she understood perfectly.

There was an understanding between Carmen and Christopher.

In case something bad were to happen…

She watched in silence Christopher dial his mother's number, eager to speak to her and dreading it at the same time.

He breathed in deep and his jaw tensed a little more at every ring.

"I'll be outside" Isabella said, as she stood.

Christopher held on to her hand and shook his head.

"I'll be back when you are done" Isabella smiled and walked to the door.

She decided it was a private moment, something so personal between him and his mother, that it deserved privacy. She couldn't possibly imagine what it felt like for Carmen to receive that phone call, what it felt like for Christopher to try and convince his mother that he was okay from a hospital bed.

No, speaking before the race hadn't been their last time. He was still here. He was safe and it wasn't happening all over again, like many years ago.

Like with James, Isabella cringed at the thought, as her eyes set on Christopher's serious stare.

Before he could say anything back to Isabella, his mother picked up.

"Hola mamà, soy yo" he said and Isabella saw him close his eyes. "Mamà, estoy bien. No llores"

Don't cry, Isabella translated in her head. She felt the tears in her eyes again.

Poor woman, Isabella thought. How painful it must have been, to watch her only child crash against a barrier, fate -so infamous and vile- wanted it to be the same circuit where her husband had lost his life many years before.

She must have relived the desperation, the panic all over again.

Slowly, Isabella closed the door behind her, to the sound of Christopher's soothing voice.

Chapter 2

Walking back to the waiting room was like walking into the boxes during race weekend.

From the glass window above the emergency and accidents door, Isabella saw that the waiting room was crowded. Packed.

There were people in MB uniforms everywhere and every driver in First Category racing, as well as many team managers, like Mr. Johnson.

Isabella smiled at the sight of them all standing near the wall, exchanging news about Christopher conditions. Everyone was there, everyone that cared, everyone that knew him.

It could have been anyone of them, Isabella realized, watching the tense expressions on the drivers' faces.

They were all there, waiting to hear about Christopher and they had no intention of leaving until news were out, despite Mr. Johnson and Hillary were telling everyone he was okay.

Isabella stepped into the room smiling, her heart so full of joy she couldn't contain her happiness.

All eyes were on Isabella in an instant, as Hillary walked up to her and her eyes lit up expectantly.

"He's okay. I just spoke to him. He's doing fine" Isabella nodded and watched the relief on everyone's face.

She explained everything the doctor had told her and that Christopher was going to be held up in the hospital overnight- as an extra precaution- but he was fine. No broken bones, no internal bleeding.

"Thank god for that" Hillary smiled wide and turned to Mr. Johnson.

"We should speak to the press outside before we go see him" he advised and Hillary quickly gathered her things, to walk out with Mr. Johnson.

"Do you need me to do anything?" Isabella asked, helping her with her bags.

"No, darling. Everything is under control. He needs you. Go back to him" Hillary smiled and walked out of the room.

"So, when can we see him?" Pietro Tommasini asked, stepping forward a little.

Isabella looked around the room as everyone stared at her, counting in her head how many people were there.

Twenty-five, she reckoned as she spotted Robert, Christopher's engineer at the far back of the room.

Isabella eyed the receptionist, who seemed quite busy on the phone, and her mind began to work out a plan. A diabolic plan.

He really wanted to go back to the race, back to the boxes and reassure everyone that he was okay, Isabella reasoned.

She had seen how disappointed Christopher had been, when the doctor had informed him he had to stay in the hospital overnight.

Isabella looked around the room again and nodded to Pietro Tommasini, a sly smile on her lips.

I am so going to get into trouble for this.

They had been inside Christopher's room a good ten minutes when a loud knock on the door, made everyone go quiet.

"Shit" Isabella said and bit her lip, her eyes wide as most of the drivers in the room chuckled.

"Shhh" she said and giggled a little, walking slowly to the door.

"Exactly how many nurses and doctors did you bribe to sneak all these people in here?" from his bed, Christopher joined in the chucking with the others.

"Not a single one" Isabella made a face and then grinned, as her hand rested on the door handle "I might have promised a few autographs, though"

When she pushed the door open she gaped, a little speechless at Noah standing before her.

"Hi" he said to everyone in the room and stood there, at the entrance, a bag – Christopher's bag – tight in his hands.

"Hi" Christopher said, doing very little to hide his surprise.

They stared at each other in silence, while Noah closed the door and kept his distance, standing at the far back of the room, despite the empty chairs around Christopher's bed.

"Could we have a moment?" Noah asked, breaking the embarrassing silence in the room.

Isabella turned to Christopher, who nodded to let her know he was okay with it.

Of all people to turn up at the Hospital, he wasn't surely expecting Noah- not after their last, heated discussion in Toronto- but Christopher wasn't going to send him out.

He was going to listen. And then eventually kick him out.

"We'll wait outside" Harold from Chiellini said, patting Christopher's shoulder gently.

"No, don't guys. I am fine, really. It's seven o'clock. Go back to the hotel. Go have a drink" Christopher's eyes went to Isabella. "You too. Go sleep. I'll see you tomorrow" he reached for her hand, as Isabella moved closer to the bed and leaned forward, their lips brushing briefly against one another, while the others started to walk outside.

"Thank you for doing this for me" he brushed his fingers against her soft, voluptuous lips.

"That smile. Priceless, like a kid at Disneyland" Isabella said, quoting Christopher's words the day he had surprised her with the visit to the Aquarium in Toronto.

She squeezed his hand a little. "Sleep now. I'll see you tomorrow"

"I will. Thank you all for coming" Christopher said, raising his voice now, as some of the drivers turned to wave. He kept his eyes on his friends until Isabella, the last one of them, was out.

"You can take a seat" Christopher gestured to the empty chairs by his bed.

Noah walked over to them and placed Christopher's bag on the one to his left.

"It's your clean change, the one you took to the track for after the race. Your phone is in there somewhere, too"

"Thank you, you didn't have to do that. I could have sent someone to get it for me" Christopher said, as Noah finally took a seat next to him.

"I wanted to see how you were doing"

"I am okay" Christopher sat up straight and winced a little, a pain as sharp as a blade pierced through his chest. He sucked in a breath and his face hardened "I managed to push myself off track without your help this time, but no worries. I'll be back next race weekend"

"Actually, I am here to apologize" Noah told him, his voice serious, his face unreadable.

Christopher stared at him a moment longer, until he let out a small laugh and shook his head.

"You know, I really don't get you anymore"

Noah nodded and leaned forward, his arms resting on his lap- one hand over his mouth- while he seemed to think carefully of what to say next.

"I'm trying to do the right thing…"

"Two weeks ago, you said you didn't see me coming. You waved it off, like nothing happened, but you sent me flying out, off the track. Today, you come to me to apologize" Christopher shook his head again.

"I wasn't thinking straight"

"No, you weren't" Christopher said "We've known each other for years. Years, Noah. We've raced against each other since we were kids. What the hell is wrong with you?"

"A lot of shit has been going on. But I am trying to do the right thing here" Noah straightened up and shifted in his seat. "I made a mistake and I came here to say I am sorry. Seeing you injured like that today, seeing you here in the hospital, made me want to apologize for Cannes, for Toronto"

"Is that it?" Christopher brows went up.

Noah stared at him for a moment and then shook his head. "We are not so different you and me. All we want is to win. To be the top driver and win the championship"

"You are wrong. We are different. So different. I put my foot down on that throttle when I know I can do it. I never put anyone's life in danger but my own" Christopher rebutted.

"And how is that any different? Isn't your life important? Is there anything dearer to you than your own life?" Noah paused. "Who are you racing against, Christopher? Not me, not Tommasini or anyone else on that damn track. Are you?" he questioned him and Christopher went quiet, his eyes dark.

Noah's words surged through him like a thousand needles.

Who was Christopher racing against? What was he desperately trying to achieve?

James' name was never spoken between them, but it didn't need to be. They both knew.

Noah knew since the first day they had met, when they were just kids and racing go karts, that Christopher's battle was going to be different from his.

I may be striving to make a name for myself, but Christopher is after the impossible.

How do you win against a ghost? How do you step out of its spotlight and manage to shine of your own? Noah had always thought, seeing Christopher's ache to win. *To win like his father, more than his father.*

"Look Christopher, all I am trying to say is that I know how important Berlin is to you and I am sorry you didn't win" Noah went on.

Christopher was quiet, his face serious.

Yes, Berlin was important to him. The victory had almost been his.

For a moment, a few laps before the crash, Christopher had almost felt that trophy in his hands. And then he had seen it slip from his grip, as the sound of the car hitting the barriers drove violently into his head.

"I am sorry I put your life in danger, mate"

"Our lives in danger" Christopher corrected him.

"Our lives in danger" Noah repeated his team mate's words. "Get your ass back on that car" and he outstretched his hand.

Christopher took it and held it tight.

"You bet" Christopher said and smiled, a wicked smile. "You think I am going to let you win the championship that easily?"

"No and I would be disappointed if you did" Noah said, as he stood up. "Championship or no championship, the last thing I want is to lose my number one rival"

"I am not your number one rival. I am the privileged one, remember?" Christopher teased, referring to Noah's latest interview in Toronto.

His words hadn't struck a nerve that time, Christopher had let them wash down until Noah had pushed him out, off the track during the race. The resentment had built up inside him, Christopher remembered the rage when he had walked to the boxes to confront Noah.

"You are the number one rival. Why do you think everyone was here today? To see you?" Noah asked and watched Christopher shrug.

Maybe because he was nice to everyone in the boxes. Maybe because Christopher spoke to everyone, knew everyone. At least that was what Christopher assumed.

"It's not just that" Noah said. "What happened to you today could have happened to anyone of us, but it happened to you and we all came to see you. Because you would have come to see us- if it had been one of us. Because you are strong, you don't fear anyone. You respect everyone and fear no one. Your determination defeats us all.

You are the one to beat and if you are out of the game, what kind of game is it?"

Noah turned his back to Christopher, with a smug smile on his face and walked to the door.

"That journalist was right you know. It's easy to win when the other fast car is out of the game. But I want to win while you are still in the game. You are the man to beat" Noah added and closed the door behind him, leaving Christopher alone and in silence, lost in his own thoughts.

What is the word I am looking for? Isabella looked around the table again.

Awkward.

Awkward was the word.

Isabella brows went up, as she looked down at her plate.

So far, all eyes had been on her, constantly throughout dinner.

Isabella had tried her best to ignore the stares, the glances across the table.

It's like I am on that creaking, old stage and it is middle school all over again, she thought recalling the moments she had loathed with all her strength during school.

Recitals, plays, Christmas shows.

If it wasn't for the folklore of the German beer house they were in, Isabella would have thought she was really back on that stage again, everyone staring and no words coming out of her mouth. Like she had forgotten that song in the school play all over again.

And this is just a preview of what is to come, can't wait for the press to have a field trip with me.

Isabella cleared her throat and reached out for her glass.

Keep drinking beer, the glass is my friend, the glass is my friend.

She took another sip and she caught Hillary staring at her. *Again.*

The waiters kept bringing them food and topping up their glasses.

Someone laughed hard at the other side of the table and Isabella's head turned to the sound.

One of Noah's mechanics- his name must have been Joshua, Isabella wasn't sure- had probably had one too many glasses.

Despite everything that had happened that weekend, despite Christopher's crash, things seemed back to normal at MB. The atmosphere was relaxed that night and for the first time since Toronto.

Except Christopher isn't here with us.

She sighed thinking of him, laying in the bed alone. Isabella would have given anything to sneak up to his room and slid in bed with him.

And maybe tease him a little, to make him feel better about himself.

He had wanted to win that race more than anything, more than any other race in the championship.

"There's always next year" Isabella had reassured him but she knew what was going on in his head.

Christopher knew what was going to happen once the press got a hold of him.

Questions about his accident, similarities with his father's crash...

"People, one moment please" Mr. Johnson stood up, a pint of beer secured in his hand.

He patted his chest, right over his heart and looked around. The table went quiet, but the room was still loud- the house of beer was packed with people.

"First of all, congratulations to every single one of you here. Today wasn't easy. We had a hard time. It was a mess and the odds were against us but despite the difficulties, we reacted like only the greatest team in First Category Racing would. Well done for holding on" the guys cheered and clapped hands, some raised their glasses to Noah – for saving the car and taking a few points home.

He waved briefly in their direction but sat there in silence, waiting for Mr. Johnson to carry on with his speech.

"But we have so much more to celebrate today. Christopher is doing well, he's not injured and he will be back on his feet I am sure for the next race in two weeks" everyone clapped and cheered.

Glasses clanged and Isabella heard Christopher's name being mentioned around the table, but didn't quite grasp the whole sentence.

"I didn't fly out tonight because I wanted to spend this evening with the number one team in First Category Racing. Because even if the results today didn't reflect our potential, we are still on that top chart, we are still number one in the Championship as a team and we still have one great race ahead before the summer break. Rome will be our comeback" everyone cheered and Isabella couldn't help but smile, feeling the passion and energy at the table, for being part of the big extended family that was MB Racing Team.

"To Christopher and Noah" Fred said raising his glass and everyone repeated after him.

A few moments later, the chit chatter was back at the table. Some guys stood, glass in hand again, doing their own cheering, laughing hard and trying to relax.

It had been a bad day, for everyone. All the people sitting there looked tired, Isabella realized.

Tired and in desperate need to turn page.

Back in that box there was a car to fix, a new strategy to plan for the next race weekend, more training, new set ups for the cars. But that evening, in that beer house it was the time to file the bad day, relax and get back to work in London with a clear mind.

With the MB racing determination, Isabella smiled at the guys' rowdiness.

They were happy, relieved and so was she. She was relieved that everything had turned out fine.

"So, it was Christopher then. The man you were seeing"? John, who was sitting right next to her, was brave enough to ask.

He smiled a little as he spoke, his voice low, while the laughter carried on at the table.

"Yes. It was Christopher" Isabella confirmed.

John nodded, his brows up.

"Well, I hope he won't hurt you or anything. If he breaks your heart, I might have to kill him" he said, but was quick to add "Well, seeing the size of him, I might have to kick him and run like hell"

Isabella stiffened a giggle and gave him her best smile.

"That's very sweet of you John, thank you" she patted his shoulder, holding back a smile and added "I admit, it would be a funny thing to watch"

He winked, just before Robert called out for him and he was sucked into one of the loud conversations at the table.

Isabella's attention was back on her food. She had picked up a chip and had taken it to her mouth, when she realized Hillary was staring at her from across the table.

She chewed and swallowed the food in her mouth, smiling a little, not sure of what that look meant. Hillary smiled back and nudged with her head.

"Would you like to go out with me for a smoke?" her manager asked.

It was one of those requests that you couldn't say no to- not really anyway -Isabella was sure of that. She nodded and stood.

Here it goes.

They walked through the crowd of people in the beer house, until they reached one of the side doors of the big room and stepped outside.

It wasn't raining anymore. The sky was deep blue but the city lights made it impossible for the stars to be seen.

"How are you?" Hillary asked and then lit her cigarette.

She offered Isabella one, but she kindly declined the offer.

"I'm okay now… thanks"

"So, how long have you guys been seeing each other?" Hillary asked, her voice calm and understanding, not the least bit bothered.

If anyone, Hillary knew what it was like, to have a secret affair. She knew how difficult it was to talk about it, to open up to somebody and make the affair go from secret to real.

Isabella let out a sigh.

How long have we been seeing each other? Well, I don't know. Since our eyes met the first time and then we flirted every single chance we had from then on.

"Three or four months. But It's complicated. It just became 'something more'" Isabella said and took a deep breath. Then she looked up at her manager "I'm sorry I didn't tell you"

"Nothing to be sorry about" she waved it off and went on "I understand why you didn't. I can relate to that, I think"

Hillary inhaled from her cigarette and then let the smoke out slowly, squinting a little as she did.

"I never noticed anything between you two. But today when he crashed, that look on your face when you saw he wasn't moving, that he wasn't conscious… It was more than worry, you were desperate" Hillary took another drag.

"I was" Isabella looked down at her feet, her cheeks flushed "I just want you to know I didn't see it coming, this thing between me and Christopher. I didn't even want it to happen…"

"Darling, it's none of my business. It's nobody's business" Hillary reassured her. "You guys are free to do whatever you want. I just hope you know what it means to work and sleep with someone at the same time"

I think I just had a small preview in there, Isabella thought looking back inside the beer house.

"We won't let this get in the way of things..." Isabella said, knowing it was true.

That is until Mr. Jenkins finds out and has a fit.

"I hope you are right. It's very hard, I'll tell you" Hillary said.

Her boss knew what she was talking about, having recently ended an affair with a person she worked with.

Mr. Jenkins.

The situation had been completely different though, Alfred was a married man. But what was Christopher? A lady's man. Not exactly the best of reputations.

There were many rumors about him in the field, that went from a different woman every night to threesomes and broken hearts all around the world.

A different one in every country, at every race, tabloids wrote about him and his phone, Isabella had noticed a few times, was always ringing.

Hillary eyed Isabella to the side, as she took another drag of her cigarette and thought of her assistant's words.

Isabella was a lovely girl, very young but also a very smart woman. Her head was exactly where it was supposed to be- on her shoulders. Hillary was sure she knew what she was doing.

"Now I get it. I understand where that constant smile on your face was coming from and the heart shaped eyes all the time. The spaced-out moments..." she elbowed her gently and winked. "I bet it's because he's as good as they say"

Isabella laughed nervously and relaxed a little, as the conversation became lighter and so did her chest.

Chapter 3

After dinner, the hospital went quiet and the lights dimmed.
Eleven pm.
Christopher checked the clock on the wall, opposite his bed.
"Rest, catch some sleep" a nurse had said to Christopher earlier,
after checking on him and handing out another dose of painkillers
for his chest.
He tried to give in to sleep and let his body recover from the crash –
his limbs ached, as if he had just run a marathon- but the adrenaline
still pulsing in his veins since the impact, wouldn't hear of shutting
his mind down.
Christopher tossed and turned alone in his room, unable to give it a
rest.
It was exactly half past eleven when his eyes finally closed.
And they were wide open again within instants.
Shit, he panted and ran a hand over his mouth, as flashes of the
accident went by before his eyes.
Maybe his body needed sleep, but his mind was wide open, wide
awake.
He tried to calm down and turned to the side, his eyes resting on the
whiteness of his room.
Curtains white, wall white, bed linen white, so Christopher tried to
empty his head, tried to think about nothing besides the whiteness
that surrounded him.
He was just tired, he just needed to rest and put everything behind
him- the accident, the race in Berlin, the trophy, the anniversary of
his father's death.
Everything. And possibly ignore every single word the press was
saying about the situation.
Focus, you know how to keep your mind off things, he willed
himself.
After all Christopher had always been good at keeping his mind
thought-free.
Slowly, his grip on the white pillow loosened and Christopher's eyes
finally given in to the darkness.
For what felt like a second.

The sound of bending metal filled his ears, clawed its way into his mind, while his head moved sideways and the car hit the barriers. A flash of his father's limp body, made him sit up on his bed, panting. Christopher's eyes were wide open again.

"Shh" his mother reached for his hand and held it tight.

Carmen smiled, a tired empty smile, and leaned a little forward on her chair, getting as close as possible to Christopher.

"Mom?" he whispered, a little drowsy from his sleep.

"Shh" she hushed again. "It's just a bad dream. Go back to sleep" she willed him, but Christopher's eyes were wide open now.

When did she get here?

He checked the watch again and it was two in the morning.

Christopher blinked at his mother, struggling to understand if she was real, if he wasn't just dreaming.

Her pale face stared back at him with tired and worried eyes. Mascara lines ran down her cheeks, as her lips were set in a thin line. It was the face of a person who hadn't slept all night, who had forgotten how to breath, how to smile. It was the face of a person that had rushed over to see her son and suffered every instant that separated her from him. It was as though the lines on her skin were the parts of her that almost broke, that almost fell apart.

"When did you get here?" he asked and smiled wide, feeling the bruise on his cheek pulse to life.

"About an hour ago. Did I wake you?" she smiled back, Christopher's smile too catchy not to reciprocate.

"No" he shook his head. "I'm sorry"

"Go back to sleep" she nodded in a haste, her voice too shaky to trust herself to say more.

It was no mystery, it was written all over her face.

Carmen had been crying. She had screamed and wept over the footage of Christopher's limp arm dangling from the stretcher after the crash.

Her heart beat hadn't slowed down, until she had seen him there, sleeping peacefully in bed, no matter how many times Hillary had assured her he was okay.

As Carmen stared at Christopher's bruised face, she realized her heart beat would never slow down again. It never truly had slowed down since James' crash and it never would.

"I'm sorry it happened. I'm sorry I did this to you" Christopher went on. "I'm sorry I am giving you a hard time with the book coming out, with this" he pointed to himself, laying there in that bed and watched her mother shake her head in silence.

"I am stronger than you think" Carmen said and kissed his hand, his rough warm hand.

Her eyes stared blankly at it for a moment, realizing how different it all was. It was completely different this time. It was nothing like what had happened to James.

Christopher's hand was warm, it wasn't bruised. It was pulsing and alive. He was okay, Christopher was alive.

"I know you are strong" Christopher nodded, never questioning his mother's personality.

Only a woman with character and will power, could have dealt with someone like his father James all those years.

James had been one in a million, he had been an artist, a calculator, a perfectionist. James had been the front man on the stage, with all the consequences that came with it.

"Go back to sleep" she said again and smiled, this time it reached her eyes.

"How long are you staying?" he mumbled, placing his other hand over hers.

"I'm leaving tomorrow morning, before the journalists get here. I am going back to Madrid. The nurses told me you are good to leave tomorrow"

"Yeah. I am going home tomorrow. Come to London"

"I will, but not now" she shook her head and looked down, afraid to meet her son's intense stare. "I can't stand this" she added and Christopher understood.

Carmen didn't have to explain. It was all so painful, not just him being injured, but everything that came with it- the caravan of questions, the attention but mostly the tragic memories that wouldn't stop haunting his mother, despite her daily iron shield.

"Go back to sleep" she said once more and Christopher nodded, his eyes soggy again.

He kept his hands on his mother's and slowly drifted into a dreamless sleep.

He was out in a few minutes, the last pills of painkillers finally kicking in.

When his grip loosened around her skin, Carmen took in a deep breath and covered her mouth.

"What is it that you are looking for, Christopher?" she whispered in the dark, silent room.

It was bright and early, when Isabella left the hotel room the following morning.

While the rest of the team drove to the airport, she crossed the city in a haste - in one of the black MB cars Hillary had arranged for Christopher- tired, after a sleepless night.

Flashes of the accident had kept coming back to her.

I hope he's feeling better today, she thought, her eyes scanning the outside world from the car window, her mind recalling his cringed face every time he had taken in a deep breath.

His face would still be bruised and scratched.

He might still have pain in his chest, she mentally prepared herself.

But Isabella tried to see the positive side of it all. Christopher was going to walk out of the hospital on his own two feet and that was surely a blessing.

Her phone rang then, just as the car stopped at a traffic light.

"Ciao mamma" she said and smiled relieved.

"Honey, I've been trying to reach you since yesterday. How are you?" her mother's first question was.

"I am… okay" Isabella reassured her "Sorry, it got really busy yesterday"

"I saw what happened during the race. How is he?" her mother cut in.

"He's good" Isabella smiled.

"I know everything"

"Oh" Isabella mumbled under her breath.

"Emilia told me everything over lunch" her mother blurted out.

"She did?" Isabella hesitated, the butterflies in her stomach were back.

"Well, we were all eating lunch when it happened and she screamed. She cried and Giovanni explained why. I know about you and that driver. Christopher is his name, right?"

"Yes, it's Christopher" Isabella stared ahead, a crooked smile stamped on her face.

"You must have been so scared for him" her mother's voice was calm, prudent and soothing.

"I was terrified" Isabella said and her eyes darkened.

She had never been so scared before. She had never been so close to losing someone she cared so much about. Until the other day, until she had seen Christopher lifeless, being pulled out of the car. It had felt like she had lost everything, like a part of her had died in that accident. Feeling hopeless and lost had changed her.

Something felt different inside.

There were no more doubts, no more holding back. It was as though the missing parts of the puzzle had finally found its place.

"But he's fine now, right?" her mother continued.

Isabella nodded, as if her mother could see her, and ran a hand through her lose hair. She was tired still, but restless to be by his side.

"How come you never spoke to me about him?" her mother wondered.

"I was going to, mom. I just wasn't sure what was going on between us"

But now I know. Isabella let out a deep breath.

"Your sister is getting married"

"I know" Isabella nodded again.

"You knew?" her mother asked, surprised.

"They came to visit weeks ago and they told me" Isabella admitted.

Now shut up and don't say anything else, nothing about them living together already.

"My girls don't talk to me anymore" Isabella heard her mother mumble under her breath.

"Mom, you are not going to cry, are you?" Isabella asked and touched her forehead, sensing a headache on its way.

"No, I am not. But it hurts, you'll see one day when your kids will go from telling you everything and I mean everything- every time they need to pee- to not even telling you they want to get married or they are dating someone new" she made her point and then went silent.

Isabella bit her lip and gathered her thoughts.

How was she going to explain to her mother why she hadn't talked about Christopher before?

Had her mother ever been in that situation, had she ever been in love with someone that felt so wrong and right at the same time? So wrong and right, to the point that it scared her so much?

Had she ever been in love with someone that lived his life to the fullest- so exciting, so restless and intense- like Christopher?

"I just wasn't sure it was something serious. I didn't want to disappoint you after breaking up with Salvo and I am sure Emilia wanted to be sure, too"

"You think you disappointed me because you broke up with Salvo?" her mother asked.

"Well" Isabella began "We were together for three years, I am over thirty and I know you guys wanted me settled and all. And what do I do? I quit everything to take on a crazy job around the world"

Which is exactly what uncle Franco has been saying since December.

"You could never disappoint me, Isabella. Not even in a million years. I am so proud of you, always. You are my wonder woman, always have been and always will" for the first time during their phone call, her mother's voice wasn't soft, it wasn't calm.

It was strong and determined. She meant every word.

"Thanks, mom" Isabella smiled and her eyes were back on the city streets they crossed. "What did dad say? I mean, about Emilia getting married"

There was a sound –like a soft gasp- and then nothing, it all went quiet on the other end.

"Mom? Are you still there?"

"Yes, honey I am here. It's just, you haven't asked about your dad for a long time" her mother mumbled.

"I know" Isabella pursed her lips.

She hadn't spoken to her father for years. She hadn't even mentioned her father for years and the word 'dad' coming from her mouth had sounded weird just then, foreign and painful at the same time.

Was she starting to forget, starting to forgive her father's unfaithfulness?

No, I will never forget.

And Isabella knew it to be true. Some things were just impossible to eradicate from one's mind, even though something had changed.

Spending time with Christopher had given her a new perspective of things.

Did she really want to live her life with a heavy weight on her shoulders? Without ever speaking to her father again?

Could she someday live with the regret of having shut out someone so important in her family?

Maybe Christopher was right about living without regrets, without thinking too much about things.

Isabella wasn't sure how she felt about her father, but she knew what she didn't want in her life. Regrets.

"He was a little shocked, Emilia is so young. But he's happy, for both of you"

Isabella cleared her throat and her eyes grew wide, as she saw the hospital not too far ahead.

Her stomach tied into a knot, as she heard her mother speak again.

"Now make it up to me. Tell me everything about him"

Chapter 4

Christopher stood and walked over to the small mirror near the sink. The smell of burnt tires was finally out of his system, he could now smell detergent and disinfectant.

He stared at his bruised face for a while – how tired and upset his eyes were- before walking to his phone. It was ringing.

"Hello?" his voice was a little rough and muffled, like he had been sleeping.

"I am happy you are okay" Christopher recognized the voice immediately.

"Call my lawyer" he grumbled and was about to put down, when he heard the familiar voice again.

"I just wanted to check on you, make sure you were okay" she said softly.

Jackal, he thought, his hand curled up into a fist.

"I thought I made myself clear, don't call me" Christopher told her.

"I thought this was the right moment to try and reason with you"

"I don't reason with people like you" he cut in, his voice dry.

"You loved to reason with me once upon a time. In fact, we *'reasoned'* quite a lot, everywhere and anytime we felt like it" she purred. "We used to be friends" she added and she heard him make a sound of disapproval on the other end.

"We are not friends. I don't call *friends* people that try to blackmail me"

There was a pause and then a sigh.

"You brought that on yourself. We had an agreement"

"I had an agreement with a friend. That friend is dead to me. No more agreements. I am hanging up. Talk to my lawyer, we are done here"

"Wait!" she shouted and her voice so different now- so tense, not smooth like before- it made Christopher smile.

She sounded nervous, upset.

Good, Christopher thought.

"Cut the bullshit. Why did you call me?"

"I don't want to fight. I want a new agreement" she finally went to the point.

Christopher held the phone tight to his ear and looked at his reflection in the mirror again.

"Authorize the biography and I will reevaluate the content. I won't go so rough on you and your story. I'll use less… let's say details. Think about it. It works both ways" she said and Christopher imagined her face, her sly smile and small eyes.

She wants my authorization to make it a big success, a bigger deal, he thought.

That could have been the only reason why she had called. Christopher knew her very well, he knew how smart she was and how her mind worked. He had hit his head hard once, for how calculating and manipulative she was.

In a way, a new agreement would mean to have some sort of control on the content of the book. A new agreement would mean limit the damage.

It was the easiest way out, but it was a deal with a person that had betrayed his trust.

Christopher looked at his reflection in the mirror again and thought if he could ever look at himself again – with no regrets, no fear- if he said yes to her proposal.

I'd be crazy to say no to a new agreement, to say no to walking away with little if any damage, Christopher thought.

His lips curled up in a smile.

I guess I am crazy.

"Not even if you beg" he said, enjoying every single word that came out of his mouth.

"You are such a fool. I don't even know why I called" her voice changed, letting out all her frustration.

"Me neither. I don't negotiate with scum like you" he told her, his voice smug.

"You act like you don't care, like you are not bothered about the biography" she pressed on, her voice angry. "But you are and you will be, when the press will be onto you"

"Do you really think I care? When have I ever cared about anyone or anything? When have I ever cared about you?" he said the words with all the bitterness he could manage.

"Think of what your mother is going to say, your father's legacy, your reputation. What will your girlfriend say about my story?"

"I would be more worried about your reputation, if I were you. What happens to me and my loved ones is none of your business. It never was. You were never part of that" his words were so crude, he could tell they were hitting a soft spot.

"This was your last way out" she informed him, holding back the bitterness inside her.

Her attempt to mediate the situation had failed. Christopher was hard to break, hard to convince. But she wasn't giving up. She still had a few cards up her sleeve and she wasn't going to let this go so easily.

"I don't need a way out. I don't need a solution. You are not a problem to me, you see why we can't reason? You and I?" Christopher said. "I don't care what you do. It doesn't concern me. You will write your book full of crap and I'll ignore it. Every question the press will have for me, I'll ignore it. You don't exist, in fact I am hanging up now" and just like that he ended the call and threw his cell on the bed.

Christopher rested his strong, tired arms over the sink and looked at himself in the mirror again.

He had bruises, he had scars. So far, he had lived a crazy life and an even crazier love life. No strings, no relationship, no distractions.

For his entire life, Christopher had bared a heavy weight over his shoulders – his father's strong personality and talent- but he had managed just fine.

Head down, no distractions, no thinking about the past.

So his private life was about to be written and sold to the highest bidder on the publishing market.

But Christopher could still look at himself in the mirror, despite his mistakes.

It was just something no agreement, no amount of money could provide.

Isabella will understand.

"Okay" Isabella mumbled to herself.

It was okay, she could do it.

No, wait, she kept her hand on the door handle, but sat still in the car.

A hive of journalists lingered around the main entrance of Berlin's General Hospital.

Shit.

Her eyes counted at least two dozen journalists.

Fuck it. I am going in. She mentally prepared for the assault.

It wasn't such big of a problem to walk in the hospital- after all she was a nobody.

True, she had been on camera holding Christopher's hand while on the stretcher and yes, she may have even kissed his hand before the paramedics had closed the door of the ambulance, but she wasn't exactly a celebrity. Not even close.

I am not even wearing my MB uniform today.

Isabella covered her face for a moment, realizing how it would be to step out with Christopher.

Maybe there's a side door we can use like in the movies.

"Danke schön" she said to the driver, after asking him to wait for her and Christopher on the left-hand side of the hospital entrance.

Then she stepped out and, to Isabella's relief, nothing happened.

Nobody noticed her, nobody turned to look at her. Journalists were too focused on who was coming out of the hospital more than who was walking in.

Isabella sneaked by, in her dark blue jeans and white t-shirt- a stripy white and blue jumper on her shoulders- holding on tight to her bag, her fingers digging into the fabric.

As the elevator doors opened on Christopher's floor, Isabella felt her pulse pick up- the butterflies in her stomach went wild, every step she took towards his door.

"Buongiorno, signorina" Christopher's deep voice filled the room.

He was up and looking much better than the day before. He was in his jeans and holding a t-shirt in his hands, his fit, tattooed chest bare. He took her in his arms and bent down to kiss her hard.

Christopher's mouth claimed hers, like they had been apart for days.

Isabella smiled as they kissed, her teeth pulling Christopher's lower lip a little.

As her hands moved along his back, she closed her eyes, enjoying the feeling of his strong, muscular arms wrapped around her, drunken by his scent.

That morning Christopher smelled of eucalyptus and lemon zest, his beard had been cut a little and the bruise under his eye was more visible now.

And still he was the sexiest man she had ever seen.

"Good morning to you, too" she said and reached up to kiss him quickly again, as her stomach clenched "You did this on purpose, didn't you? Wait for me without your shirt on, just to flex your muscles and try to impress me?" she winked and bit her lip, as she ran both hands over his chest.

"Seems to be working quite well. I might even get lucky tonight" he mumbled and dropped his hands down to Isabella's hips.

Just as they slipped behind her lower back, Isabella grabbed a hold of them.

"Let's get you out of here" she said and backed a little.

"Fine" he held his hands up and smiled, one of his best, sexy smiles. *Hot!*

"Could you please help me with this? I can't lift my arms up properly, they feel heavy" he winced, as he tried to slip in his shirt.

"Did you tell the doctors?" Isabella asked while she helped him.

Christopher nodded. "They said it's nothing serious, I need to rest and take it easy"

"Then rest and take it easy. I'm here to help" Isabella smiled.

"Mmmm. Are you going to wear one of those sexy nurse outfits for me?" he smirked.

"Maybe, If you behave" she eyed him to the side. "Come on, let's get out of here"

Christopher took his bag and they walked to the elevator, down to the hospital entrance, Isabella's mind back on the same page as before entering Christopher's room.

The journalists. The flashes, the questions…the journalists!

"What's the matter?" he asked, feeling her body tense.

Christopher pulled at Isabella's hand a little and stared at her, amused as always as a series of emotions seemed to cross her absolutely, wonderful face.

She wrinkled her nose a little and he loved how her small, tiny freckles seemed to disappear for a moment under her golden, brown eyes.

"Nothing. Just looking for something hard to smash on the journalists' heads" she laughed "I'm okay. I'm just freaking out a little" she shrugged and looked towards the glass doors at the entrance.

I am freaking out alright, she looked back at Christopher again. *But not about what's happening between us.*

There were no more doubts.

She knew it was real, what they had. She could feel, just standing beside him hand in hand, that they were real.

Even if it was crazy, even if it still made no sense – to why Christopher was so interested in her- Isabella knew it was there, the connection, the attraction between them. It was so strong and impossible to ignore.

And I don't want to ignore it. I don't want to give it up. I want him. I want to be with him. I want it all.

What she had felt seeing him crash and unconscious, had opened her eyes to what they had become. It had felt as if she had crashed herself, like it had been her in that car. Isabella had felt hurt and helpless.

I don't want regrets, I want to live without regrets.

She looked at the door again.

From where they were standing, they could already see journalists shuffling around, stretching their arms up in the air- people holding cameras and recorders. There was commotion. Someone had spotted Christopher already.

"No worries, luv. It's the same as always. They'll ask me questions, some of which good, some stupid. Just let me talk as usual. You can let go of my hand and walk next to me. If they ask, I'll say you are here for work, as my press agent" he said and smiled at her reassuringly. "I'll just say you were worried and emotional the other day, seeing a coworker injured like that" he went on and started to let go of her hand.

His fingers had almost slipped out of her hand, when Isabella grabbed them and held on tight. Slowly, she moved her hand back into his.

"That was very diplomatic of you, Mr. Taylor. As your press agent, all I can say is bravo!" Isabella smiled and went on "But there is a problem with what you just said" she pursed her lips and looked down at their hands, their fingers entwined.

"I am not here as your press agent. I am here… for you. I don't want to let go" the warm feeling spread through her stomach, her entire body, as she said the words, her eyes back on their fingers.

And I just jumped, I just took my leap of faith.

She swallowed hard and smiled, terrified and happy at the same time for putting her cards on the table.

There was no going back, no intention of a coward retreat.

Isabella looked up again, straight into his deep green eyes and felt no regret, no fear.

This was what she wanted and it didn't matter how it would end. For the first time in her life she was risking everything – her job, her heart- and she had never felt better. She had never felt so alive.

Christopher reached for Isabella's soft lips with his other hand and smiled.

"Are you sure?" he smiled to the side, surprised.

Isabella nodded "I am just trying to figure out how to cope with all the unwanted attention" she laughed nervously again, as she caught sight of another flash through the large window near the main entrance of the hospital.

Christopher smiled wide and the bruise moved slightly up to the side, almost disappearing from his face.

"You've got to dance like there's nobody watching, Bresciani" he kissed the back of her hand.

You make everything seem so easy, she thought.

Maybe it was, though. Easy. Just like it had been easy to fall for him, to feel something for him.

Going out with someone like Christopher, trusting him, had been the riskiest thing Isabella had ever done in her life. She could face the spotlight and everything that came along with it.

He held on tight to her hand. "Let's go baby"

Then, they stepped outside.

And the questions began.

Gossip was something Isabella was very familiar with – even if on a small scale.

Small town, huge mouths.

That's what she had discovered growing up in her hometown. If there was something she had been good at all her life, was to keep out of any sort of rumor. Isabella had mastered the ability of being invisible- no chit chatter, no sticking nose into other people's business, no public display of any sort.

The iron lady, she was aware of what some people called her.

"The iron lady is keeping her sister out of trouble" every time Isabella had saved Emilia's butt from her parents, as a teen.

"No wonder they broke up, she is the iron lady" had been one of her all-time favorites, like they knew her so well, every detail of her love stories.

Pathetic. Yes, it was all so pathetic. Gossip.

But It was fine, she was totally okay with it. Some people her age had been given worse nicknames. To Isabella, it was way better to be seen as cold, rather than slutty or snob.

However, gossip on an international level was a whole other matter.

Gossip, real gossip travelled faster than cars, faster than speed train, faster than airplanes too apparently.

It took Christopher and Isabella exactly three hours to go to Berlin airport and fly back to London.

Three hours.

In that amount of time, news about Christopher's recovery and gossip about his love life, had travelled at a supersonic speed the distance between countries.

When the cab stopped in front of Isabella's house on Queensway road, the sidewalk was packed with journalists.

Isabella gaped at the crowd gathered around her front door, like she was some famous rock star.

It was going to be hell, to walk through them.

What the....

"What do they want?" she stared blankly at Christopher.

"Pictures. Declarations of love. Me walking with a hand stamped on your ass" Christopher mocked her.

"You find this funny, don't you?" Isabella asked, one brow up and unable to stop the smile from spreading on her face.

"I find it entertaining, like everything that seems to terrify you" he smirked.

"What's the big news, anyway? You have dated so many famous women… and how the hell do they know where I live? Me? How?" Isabella was incredulous.

"I don't know how they do it" he shook his head. "Let's go to my house"

"I need a change of clothes" Isabella sighed, her nose brushing against the passenger window.

She needed clean clothes, she craved a shower, a lazy evening.

I smell public transport on me!

"Since when do you wear clothes at my house?" he looked ahead- not meeting Isabella's stare on purpose- and started talking to the cab driver, as If he hadn't just said what he had said.

Isabella saw the driver chuckle from the rearview mirror.

I bet these taxi drivers have heard and seen a lot in their lives. If these cabs could talk…

"Don't listen to him, sir. I wear clothes in people's houses" she gave Christopher a dirty look.

The man laughed, this time openly and raised his hands up, like it wasn't his business.

Christopher was laughing, too, right in Isabella's face. He looked at her amused as always, her red cheeks and wide eyes were so entertaining to watch.

"Well" Isabella tried to get it back together "what makes you think they haven't surrounded your place, too?"

"It's not what I think" he said and told the driver their next stop. Maida Vale.

The cab moved slowly through traffic, uphill towards Paddington Station and then turned left at the bridge to cross the small river of Little Venice.

"I know they aren't anywhere close to my house" his mouth moved up to the side and Isabella stared at him puzzled.

"They have my Mayfair studio address, not the other one"

"Ah" Isabella understood perfectly well.

The press knew where to find him, when he usually went out with a woman. The place where Christopher met his one night stands, when he was out and about in town, partying and clubbing.

His love nest in Mayfair, Isabella frowned. *Sleeping with this girl, that girl…*

"What's the matter, Bresciani?" he leaned forward a little and searched her face, taking her chin into his big, right hand.

His touch made her shiver.

"Nothing" she shook off any negative thought.

Christopher had been straightforward and honest from the beginning. Plus, she had been the only woman he had taken to his home, his real home in Maida Vale. That meant more than any one night stand in a Mayfair studio apartment.

"I still need to go home" she pouted a little and then smiled, feeling his eyes on her again.

"What for?"

"I've been away for almost a week…" she looked his way, a soft smile on her lips.

"Backing out from your promise to be my sexy nurse for the next few days?" he smirked.

"I said I'd take care of you, the nurse bit was all your dirty mind thinking" she held his stare, pulling off her best smug face.

"Just stay with me for a few days" he said as they drove up the road, Christopher's house was already in sight.

He moved closer and kissed her hard- one hand in her hair, the other one slipping down, between her thighs- making Isabella gasp against his lips.

It was Christopher's way of stressing the point, of winning the argument.

When he's right, he's right. Isabella giggled in the back of the cab.

Chapter 5

First gear in. Foot ready on the gas. Red lights out. Go!
The car skidded forward, fast as a bullet, straight into the first turn-
the familiar smell of burnt tires filled Christopher's helmet.
Second gear, third gear, fourth…
His grip on the wheel tightened, as he pushed hard on the brake and
turned left, driving through the first turn, his eyes fixed on its exit.
See the exit, always focus on the exit of the turn.
Christopher gave gas again and concentrated on the car ahead.
He knew it was absolutely mandatory to overtake it as fast as
possible, to work his way up to the front of the race.
He may have started at the far back, but he was going to end up on
that podium.
I am going to win this today, he thought passing the first car just
before the next curb and went straight on, breaking last minute, as he
focused on his next target- the next car ahead.
I need to speed up.
"Easy on the throttle, Chris. Tarmac is soaked in two sectors of the
track already" Robert's voice echoed in his ears.
"Car is good" he said to his engineer, keeping his eyes ahead.
He was so close to the car in front of him now, he could hardly see
anything at all- the slipstream of water coming from its tires,
splashing on his helmet.
Three hundred and ten, his speed was incredible, the car felt perfect.
They almost entered the next curb side by side, Christopher's foot
heavy on the throttle, until they were out, onto another straight and
Christopher made his move.
The two cars were so close, the tires nearly touched, as Christopher
launched forward and was about to close in, in front of his opponent.
Keep your eyes ahead, he reminded himself, but he didn't.
Christopher glanced to the side, just as his car moved ahead and
something caught his eye.
He recognized the black and red helmet immediately.
James Taylor, it said on the left-hand side.
"What the…"
"You are just his son" he heard a voice on the radio, but it wasn't
Robert's.
"You live in his shadow" the same voice went on.

"It's not real" Christopher mumbled under his breath.

He kept staring at his father, at the man he was overtaking, as he waved briefly at him and Christopher gaped.

"What the fuck…" he mumbled under his breath again and then Robert's voice was back, full on, screaming to the top of his lungs.

"WATCH OUT!"

Christopher looked up, his eyes back on the road, only a fraction of a second before he hit the barriers and his body began to shake, as if struck by a lighting.

He sat up in bed panting, his heart thumping wild across his naked chest.

"What's wrong? Are you in pain?" Isabella asked and jolted up.

Even in the darkness of his bedroom, Christopher could see her eyes were wide. She was scared, just as much as he was disorientated.

"Sorry" he mumbled, his heartbeat slowly going back to normal.

He caressed her cheek and kissed her lips softly. "I just had a bad dream"

"Are you okay?" she asked, holding on to his hand a moment longer, but Christopher slipped out of her reach and pushed the sheets away.

"Yeah, I am just going to get some water downstairs. Go back to sleep, luv" he stood and, without saying another word, Christopher walked out of the room, his face serious and unreadable.

Isabella stayed exactly where she was, sitting up on the bed, unsure of what had just happened.

She watched him walk downstairs and laid back on the bed, only once he was out of sight.

What's going on in your head, Christopher?

He had seemed okay the day before, when they had arrived in London.

Even with the press, Christopher had seemed not at all bothered by their questions and their intruding.

That's just the problem, Isabella thought. *He's so good at guarding his feelings from the public, I don't have a clue what's really going on under that cool façade.*

She let out a deep breath and kept her eyes on the ceiling a moment longer.

She thought about what some journalists had asked Christopher, the minute he had stepped outside the hospital. She tried to recall his face when one of them had attempted to bring his father in the conversation. Some simile, some anecdote.

Half an hour had already gone by, when Isabella's eyes snapped back open.

Did I fall asleep again?

She looked around. Someone –obviously Christopher- had pulled the covers on her and she was no longer on one side of the bed. Isabella had sprawled out, one leg curled on Christopher's side.

No sign of Christopher.

She sat up quickly and caught a glimpse of the light coming from the big wooden window near the bed. It looked like the sun was about to rise.

Christopher?

Isabella wondered in the corridor and down the stairs, making the floor creak every time she took a step. Her bare feet touched the carpet on the ground floor and she welcomed the softness and warmth of the material for just a moment, just before peeking in the quiet, dark living room and stepping on the rough, cold, wooden floor near the fire place.

Both the living room and the kitchen were in sight.

Empty.

A shiver ran down her spine then, as she turned around and moved towards the back of the house- in the music room, in his study, then in the gym and all the way to a part of the house she wasn't familiar with.

It was right in front of the garden patio, she could just barely make out the shape of the garage from one of the curtains of the large windows of the room. There was a hot tub, a sauna right next to it and then a small corridor that led to the farthest corner of the house.

There was a door to her right. She went through it, stumbling into the darkness as she did, and found herself in a wide room she had never seen before.

The curtains were drawn and the only light came from a lamp at the far back.

All Isabella could see were shelves, a wall full of shelves. And trophies, trophies covered the entire wall, together with awards, pictures and worn racing gear. Pictures were neatly dispersed on one side, some black and white.

They were in no particular order, but they seemed to have a voice of their own, an important story to tell.

A boy on a kart, same boy on a podium, a boy crying and hugging his helmet after a race, his cheeks red and covered in dirt. In some pictures, his hair seemed lighter, but those deep, green eyes were impossible to mistaken.

Christopher, Isabella smiled and her eyes moved ahead, to the pictures that followed.

There were several men and women in them, too. A very young Carmen – Isabella later realized- and a very handsome, the legend of auto racing, James Taylor.

It was a collection of everything Christopher was, everything he kept inside and kept away from the spotlight. It was all that he kept to himself, that he jealously held on to. Nothing there had ever been sold to newspapers. Nothing on that wall had ever gone public.

In the darkest corner of the room stood Christopher, his back to the door, his eyes focused on the target ahead. He was shirtless, Isabella could see his back a little shiny from the sweat.

He was holding his hands up to his face, curled into fists, covered in white and black leather gloves.

Isabella stood there near the shelves, not making a sound, deafened by the silence in the room.

She watched Christopher hit the sack in front of him with his right hand, then his left, each time faster. He slowed down, only to walk around the sack hanging from the ceiling, and then he was back on the target again.

Fast. Punch after punch. He went down hard, as hard as he could and stopped only to steady the sack, so he could hit it again.

The place was silent like the night, Christopher's heavy breathing the only sound in the room.

Isabella noticed his jaw, how it seemed tense, his face contrived. She stared at his dark unemotional eyes, how focused they were, spaced out.

Tell me what's wrong, what's bothering you so much?

It wasn't until he had walked around the sack a second time that he saw Isabella, in her white shorts and top, standing near the door, her arms over her chest, holding on tight to her shoulders.

Her hair was up, tied behind her head and even from that distance, Christopher could see the sinuous lines of her neck, how they meshed into her small, shoulders. A stray strand of hair dangled down just over her shoulder blade, but it was her worried stare that caught his attention.

"Hey" she smiled, but it didn't reach her honey brown eyes. "What are you doing here?" she crossed the room slowly, never looking away from him.

She walked all the way down to the corner and hesitated, stopping just beside a dark gray armchair, next to one of the bay windows.

"I couldn't sleep" he told her, his voice as low as a whisper, like the voice of someone who hadn't spoken to anyone in a while.

Isabella's stare wandered around the big, decorated room and noticed Christopher's black leather jacket on one of the chairs.

He followed her stare.

"Did you go out?"

"I took a walk around the block, I needed some fresh air" he said and rubbed his chin.

"Chris" she hesitated "The doctor said to take it slow" Isabella reminded him, her voice gentle.

"I don't need to take it slow. I am okay" he said but looked down at his hands, at his gloves again, knowing he was in the wrong.

The doctor had been pretty straight-forward.

No strong, physical activity until the checkup in London. It was mandatory. It was for his own good.

Only two days had gone by since the accident and it was Christopher's first day without pain killers, but his mind was what kept torturing him. It was all in his head -the ache, the frustration.

He couldn't stop thinking.

No matter how hard he had tried, he just couldn't stop thinking.

The crash, his father's death, the book coming out about their lives.

How did I let all of this happen? Christopher wondered.

It seemed as though things had slipped out of his hands and he had lost control of his own fate.

It was only a matter of months, his story- their story- was about to go public.

Christopher eyed Isabella and then looked back at the sack. He needed the sack.

He needed to hit it, he needed the distraction, craved to have a thought free mind for just a night. No nightmares, no resentment, no worries for a night. He needed to shove the negative thoughts back in where they had come from, back in his head.

"You are not okay" Isabella spoke up, her heart beating faster and faster, while all the tension build up over the past weeks resurfaced. *The blackmailing, the friction in the team, the accident.* It was all too overwhelming, so many words left unsaid. *And confusing, so damn confusing.*

"I just needed to clear my mind a little" he avoided her stare and looked down at his gloves. "I'm sorry I woke you up, baby"

"You didn't" she shook her head and bit her lip, daring to ask. "What's going on, Chris?"

"Nothing. I told you, I am a little tense. I need a distraction" *Something that will stop the nightmares, the questions and the doubts in my head,* Christopher thought but kept these last words to himself.

He turned away from her, his eyes were back on the sack.

The frustrated tone of his voice made Isabella jump a little, but she pressed on knowing it was now or never. She had to know, she had to find out what was wrong.

"I overheard you speaking to Mr. Jenkins…" she blurted out, knowing it was the moment to come clean, to set the cards on the table.

I hate lying, I hate secrets.

Christopher kept his back to her, but eyed her to the side.

"What did you hear?" his voice calmer now.

"I didn't mean to overhear you, I was in the stairwell…it doesn't matter what I heard. You can't always block your thoughts, Christopher. You can't just stop thinking about it and think that problems go away. It doesn't work that way"

"It works for me" he snapped, his head turned her way again. "This is how I deal with things, I stop giving them a meaning, a reason to affect me. I delete them from my head"

"No, you are just pushing them away, but they are still there. They come back for you. Just like your father's death" Isabella almost mumbled the last part.

She watched his face change- by just mentioning James- and pressed on.

"Just let it out, let it all out. Those thoughts can't haunt you anymore, if you let them out" Isabella took a few steps forward but stopped when she heard him speak again.

"I said I am okay" his voice was tense but his eyes seemed to soften, seeing Isabella's stunned face. "Just go back to bed. I'll join you soon"

Isabella's stomach clenched and her mouth dropped open.

Talking was no use. That conversation was over, it had never even started because Christopher wasn't listening. He wasn't going to open up, he wasn't going to face his troubles.

Not trusting herself to speak, Isabella turned on her heels and walked out of the room.

Her chest felt heavy, her stomach hurt.

Shit, Christopher's eyes went to the door, just as Isabella disappeared in the hall and cursed under his breath.

What the fuck am I doing?

Quickly, he bit the straps off the gloves and tossed them on the floor, while making his way out of the room.

A glass of water, Isabella moved swiftly to the front of the house, her footsteps a soft hum that broke the silence.

She walked into the kitchen and let the water run a little before grabbing a clean glass. She watched the water fill it up and got lost in her own thoughts again.

He won't talk to me, Isabella thought and welcomed the freshness in her mouth, as she took sips from the glass.

One minute we are so close, the next so far away. Why would he share so much with me- his house, his time, his bed- and then keep me in the dark like this?

She placed both hands around the sink and leaned a little over the kitchen counter, trying to regain control of herself and to calm her nerves.

A sound behind her, made Isabella turn in a haste.

With her back now to the kitchen counter, she took in a breath seeing Christopher walk in the room, his arms lose along his body, his wrists a little red and sore where the gloves had been fastened.

He walked around the kitchen isle, to where Isabella was standing, slowly, his pace steady, his lips sealed in a thin line.

"I am sorry" he said and stopped inches from her.

"I'm going to bed" Isabella started to move but he took her arm and Isabella froze into place.

"I am sorry"

"You said that already" she tilted her head to the side and tried to keep her face straight, but her eyes gleamed, as his hand reached up to cup her cheek.

He wasn't just telling her he was sorry. Christopher looked sorry.

Good, she thought for a moment, the tone of his voice from before replaying in her head.

But then his hand slipped down her neck and he moved in to kiss her lips, slowly but with a certain rush, a certain need.

His dark eyes stayed open, like he had to see for himself that Isabella was still there with him and he hadn't messed it all up, by shutting her out moments before.

Sharing was something he wasn't used to- he didn't know how to- but his hands, his body knew exactly he had to keep Isabella by his side.

She let him kiss her but her hands stayed behind her back, holding on to the kitchen counter.

"I was a wanker" he mumbled in between kisses.

"Uno stronzo" *"An asshole"*

"Uno stronzo" *"An asshole"* he nodded and smiled a little to the side, getting lost in her warm, honey brown eyes.

"It's not easy for me, to talk about certain things" he began to say.

"It's not easy for me either, to be with you and not being able to help" Isabella told him and watched him nod.

"I know it isn't. There is so much you don't know about me. It's just very hard for me to let certain things, certain issues resurface. There are things I cannot deal with"

"Yes, you can"

"No, I can't Isabella. I don't want to. I don't want those memories to come back, I don't want to feel the pain again" Christopher said cautiously, like he was weighting every word, being careful not to say too much, not to let his ghosts loose.

"You are strong enough to deal with anything. You can't keep pushing your worries away. They'll come back for you"

"They won't leave me. Not even If I face them, Isabella. I know there are certain issues I'll have to live with forever, but I don't want them to be part of my present. I choose to leave them where they are, somewhere remote in my mind" he held her stare and ran a hand through her hair, his fingers playing with her soft curls.

Isabella shook her head slightly and closed her eyes, savoring his big, warm hands as they now both travelled to her cheeks. Christopher cupped her face and she couldn't hold the grudge a second longer. She stood on her toes and reached for his face.

"Tell me what's wrong, please Chris. What's wrong? Let me in, let me help you" Isabella pleaded- her eyes a little watery, her pulse picking up as she spoke.

It hurt deep inside, all the way down her chest, to see Christopher so troubled and distant.

She held his stare, in search of an answer, pleading her way into his mind.

She needs to know about the book. I have to tell her, Christopher repeated in his head, like he had been doing for some time now.

He searched, in Isabella's big, honey brown eyes, that courage he seemed to lack, the strength to trust and open up to her. She looked worried and confused, her red lips half parted in anticipation.

She already knew something was up. She had overheard him and Alfred. And Isabella could see it then, in his worried eyes, the angst. Way beyond his bullshit, his public shield. It was there and she could see it. Because she wanted to know everything about him. Him. Christopher. Not the race driver. Not the son of James Taylor.

She cares, he realized as he stroked her hair.

He contemplated telling her, telling her everything.

How his father's memory haunted him every day, how images of James' accident kept coming back to him over the years. Christopher contemplated telling Isabella the mistakes he had made growing up in his father's shadows.

Looking into her eyes a moment longer, Christopher thought about telling her how the constant battle to try and beat his father, was slowly consuming all the energy within him.

Never stopping to think things through, had been his only salvation until now.

Not only the book was going to put his private life in the hands of the public and the media, it was also going to force him to face his mistakes, all of them, his weakness and his biggest fear- being compared to his father James.

'Like father, like son', that was the title of the book.

Memoirs of legend race driver James Taylor and the ultimate 'son of' read the subtitle.

Christopher had seen the cover, 'the leech' had been brave enough to email it to him.

It was a masterpiece of real life and fiction, perfectly crafted into a bestseller.

The story reeked with private moments of his life, gossip and betrayal.

Each and every stupid thing he had done in the past, every little crazy idea he had had- his past affairs, his weaknesses, his constant strive to be worthy of his surname- was going to be written in black ink- on paper- pungently tailored with a load of gossip, by one of the best reporters in the field. A person that was not only a professional in the sport, but a person he had met and trusted. And became intimate with.

What they will see is an arrogant, demanding champion and his trophy wife- a real wizard on track, a perfectionist. And then his son, a sloppy copy of his father, a mare number two, a lady's man, a tormented soul, a perfectionist, doomed to never succeed because of his nature.

Just a number two.

He had to tell Isabella about the book, about who was behind all of it and how it was going to hurt everyone around him. But mostly how it was going to hurt him and his father's memory.

How will she see me after I tell her? After I tell her we'll have the press on our backs?

Christopher looked down at Isabella in silence, at her perfect half naked body in the dim light and the words just wouldn't come out.

What if I lose her? What if she can't stand all this? The thought crossed his mind a second later.

"I want to tell you" he murmured. "But not now. I don't want to talk now"

He stroked her hair, enjoying her sudden heavy breathing, as his other hand moved down to her shorts.

Slowly, he traced the length of her thigh, all the way up to her waist, while his eyes contemplated her perfectly round, smooth hips.

"You are so beautiful" he mumbled under his breath, looking up at her. "I don't want to think, I don't want to sleep…I just want to touch you all night"

He kept his eyes on her a moment longer, as his strong arms wrapped around her back and he lifted her up on the kitchen counter. Isabella gasped, her legs tightening around his waist, while Christopher's hands moved to her shoulders in an instant, pulling down the straps over her arms.

"Kiss me" she moaned, her cheeks on fire, while her hands travelled to his waist.

She unbuttoned his dark pants in a haste, the fire in her stomach spreading quickly across her entire body.

Kiss me all night, her eyes begged him then.

His lips pressed hard against her mouth, harder as he cupped her behind and guided her closer to him.

Closer, he thought, *I want you closer.*

He let his pants drop to the floor, his hands lingering around her breasts.

No bra, he realized and felt his stomach clench, easing her out of her tank top.

In the dark, Christopher moved down to kiss Isabella's full round breasts, while his hands explored every single inch of her skin.

"I want you" he groaned and grabbed Isabella's leg, holding it up, over his shoulder.

"Chris" she gasped, as her body shivered with pleasure, her fingers clawing behind his back.

Her heart was racing, it hummed inside her chest begging for more.

"More" she whispered and saw a light cross his eyes.

She saw it in his stare, she felt it how he was touching her, how his hands craved her skin.

He too wanted more.

We are not talking. Talking is what we should be doing, her head reminded her, but in a way it was as If they were.

Their bodies were speaking the only language they knew- a touch, a whispered word in between kisses, the pressure on each other's skin, the sparks every time their lips brushed.

He watched her in awe, as she tilted her head back in delight, his thumb over her soft, red lips just as Isabella opened her mouth to let out a moan.

Their bodies swayed in the dark silence, their breathing the only sound in the room.

I can't get enough of her, he thought and his hand went behind her head, through her hair, as he breathed in deep and took in her incredible, sweet scent.

He held on tighter, tight to her body and to that feeling – the feeling of getting lost in someone else and wanting to never be found again.

"I want to lose myself in you" he breathed out and lifted her up a little roughly.

Isabella's body quivered in his arms like never before, as a soft moan escaped her parted lips.

He turned around – her legs safely wrapped around his body- and lowered her onto the floor in a haste. He took hold of one her wrists and pinned it down on the hard wood floor.

Isabella's breathing quickened, while her free hand snaked up his abs, her eyes lost into his. Their noses almost touched, for how close they were then.

"Tell me you are mine" he groaned, moving deeper into her.

From the moment I saw you, Isabella realized for the first time, as she arched her back.

It had been instant- their connection -their passion uncontrollable and consuming, to the point it had been impossible to stay away from one another.

Maybe I will end up burned. Maybe this relationship will leave me empty and stranded, but I've never felt so good. I've never been so high.

"I am yours" she whispered against his ear and rolled on top, Christopher's eyes shining with desire.

Chapter 6

"You have one hell of a wall of fame" Isabella brushed her fingers against Christopher's forehead and kept her eyes on the wall, on the trophies ahead.

They were back in the room where their conversation had started, next to the sack, Christopher's gloves and gear spread across the floor.

They were sitting on an armchair, Isabella at ease on his lap, her legs dangling to the side, looking good in Christopher's white t-shirt.

His head was resting on the seatback, a hint of a smile on his face.

He looked like Christopher again- relaxed, not the least bit tormented like he was before.

Before we did it on kitchen floor…

"A what?" he asked, looking straight at her- Isabella could see his lips twitch in a half smile.

"A wall of fame. You know, the place where we all keep our successes and happy memories" Isabella turned to look at him.

"Do you have a wall of fame?" Christopher's eyebrows went up.

"Of course" she gave him one of those 'obviously I do, who doesn't?' look. "Only mine involves nursery handcrafts and pictures of birthday parties and first communion"

Pictures of me and my siblings, sticking our faces into huge ice cream cones.

Isabella kept her face serious, until she met Christopher's eyes and then she couldn't resist any longer. She laughed and wrapped her arms around his neck.

The light coming from the garden patio was strong now. Sun was up.

"Your wall of fame is about different things. Mine is only about racing and car related accessories" Christopher said and then chuckled, Isabella's face so funny just then.

"Is that supposed to make me feel better?" she raised a brow and then kissed him on the nose quickly. "Your wall here just kissed my sweet, little wall of fame's ass"

"You do have one sweet ass" his hands slid down to the lower part of her body, to stress the point and took a quick peep.

Isabella giggled and wrapped her arms around his neck even tighter, snuggling up beside him.

"You are really something, do you know that signorina" the grip on her behind tightened, as Christopher moved in to kiss her hard.

"Thank you" she said, after biting his lower lip. "You are not so bad either" she grinned and watched Christopher smile back.

"I've been told I was bad, several times actually" he said as a matter of fact and it didn't surprise Isabella one bit.

Flirt, ladies' man.

"You know, I don't have trouble believing that"

He chuckled and laid his head back on the armchair again. He stared ahead, his attention back to the wall where all his successes and his memories hung before him, and the smile on his lips slowly began to fade.

"I had a dream about the crash" he said of his own will.

Isabella held his stare.

That was what the nightmare was about.

"What happened in the dream?" she asked.

"It was about Berlin, about the crash. It was me driving but it wasn't how I crashed"

"What do you mean?" Isabella pressed on, holding in her breath for a moment.

"It was me driving, but I dreamt exactly what happened to my father. I think you remember how it happened" he looked down at her and Isabella simply nodded.

Of course, she did.

Everyone remembers when a legend like James Taylor dies.

"It was raining hard and I was at the far back of the race. I was making my way to the front, ignoring the rain, not bothered about anything but overtaking every single car in front of me. I felt great, I felt like I could win. The car was running smoothly, despite the wet tarmac. When I was about to pass the second car, I saw it was my father driving it. I turned to look at him, and I went off track, straight onto the barriers. Then I woke up. But I remember exactly how it goes from there. My father almost flew out of the car- despite the safety belts- for how strong the impact was. His body moved sideways like it wasn't real, like he was a dummy. I will never forget that. Every time I close my eyes, after crashing in Berlin, I see that. I see his head moving, like it has been snapped off his neck"

"Chris…" Isabella covered her mouth, but didn't say anything more.

She waited for him to carry on with his thoughts, as he looked down at her again.

"It's a recurrent dream of mine. It comes and goes. It has been with me since he died and it will be with me forever. I know I can't change that, some things are impossible to forget. And when I try to forget, to set them aside, circumstances push the memories back in my head. I don't need this, all of this in my head. I need to stay focused. What's done is done, I cannot change it and It cannot affect me"

"I can't imagine what that is like" her voice shook a little, Isabella's feelings all over the place, as she wondered how tormenting it was for Christopher, to be haunted by the same, reoccurring nightmare

"Thank you for telling me, for telling me what the dream was about" they locked eyes and Isabella kissed him gently, her stare stayed on him as Christopher spoke again.

"It's ironic, if you think about it. Since I started racing I've been acting like I am nothing like my father and what do I do? I crash, on the same track where my father died over twenty years before. Absolutely, fucking ironic" he snorted.

"You just did what your instinct told you was right. You took your chances, that's what you do in that car every race"

"I fucked it up, Isabella. I let my guard down. I lost my concentration, just like my father did."

And for what? Christopher thought. *For a lunatic that hoped I would die during the race – and I nearly served him my death on a silver plate? For a book about me and my father, written by a leech, desperate for money and fame?*

"Hey, look at me" Isabella cupped his face. "The track was slippery, you did what you thought was right. You know your strategy could have been a real success. And it nearly was. You were right about changing the tires at the end, you were just unlucky in that turn." Isabella's fingers brushed gently against his bruised cheek and Christopher stopped moving, his body tensed under her touch.

"Does it hurt?" she asked, her hands frozen in place.

"No, not my cheek, nor my legs, my arms. I am okay, Isabella" he shook his head slowly "But my mind… my mind is scarred. I can't stop thinking about the crash, about my father"

"Does it…" Isabella searched for the right words and realized there were none. It wasn't easy to say, what she wanted to say out loud. "Does it scare you, to get back in the car after the accident?"

Isabella bit her lip and kept her eyes on Christopher.

She watched him shake his head, his face unreadable.

"No. I am not scared. I'm not scared of racing. I fall and I get back up, that's what I do" he turned her way. "Not being able to race is what scares me"

"You are fine. You said it yourself"

He nodded absent mindedly, his eyes focused on something far away, at the back of the room.

"You'll get your chance Christopher, you came this close. Next time it's a sure hit"

"Or maybe I won't. Maybe I won't get what I am striving for. Maybe I will end up just like him, searching for something and losing my life, my everything while I try"

Isabella shuddered as she heard him speak- his voice so dark and crude just then, it shook her to the core- but her face didn't break. She kept it together and spoke up.

"Listen to me. You are not James Taylor. You are Christopher Taylor. You achieved so much, you already won more than your father has. You'll get your chance in Berlin. You will take that trophy home, you will show everyone what a fantastic, brave, strong and absolutely crazy race driver you are"

His eyes burnt into hers then and his hands went up her neck, in her hair and Christopher kissed her hard, but slowly, like he was claiming every little inch of her lips.

"Thank you" he said, looking into her eyes.

Isabella smiled and placed her hand over his, behind her head.

"I mean every word"

"I know you do" he nodded to Isabella's words but his eyes were back on the wall a moment later, back to the pictures and the trophies.

Gently, Christopher helped her up and they both stood, only to move towards the wall, towards the shelves filled with trophies.

He stopped right in front of an old picture hanging on the wall.

It was one of him holding up a cup together with his dad. He still remembered that day perfectly. His dad had been so proud of him, for winning the hardest race in the junior championship- after months and months of training.

Christopher must have been eight or nine years old.

But it wasn't always like that. There weren't only happy moments in his memories.

He remembered every victory, every achievement and every disappointment. Christopher had only started driving go-karts when his father had died, but he could recall every single word his father had shouted in his face on more than one occasion.

"You lost your focus" he had said often enough after a race or a training session. *"Where is your head? Feel the engine, you weren't feeling the car. It was telling you to change gear, You didn't and it slowed you down. Focus, focus!"*

It was only years later that he had understood, the force that was consuming his father, that had lead him to make that mistake during the race, the day he died. James was after perfection, he was after the impossible.

I am my worst enemy, he kept the thought to himself.

All those years in auto racing, Christopher never had rivals. Only one. His father James.

It wasn't the comparison with other drivers that hit him, it was the constant invisible battle with his father, with a legend of the past. A ghost.

How can I win against someone that's not here anymore? How do you win against a legend?

"They are writing a lot of crap about me" he said, breaking the silence.

"What have you read?" Isabella asked.

"I don't need to read anything. I know they are" she felt him smile, a tired smile.

"Not more than what we expected" Isabella told him and cleared her throat, secretly wishing she didn't have to admit that.

She wished she could have said no.

No, they aren't writing about you and your father, how you both crashed on the same track. No, they are not saying that you brought it upon yourself with that risky strategy of staying out with dry tires, when the tarmac was soaked with water.

Out of nowhere, a memory came back to Isabella.

"It's going to be worth millions if you die like your father" those words, cold and piercing like ice, made Isabella shiver. She recalled that lunatic, the crazy man on the stands – his eyes gleaming at Christopher's autograph- and the words he had said to Christopher just a few hours before the race.

"What if I told you that there will be more?" Christopher said.

"More of what?" Isabella moved forward and stood right behind him.

She gently reached for him, for his skin, his broad shoulders and Christopher turned his head to the side but kept his back to her.

He let Isabella wrap her arms around his waist and he placed his strong arms over hers, making sure she stayed right where she was.

Tell her, tell her, just tell her.

"Of everything. This won't be the last time I fail, this won't be the last time I crash trying to achieve something. You know that, right?" he paused. "There's a book coming out. About me, about my father…People will say things, bad things about me, about my family. Can you stand all that?"

A book, Isabella took in a breath, as her mind raced.

"Chris" she began, her head shaking a little "I don't know what's going on, but I want you to know something. Whatever it is they are threatening you with, It won't change the way I feel about you" Isabella said, her voice determined. "Tabloids can write all the crap they want, Christopher. You know what I cannot stand?" Her eyebrows went up and Christopher shook his head, waiting for Isabella to carry on.

"You on a stretcher with your arms limp, not responding to the paramedics. I nearly died, I couldn't breathe or think straight. But you know what I knew, what I never doubted for a second?"

Christopher shook his head again and listened carefully.

"I knew where I had to be. Right by your side. Like now. I am right here and I don't want to be anywhere else"

The glimpse of a smile appeared on Christopher's face, as he looked down at Isabella, his eyes on her blushed cheeks.

"Is that what it takes, signorina? I have to injure myself to have you here with me?"

"It's not funny, Chris" she shook her head. "I nearly lost it. I pushed around a dozen journalists to get in to see you" Isabella frowned.

Christopher smiled wide then. He chuckled and the sound of his laughter overcame the heaviness that surrounded them.

His body relaxed, as he stared at her and grinned, like Isabella had just told him the best news ever. Journalists being shoved around, journalists being molested – getting a little reality check, a little taste of their own medicine.

"You are welcome" Isabella smiled back, picking up on his thoughts. *Yes, he is back, flirty, easygoing Christopher is back.* Isabella breathed out, relieved.

He turned around and took hold of her chin, smiling wickedly and going for her lips.

Isabella pulled back a little, escaping from his hold, only to giggle one second later, as Christopher's arms wrapped around her again and pulled her against his chest.

"Are you hungry? I bought you breakfast, when I was out" he smiled to the side and studied her face.

Isabella's eyes went wide with joy.

"You know how to win a woman's heart" she said and they started to walk out of the room and into the long corridor, half naked – Isabella wearing his shirt and Christopher in his pants- their fingers intertwined.

Something happened back there, Isabella had that distinct feeling, as they made their way to the kitchen in silence.

Maybe there were still many unspoken words between them- things kept safely inside, too afraid to reveal, too afraid to be let down- but Isabella had never felt so close to someone before like she did with Christopher.

Walking away from the private moment they had shared, Isabella had realized she and Christopher were more similar than she had thought.

It took them both time to open up and trust someone, but once they did it was all or nothing. They chose they wanted it all.

She eyed him to the side and smiled.

I did the right thing, coming to stay with him a few days, she thought once they had reached the kitchen.

On the dark wooden counter, there were two bags of puff pastries, cookies, granola and even – Isabella took a glimpse- pancakes and waffles.

"Fantastic, what are you having?" she glanced cheekily his way, the small freckles on her cheeks giving her an extra naughty look.

"You, Bresciani" Christopher said, moving to stand behind her to nibble her neck. "I am having you"

Chapter 7

Wednesday morning Isabella opened her eyes and doubted she had woken up in London.

Wait a minute, she had looked around the big, empty wooden bed and it had all come back to her. Yes, she was in fact in London – in Christopher's bed.

And I'm confused!

There was a good explanation to why she had felt so disorientated.

The sun coming from the windows was strangely hot and incredibly shiny. But the best news was that the sky was clear blue and there were no clouds in sight.

No clouds in sight, she played with the words in her head for a while, as she set her breakfast to the side and started working on her laptop.

Isabella busied herself – she had a few things to post but it would only take her about half an hour, just the amount of time for Christopher to shower and get dressed. They were going out, making use of the beautiful day to spend some time outside.

Third and last day in the house of Taylor's, Isabella looked around the room and smiled to herself.

No women's stuff detected, no skeletons in the closet. She giggled to herself and took another spoonful of yoghurt.

Three days had gone by in the blink of an eye and everything seemed back to normal.

Despite the first rocky night, Christopher's mood had brightened up from then on. No more nightmares, no more sadness or spaced out moments.

Just like that Wednesday's morning blue sky, there were no clouds in sight and Christopher was back to being himself.

She leaned backwards in her stool and reached for the cream-colored curtains, to get a better glimpse outside.

"Ding", her laptop made the first sound of the day and on the screen Isabella saw Mr. Jenkins' first email- first email after Christopher's accident, first email after their relationship going public.

Ding, ding, ding, the sound echoed in her ears, as his name popped on the screen.

You have three new emails from Alfred Jenkins, her email account kept reminding her.

Here come the clouds, Isabella frowned but kept writing her blog post about Christopher's Drivers Academy and attaching pictures, she had personally taken the other day on the spot. In the end, she had given in. Isabella had agreed to help him promote his project, despite her initial doubts- her initial doubts being pissing off Mr. Jenkins with her intrusion in the project.

Oh well. He's probably already pissed off that we are seeing each other so… Isabella thought while working on the final touches to the post. She gave another quick look at the pictures – if they needed more filters and editing- and was mesmerized by one in particular, the one she had decided to add last minute. It was of Christopher, standing on the Drivers Academy's track, speaking to the person he had appointed to help him coordinate the project- Jonathan Korr, the man that once had been his father's engineer.

The light in the picture was very particular, it had been taken at sunset and the lighting around the track had just been turned on. Christopher was smiling, looking at the man and explaining something, his hands in motion and his eyes keen. He looked so focused, so concentrated on his goal- his driver's academy, his future.

He looks really happy, she realized.

The worry in his eyes since their first night in London, seemed like it had mysteriously disappeared somewhere. He wasn't hiding it, she could see he looked more relaxed- his attention only on the good result of his project and the medical check-up.

"It's because I have the best press agent by my side. And the sexiest" Christopher had commented on their way back from the academy.

Smooth talker. She smiled.

Another email from Mr. Jenkins caught her attention then and Isabella mumbled something mean under her breath.

She posted everything and then finally checked her email.

Her stomach tied in a knot after reading the first one. It wasn't about work like the rest. It was personal.

Meet me tomorrow morning. Coffee place opposite Bond Street tube station. Alfred Jenkins.

She read the sentence again.

It's official, his distrust in me has officially become personal.

Isabella took in a deep breath and stared at the screen, thinking of what to write back.

Don't let It get to you, don't let it get to you…

But Isabella couldn't hide it to herself, the worry. One thing was try and lie to others, but how could she lie to herself?

This had been one of the reasons why she hadn't wanted things to become public with Christopher from the beginning, in addition to be taken seriously for her job.

Things had taken an unplanned twist, though. There had been a turning point, a moment when she could have either turned or stopped –speaking in terms of the automobile field. Isabella had decided to take that turn and see what was at the end of the road.

Things with Christopher had been taken to another step, another level. It wasn't just a stupid fling, not after surviving what had happened in Cannes. Not after coming so close to losing him.

You are going to the meeting and you'll make him see he is wrong about you. You are not an untrustworthy person, you aren't after Christopher's anything.

Isabella bit her lip and replied to Mr. Jenkins email.

See you there at ten. Isabella Bresciani.

No hellos, no thank yous, no pleasantries. Just like he himself was used to doing. There would be no sorry, no please, no excuses.

There is nothing to be sorry about, I love him.

The thought paralyzed her.

She stopped typing. Isabella looked at the screen and breathed in deep.

She had said it. Well, not said it but she had thought about it, which meant so much more than saying it out loud. What went on in a person's head was the purest form of truth, Isabella firmly believed in that.

How did I manage to fall in love with a man like him?

As her mind kept wondering how it had all happened in just a little over four months, she heard the door of the gym open and then Christopher walked in the kitchen, his hair wet from the shower and wearing only a towel around his hips.

He walked towards her, without saying a single word. His eyes were burning into hers like fire. He reached the stool where she was sitting and wrapped his arms around her, one hand sliding under her shirt, the other wrapping around her neck. He kissed her hard, not giving her time to think.

"Hey" he mumbled, stopping to look at her for a moment.

"Hey yourself" Isabella smiled to the side and reached up to kiss him again.

She tilted her head back and reached for his nape.

It had been like that since they had stepped inside his house on Monday. They couldn't keep their hands off each other.

Like the day before, he had been in the gym, walking on the treadmill – because anything more than that, any real exercise had been strictly forbidden from the doctor in Germany, at least until Thursday- and Isabella had walked inside the room, to inform him Hillary had tried to call him.

Christopher had lifted her up and taken her on one of the benches.

Isabella's head had started spinning, his hands had driven her crazy. Just like now.

"Chris…" she whispered against his lips.

"Yes, luv?" he murmured, as his lips slowly worked their way down her neck.

She turned around with the stool and he slowly unbuttoned her yellow, short sleeved button-up shirt, his eyes on her the whole time, a soft smile played on his lips.

"I thought the doctor said no exercise" Isabella smirked and her hands stroked his abs. His skin was warm from the hot shower. "We've been doing quite a lot"

"Do I look like someone who isn't fit to 'exercise'?" he leaned forward and rested his forehead on hers, same sexy smile glued to his lips.

Isabella's hands travelled up and down his chest then, her fingers drawing circles on his tense muscles.

She shook her head absent mindedly, like she had forgotten all about her question and was thinking about something else.

Yeah, his body!

"You know, you can kiss me all you want, but I am still mad at you" Isabella made a face and reached for something behind her.

Christopher gave her the sliest smile he could manage.

"What did I do now?"

"This, remember?" she handed him a magazine and pointed to the small print beneath the picture.

The photograph had been taken in Sloane Square- opposite a department store- and it was a snapshot of them walking hand in hand, Christopher looking casual and relaxed – just a hint of a smile on his lips. They had both been wearing sunglasses- Isabella had nicked a cool pair of Christopher's shades- and she was looking at him and laughing. He had been making fun of her, of how serious she looked whenever she was busy working during race weekends. Christopher had even tried to imitate the expression on her face, every time she took pictures with her camera in the boxes and so Isabella had done the only thing that seemed right then.

The most annoying thing she could think of, to set the record straight on who was the queen of jokes.

She had taken her reflex out of the bag and had taken a snapshot of him, right there on the street as they were walking.

"This face, like this?" she had said and then she had pressed the button.

She had laughed so hard at his surprised face.

"You are annoyingly smart and super sexy. I can't decide what you are more" He had smirked, just before spotting someone on the opposite side of the street, right next to the pedestrian crossing. A photographer. He was taking pictures of them.

"You see that, Bresciani? Take a picture of him, that man with the camera. Let me see how annoying you can be" and to that, Isabella had started clicking, taking snapshot of the man. She had played the game.

They had waved and then exchanged a few words with the stunned photographer.

He had wanted to make sure he had gotten Isabella's name right for the magazine.

"Monica Trevisani" Christopher had told him and Isabella's mouth had dropped open.

Christopher had simply grinned, like it was perfectly normal to give out a false name.

A small innocent revenge for having his privacy violated on a walk around town, he had said.

Monica Trevisani, said the small print under the picture she was showing him, on the latest issues of VIP news.

"You are bad" she said and put down the photo. She moved in close again and kissed him passionately "Very naughty"

"Thank you" he smirked.

Very, very naughty. And sexy and you could get away with murder, Isabella squinted her eyes at him and then smiled.

"What time do you have your medical checkup tomorrow?"

"Nine in the morning" Christopher said and Isabella couldn't help but notice his jaw tense a little.

"Are you worried?" Isabella asked, searching his face.

"I am a little tense"

"Anything I can do, to get your mind off it?" Isabella raised an eyebrow and giggled as a look of amusement registered on Christopher's face.

"More than one thing, actually" Christopher's hands slipped down Isabella's back and straight into her jeans pocket. His hands grabbed her behind, as he gently bit her lower lip making her jump and giggle with excitement.

Her arms wrapped around his neck and she smiled.

"How about we go out for a walk somewhere? It's a beautiful day. Look at the sky. I want to look at the sky all day, so I can remember how blue it is when it will get gray and miserable and it will rain again"

Christopher chuckled and then took Isabella by the chin.

"That's what you want to do?" he asked looking into her eyes and Isabella nodded slowly.

"Let me put some clothes on and I am all yours"

"I think you are pretty fine like this" Isabella bit her finger.

"I think I would create quite a stir, walking down the city streets wearing just a towel around my waist"

"But it would help me. I'm sure it would get the attention off Monica Trevisani, your 'girl' or whatever my name is" she made a face and smiled again. Then, her face was back to being serious and her hands reached out for his hair, brushing it back gently.

"Would you like me to accompany you to the checkup tomorrow?" Isabella asked.

She wasn't sure if Christopher would have liked her to go, if he wanted anyone to go with him. The idea of having his doctor decide whether he could race or not next week, was like a heavy weight hanging over Christopher's neck. For sure.

Even if he was good at keeping his troubles to himself, Isabella couldn't help but notice how hard he had tried to avoid the subject over the past three days.

"No, that's okay" Christopher smiled. "I'll meet you later at the sponsor photoshoot. You and Hillary will both be there, right?"

Isabella nodded.

Right after I've had a chat with your manager Mr. Jenkins.

In that moment, Isabella thought about telling him and refrained from doing so.

No, Christopher had a lot on his mind already. She could deal with Mr. Jenkins on her own. She would eventually tell him, later, possibly over dinner and in the presence of a large bottle of red wine. *Make it two bottles of red wine.*

The kitchen counter began to vibrate and Maria's name popped on Isabella's phone.

She took it in her hands and Christopher took a good look at Isabella, the spitting image of happiness that she was. He could tell it was someone important to her.

"Go on, pick up" he encouraged and gently released her from his arms.

He winked, walked around the kitchen isle and then disappeared in the corridor, tossing dried fruits in his mouth.

"Ciao" Isabella said, as she poked her head in the corridor, just to make sure Christopher wasn't nearby.

"There's this picture of you on Gossip news, you look amazing. Can you believe it? You, Isabella Bresciani, my good friend on Gossip news magazine" Maria shrieked.

"What an achievement, on Gossip News magazine" Isabella frowned "Tell me at least I don't look like a complete idiot and my eyes are open"

"No, no you look beautiful, with your sunglasses on, looking casual in jeans and tank top. The headline says 'Driver Christopher Taylor out and about with his new girl'"

Isabella frowned again.

His new girl, she repeated in her head.

Of course they would say that, people had lost count of all the 'new girls' he had had. So now she didn't even deserve a name on the headline, Isabella was just a new girl, one of many nameless girls.

Monica Trevisani wasn't that bad after all.

"Where were you, by the way?" Maria asked, her voice distant, like she was reading the magazine while speaking to Isabella.

"It was probably taken while we were walking to a department store to buy clothes for me" Isabella said nonchalantly.

"Clothes?" Maria asked.

"Yes, well I haven't been home since I left for Berlin" Isabella mumbled.

"Really????" Maria screamed "You are telling me, you are living with the guy now?"

"No, no" Isabella said quickly "No, nothing like that" she paused.

It surely seemed like it. She hadn't been home at all.

Okay, so the first night they got back, her house had been surrounded by paparazzi, like she was one of the royal family being caught cheating or something like that. But then she had stayed with Christopher the following day and the one after that.

They had put it off, going back to her place.

The truth was, they had spent the best days together, sleeping in late since Christopher couldn't exercise and Isabella was off from work.

"There's another picture of you!!!!!" Maria screamed again on the other side.

Isabella touched her ear and frowned "Jesus, Maria. Stop with the screaming" she said and laughed hard, finding it so funny how Maria was getting all excited over gossip.

"Sorry. Were you at a game or something? Cricket?" she asked while scanning the page.

"Oh yeah, we went to a game yesterday" Isabella confirmed.

These tabloids are so quick with writing up their stuff, she thought. They had been to the game just the day before.

Game, Isabella frowned. If watching a cricket match could even be called a 'game', more like 'the episode' of a game.

They had sat on the stands all afternoon, sun-kissed and in the company of a light, fresh beer- luckily the weather had been wonderful- and watched the two teams throw the balls at each other.

Isabella had followed the game, feeling a little uneasy, not getting the rules at the beginning. What did Christopher say again about which team throws and when?

"So, wait who is that guy that caught the ball?" she had wondered out loud.

All the while throughout the game, Isabella had sat at the edge of her seat, doing her best to get the hang of the game. And failed.

"You are so funny" had been Christopher's answer to her question.

He had been sitting, relaxed and leaning on his back, the bruise on his cheek a little yellowy looking, his face amused as always.

"Relax, there's little action, it's more like a show"

"You are not helping me understand" Isabella had pouted a little and then had let out a sigh *"I give up on the rules"* she had leaned back at some point and let him wrap his arm around her shoulders loosely. Christopher had bent down to kiss her pouted lips then and they had made fun of the players for a while- Christopher pointing out how little athletic they were, with their tummies and slow motion running around.

Then the funniest thing had happened. The players had all walked away and people on the stands had clapped their hands and had begun to leave the stadium.

"What?" Isabella had opened her arms, palm up, in wonder. Why were they leaving? *"Did the game end like that? Where are they all going?"*

"It's tea brake. And the game is over for today" Christopher had delivered his answer with the cheekiest of grins on his lips. He knew what was coming, Isabella's hilarious outburst of sarcasm and he loved every little moment of it.

"You are kidding? Tea brake?" her eyebrows went up *"What do you mean over for today?"*

"Game lasts three days" he grinned.

"I am not coming back tomorrow" she stood up and put her hands on her hips and Christopher had made fun of her outraged face, all the way out of the stadium's gate.

She had wasted an afternoon, she had said. Isabella had at least expected to find out which team had won – and preferably understand why.

"When are you going back to your place?" Maria asked and Isabella was back to reality, back in Christopher's kitchen.

"I am going back home tomorrow, after a work thing" Isabella mumbled the last part.

It wasn't exactly about work, why Mr. Jenkins had asked to meet up but Isabella didn't feel like getting into that with Maria. With anyone. Especially not with Mr. Jenkins.

Her eyes went up to the ceiling, hearing a noise coming from upstairs. Christopher was changing. "I can't believe you read that trash"

"I read everything that has you on it"

"You should call my mother and get together sometime, form some sort of club" Isabella mocked Maria.

"Say what you want. My friend is on a tabloid with her new, famous, sexy boyfriend, I'm buying the magazine and covering the whole town with it, from wall to wall, if I want to. Salvo and Angela are going to have a fit"

"I couldn't care less" Isabella said, her voice emotionless "How are you? How are things going? Tell me about the nursery"

"Everything is good, we are just running a little late. We'll open late September"

Maria explained to Isabella how some permits they required were taking longer than expected.

"That's okay, you'll have all summer to advertise it" Isabella reassured her. It wasn't going to be a problem to postpone the opening of the nursery.

The door opened again and Christopher walked in the room, this time fully dressed and wearing black pants and a grey fitted t-shirt, a hoodie jumper casually hanging over his shoulder.

He moved around the kitchen silently, barefoot and with a certain satisfied look on his face.

Oh, I know that face, Isabella realized.

It was the look Christopher flaunted every time he had something crazy on his mind.

He checked her out, leaning on the kitchen counter, his hair still wet and ruffled, as he took a few grapes and brought them to his mouth.

His eyes locked with Isabella's and he smiled to the side.

Hot.

"Are we going out now?" she whispered, her hand over the receiver so Maria wouldn't hear.

He nodded and gave her a look- more like a smirk- so cheeky, Isabella wasn't sure what it meant.

Christopher walked around the counter again and stopped right behind Isabella. He placed both hands on the counter's surface, his chest brushing against Isabella's back- his lips inches from her shoulder- and set a small box on the table, right in front of her.

Isabella swallowed hard and her eyes grew wide.

They stayed on the box for an instant, trying to register its meaning and then turned to the side to stare at Christopher.

He glanced at her amused, curious to see her reaction.

'Open it' he mouthed the words and leaned in to kiss her briefly- the touch of his lips, like a shiver on Isabella's mouth.

"Uhm, Maria I have to go now" Isabella told her friend.

"Oh really? Why? Can't we talk a little longer?" she asked but then added "Is he there with you?"

"Yes" Isabella's wide eyes stayed on Christopher. "He just gave me a present"

"Oh, wow. What are you waiting for? Open it!"

"I am going to" Isabella laughed a little at her friend's excitement.

"Text me as soon as you can" Maria willed her.

"I will, love you"

"Love you, too"

Isabella put down the phone and eyed Christopher, who was now standing next to her, his back leaning casually on the kitchen counter, like he was cool and not bothered.

Like he didn't just give me a small box with jewelry inside.

"What is this?" Isabella took the small box in her hands.

"A late present for your birthday" he kept his face straight.

"You already got me something for my birthday and it was fantastic. Remember the visit to the aquarium?" Isabella looked up from the box and straight into his deep green eyes.

Christopher tilted his head to the side and said, "Just open it, baby"

Isabella's eyes went down to the box again and she gripped the upper part, slowly pulling it open. Her hands were shaking, the present being so unexpected and unneeded.

She had no idea what was inside of it, but already she knew it was too much.

For a moment, she didn't say a thing. Isabella just stared at its content, taking in the beautiful present Christopher had given her.

Earrings. Gorgeous small, white stone earrings.

"They are diamonds, of a rare kind. See the reflection of the light? They are slightly amber" he said, breaking the silence in the room.

"They made me think of you"

"They are so beautiful" *This is…too much,* Isabella shook her head and then turned his way.

"They are perfect for you"

Christopher took the sparkling stones out of the box and removed the ones Isabella was wearing- small white pearls.

He did everything slowly, his fingertips brushing against her cheeks, his fingers moving her hair to the side and Isabella felt the burning feeling spread in her stomach.

"They are discreet. One of a kind. Classy. Like you" he said slowly.

Christopher adjusted the second earing and, when he was done, he looked at Isabella and said:

"Absolutely perfect" he smiled content.

"They are beautiful but I can't accept them" Isabella said.

She stared at him, searching for the right thing to say but unable find the words she was looking for.

You could just say thank you, period.

"Yes, you can. They are yours" he leaned forward and kissed her gently. "It's also a thank you gift"

"Thank you gift for what?" Isabella murmured, her lips prickled against his.

"For staying here these three days, for taking care of me and putting up with me" he grinned.

"And you survived my cooking, I should be grateful" Isabella grinned, too.

She touched her left ear, her fingers drawing loops around the white stone. The earrings were absolutely gorgeous.

Christopher touched her chin, looked into her honey brown eyes and saw something that hadn't been there before.

It was something he had noticed after they had been back from Berlin, after the race, after the accident. But Christopher couldn't quite grasp its meaning, even though he was sure Isabella's eyes were trying to tell him something. Something important.

"You don't have to thank me" Isabella shook her head slightly. "These days have been incredible" she went on. "You don't have to get me presents…"

"I don't have to, Isabella" Christopher touched her chin again "I want to"

She closed her eyes and then opened them again, leaning in his hand.

I want you, I'm in love with you.

"Thank you for the earrings. Thank you for letting me stay, I had a great time" she said instead and blushed, embarrassed at herself for not having the courage to speak her mind.

Tell her to stay, tell her that having her by your side keeps all bad thoughts away. Tell her you love her, Christopher thought.

"Don't go then. Stay here with me" he suggested and Isabella smiled.

"I can't. I have a house remember. Actually no, I have my little hole waiting for me in Bayswater" she grinned a little. "Aren't you tired and bored of having me around all the time? During race weekends and in your house?"

"Impossible. You are so entertaining" he shook his head "I am anything but bored with you, especially when you hang around the house half naked"

"I don't walk around half naked" Isabella bashed her eyelids at him.

Maybe I do, just a little. I love the way he checks me out…

"I had so much fun. Apart from yesterday when you took me to the cricket game. I was so disappointed, just when I was getting the hang of the game it ended. Actually no, the first part of the game ended. So disappointing not to know the results, who won who lost…"

"We can always go again tomorrow for the final game" he grinned and then laughed at her funny face.

Isabella's stare said it all. She wasn't going to a cricket game ever again.

Not unless the tea brake they have involves cookies and scones for me as well.

"I want you to take this" Christopher said, as he gently opened Isabella's hand and placed a set of keys in it. "You can come and go as you please. Anytime you want"

Isabella looked down at their hands, at Christopher's keys and felt heat spread across her chest.

He had never had a woman over at his house- Christopher had told her the first time she had gone to his place. He had never shared his home with anyone and he was giving her free access to it.

Not the studio apartment in Mayfair, not to party, not for a quick fuck.

He wanted her to stay.

"Thank you" she smiled wide and stood on her toes, wrapping both arms around Christopher's neck.

His hands ran up and down Isabella's arms, as his deep green eyes got lost into hers. They were shining, Isabella's eyes, and smiling, like he had never seen them smile before.

"You know, I figured out how you could help me release some tension…" Christopher smirked.

"Really? How?" Isabella teased.

"Why don't you go get dressed? I'll wait for you in the kitchen" he touched her chin and leaned in for a kiss, slow and deep.

As their lips locked, his strong, big hand sneaked in Isabella's button up shirt and tickled its way up her body, lingering around her belly button.

Isabella gasped.

"You say you want me to go, you kiss me like you want me to stay" Isabella said, her hands moving slowly on Christopher's chest.

She looked up at him, with the eyes of a tease.

His kiss had left her wanting more, her lips a little swollen and prickly.

"That's because I can't get enough of you" he bent down to kiss her again and then added "Go get changed or we won't make it to the door, if you keep looking at me like that"

"Are you going to tell me where we are going this time?"

"Do I ever tell you where we are going?" Christopher smiled to the side, as he spoke.

"Are you EVER going to tell me where we are going?" Isabella asked, as she stood up from her stool defeated- knowing that she would never win that argument and get a word out of Christopher.

"Not a chance. Wear something comfortable and tie your hair up, Bresciani" he grinned "Now, let's go take a look at this fantastic blue sky"

Chapter 8

Ten minutes on the highway, Isabella let out a triumphant sound.

"Ha, got ya. We are going to the driver's academy. That's why you asked me to bring the camera with me"

Isabella changed gears – her left hand finding the movement so awkward and unusual, she failed to synchronize her movement. She grinded the gear.

Immediately, Isabella felt Christopher's alarmed eyes on her and she grinned.

"Maybe, maybe not. Maybe later" Christopher kept his voice casual. "Eyes on the road, Bresciani. This is the last time I let you drive my car"

"This is the last time I am coming with you, if you don't tell me where we are going first" Isabella scolded him.

"Nah, you are bluffing. You are too curious to pass" he said nonchalantly and Isabella mumbled something in Italian under her breath.

He figured me out already.

"Let's just say, you should be careful what you wish for" he smirked.

"What?" Isabella glanced his way, stunned.

"And you and I have unfinished business, signorina"

"Unfinished business?" she looked sideways at him. They definitely weren't on the same page. She had no idea what Christopher was talking about. "Now I am scared"

Christopher laughed hard, then placed a hand over her lap.

"I am kidding. I like messing with you Bresciani" he winked and pointed to the big sign to the left. "Take the next exit"

City Airport. Canary Wharf. M22. Isabella read the indications and got totally nothing out of it.

"Do you remember what you told me the first time we spoke?" Christopher asked.

Isabella scanned the memories, fast in her head. She remembered the event, up at the Olive garden roof restaurant in London. She recalled the moment Christopher stepped to the bar to speak to her. The conversation replayed in her head.

Yes, we flirted, flirted, flirted.

"I told you I didn't like Champagne and you nearly bribed the waiter to get me some more strawberries" she grinned.

"That's not all you said"

"I don't remember. I was too busy keeping you at a safe distance" she made a face and giggled.

Christopher chuckled, as he pointed to a gate entrance. The long dirt path seemed to lead to an old hangar.

Wherever they were, Isabella was sure of one thing. It surely wasn't the driver's academy.

She parked the car next to a SUV in the parking lot and turned to stare at Christopher, willing him to explain.

"That evening I told you I wanted to take you in the car with me, on track" Christopher told her.

"Yeah, I remember now and I elegantly told you to sod off" she took his hand and smirked.

"No, that's not what you said" Christopher shook his head and registered confusion on her face.

"I am not following you"

"This is the moment of truth, Bresciani" Christopher looked at her solemnly. "Let's see how brave you are"

"OKAY now I am terrified, Taylor" Isabella tightened her grip around his hand. "Just tell me"

"You have a choice. Get in a race car with me and go for a ride on track or… "

"Or?"

"Or follow me in that hangar and do what you told me that evening, when we met"

"I'll take my chances" she opened the car door and stepped out.

I couldn't have said anything worse than getting in a race car and drive at the speed of sound, Isabella mentally convinced herself.

Silently, they walked to the hanger side by side, Isabella couldn't help but laugh a little- nervous and excited at the same time, for what she didn't know was to come.

With his hand secured behind her back, Christopher guided Isabella through the door and her foot landed next to a colored, cloth looking object laying on the floor.

She took a step back and held her breath. Isabella looked around the room, stunned. She felt suddenly lightheaded, like all the blood in her body had rushed down to her feet.

Parachutes. Parachutes everywhere and bent down next to them, were men and women patiently folding them.

The people there barely even register them coming in, too concentrated, carrying out their tasks. Christopher said hi and they all mumbled something under their breaths.

"What the…" Isabella started to say, but a tall woman with long blonde hair greeted them.

"Hi, so good to see you again Christopher" the woman shook his hand and then turned to Isabella "Hi I am Sylvia, your instructor today" and she shook her hand, too.

"In-instructor?" Isabella stuttered.

"Your skydiving instructor" Christopher wrapped his strong arm around Isabella's shoulders and smiled wide.

"What?" Isabella laughed hard, unable to control herself.

Such a funny guy, she thought but then stopped laughing, seeing that no one else was.

"It's a joke, right?"

Christopher shook his head and smiled to the side, the dimples on his cheeks making a scene, like they were mocking Isabella.

"Do I ever joke about these things?" Christopher's eyebrow went up.

No, he doesn't. And he isn't.

"When I met you, you told me that you'd rather jump off a plane, than get in a race car with me" he started to say.

"I was joking! It was a joke, that's me joking" Isabella laughed again and stared at Christopher, gaping as he chuckled.

"So, what you are saying is that you'd rather get in a car with me instead and that you were just joking about the whole parachute thing?"

"I didn't say that either"

"You are free to change your mind" Sylvia the instructor cut in.

She told Isabella she could either listen to the briefing and how it all worked- skydiving in tandem with her, while Christopher would be by their side the whole time- or she could just say no. Either way she could back away any moment, even seconds before the jump.

"I am sorry Sylvia. Could we have a moment?" he said and Sylvia nodded.

"I'll be waiting in the briefing room, whatever you decide" she nodded and then disappeared through one of the metal doors.

Christopher turned, taking hold of Isabella's shoulder.

"You asked me earlier if there was anything you could do to help me release the tension"

"Yes, I did. I was actually referring to something not life threatening but you seem to have absolutely no limits" Isabella told him.

"It's not life threatening. You are safe with me" he said the words never losing eye contact with her. A shiver ran down Isabella's back. "You know that, right?" Christopher went on. "You are safe with me. I would never let anything happen to you"

"I know" Isabella nodded slowly, as a burning feeling spread across her chest not just for Christopher's words, but for how he was looking at her, like there wasn't anything he wouldn't do for her.

"And you are right, I have no limits" he looked up, proud.

"No, you don't" Isabella agreed, chuckling as she felt Christopher's hands move slowly up and down her shoulders.

"Limits don't exist" he raised his hand and touched her forehead. "They exist only here, in your head" his hand slid down slowly, only to linger around her shoulder blade, sending sparks all the way down Isabella's back.

"You have never skydived, I am guessing" he grinned and Isabella smiled.

"Have we met?"

She bit her lower lip and looked around the room again, at the people folding their parachutes, at how normal they all looked.

She imagined what were their everyday jobs, how they explained their unconventional hobby to their families and friends.

Bye mom, I am going to jump off a plane this afternoon, she imagined one of their conversations, like it was such an ordinary thing to do.

Normal people don't jump off planes in the afternoon, right?

She turned to Christopher again and noticed how at ease and overjoyed he looked. She could feel his energy, how excited the situation made him feel. The tense, nervous person she had seen a few days ago, seemed miles away now. Vanished somewhere. Her Christopher was back.

No, Isabella thought, *normal people don't jump off planes. Only extraordinary ones like Christopher do.*

"It's the most incredible thing I've ever done" Christopher said, interrupting her thoughts.

"How many times have you done this?" Isabella wondered and watched his crooked smile make a triumphant appearance on his lips.

"Several, I lost count"

Of course, is there anything crazy he hasn't done?

"I had no idea. I mean I knew you were absolute bonkers, but I had no idea you did this regularly"

"Nobody does" he shook his head. "Just you and the guys here. They keep my secret"

"Secret?" Isabella blinked at him.

"I am not allowed. I am breaking the rules. By contract, some of my sponsors don't want me doing this sort of things. Bungee jumping included"

"Why?" Isabella wondered out loud.

"Because to them I am worth millions, Isabella. I am a one million dollar note walking around. If I injure myself – out of the racing field- I won't be able to race. Less chances of the sponsors on my car being seen, no sponsor duties for me, less publicity, less money. I think it's best If I keep it a secret" he winked and then took her hands into his. "It is such an amazing feeling, to throw yourself into nothing. And today is the perfect day, too. Perfect weather"

"Perfect day to get ourselves killed" Isabella made a face and then smiled, as Christopher began to laugh hard- the look on Isabella's worried face too funny to resist.

Sarcasm, he thought and smiled to himself. That was the sign, the sign that she was coming through.

Isabella was giving in, slowly to the idea. She was checking the surroundings, reasoning with her fears and evaluating the pros.

"Look" he said, his deep, green eyes locked with hers. "These past few days you have been by my side, you have helped me deal with a lot of things… I trusted you, I believed you and what you said to me. I want to give something back to you. Trust me, believe in me"

"I trust you" Isabella mumbled and Christopher nodded.

"Do you trust me with your life?" he asked then and Isabella searched his face.

She nodded slowly, the butterflies in her stomach uncontrollable. Even if her feet were still on the ground, it felt like she was flying already.

"I trust you with my life"

"Then say yes. Jump with me. Do something reckless for once. Let me be responsible for both of us. Let me clear your head, ease the weight you carry on your shoulders. You've been carrying it for too long" he moved closer and brushed his lips on hers, Isabella's mouth on fire. "It's going to be great"

"I haven't said yes, yet" Isabella bit her lip again and shook her head, as Christopher took her by the hand and looked deep into her eyes, her worried and excited eyes.

"Then say it, say yes. Trust me on this. It's going to be incredible"

"My legs are shaking" Isabella let out a nervous laugh and looked around, not sure of what to say, what to do.

She saw Sylvia peak from the briefing room and smile. Isabella tried to smile back, but Christopher searched her face, his stare so intense again.

I need time to think...

"Don't say it. Don't say you have to think about it. You don't need to think about it. This is exactly the point. This is how I do things, this is what works for me. Don't say 'let's do it another time'. There is no other time. Now is the time. Together"

This is crazy, she looked down and breathed out. *Crazy like anything and everything we have done together so far.*

When she looked back up and met his stare again, Isabella knew it wasn't true.

That wasn't the craziest thing they had done. Being together was.

She had never met someone so different and yet so in harmony with her.

It was as though they were constantly taking each other by the hand, never forcing, never invading each other's space, never oppressing each other's personality, but always pushing the other to achieve more.

We compensate each other, Isabella thought and understood why he had taken her there, to that skydiving facility.

He needs this, he needs it to feel alive, to free his mind from the checkup, the races, the blackmailing... And he wants me to feel it, too. He wants me to feel free, to feel him, his soul.

"What about your health conditions? You were in hospital just three days ago"

"I feel great" he said quickly.

"No pain?"

"No pain. I feel okay." he shook his head. Then he smiled wide and lowered his voice a little "Come on, Isabella. You said you wanted to look at the sky, let's go check out the sky" Christopher winked.

"Okay" Isabella smiled and took in a deep breath, the excitement so palpable she felt her legs go soft a little. "Let's break the rules"

She raised her finger to his lips, as soon as he smiled wide. "Those hooks there better be strong enough. I am putting my life in your hands"

Christopher nodded and kissed her finger. Then, he looked up at her, as he took her by the hand, and said:

"I've never held anything so precious in my hands before"

...five, six, seven, eight, nine...

Isabella counted the people in the airplane again and again and thought that the excitement must have been playing silly tricks with her head.

She counted twelve people and it couldn't be right.

"How many on this plane?" she asked Sylvia, who was sitting right behind her -all buckled up and secured to Isabella by four, large, blue hooks.

She heard Christopher chuckle then and she shot him a dirty look.

As she looked away from him again, one of the hooks on her left shoulder caught her attention. For an instant, she thought it was unhooked.

It's fine, it's closed. I'm safe, she told herself and closed her eyes a moment.

For now, at least.

Her thoughts did absolutely nothing to calm her nerves, to ease the pain in her stomach.

So, my good sense is long lost. But what about my defense mechanisms? Quick, think of something else. Isabella looked around, hoping to find something else to focus on and found absolutely nothing.

Who was she kidding? She was flying at god only knew what speed, what altitude and with how many other crazy people like her and Christopher, waiting to jump off the plane with their pretty colorful parachutes.

I might be the craziest one of them all.

"There are twelve of us in here" Sylvia told her and explained how it was okay to be cramped inside the plane. They would all be jumping off in a few minutes.

"And I'll be all alone during landing" said the pilot up front.

"If you want company…" Isabella began to say and then grinned at the man, as he chuckled.

"Having second thoughts?" Christopher squeezed her hand and then moved a little closer, his warm breath tickled her ear. Isabella's stomach tightened.

"No. It's called 'survival instinct' but I don't think you two have met" Isabella said and saw him smile to the side.

"One minute to the launch" shouted the pilot and he turned a little, making sure they were at the exact spot planned ahead of the flight.

"Who goes first?" said Sylvia to everyone in the plane.

"US!!!" Isabella shouted and shut her eyes.

"Are you sure?" Sylvia enquired, stunned to hear her speak up first.

Isabella nodded and locked eyes with Christopher again. He was leaning forward, his chin almost brushing against her shoulder, curiosity written all over his face.

"I am scared I won't do it If I see him jump out first"

He doesn't even have an instructor with him, for crying out loud, a shiver ran down her spine. Christopher was going solo.

He had jumped several times before with an instructor and on his own. He knew how it worked and what to do.

"That's my girl" Christopher mumbled and held on to her hand a moment longer.

Then the sliding door opened and Sylvia did exactly what she said she would do in the briefing.

She pushed forward with her pelvis, all the way to the door, until Isabella was sitting on the edge of the plane- her legs safely pinned under the plane, like instructed.

Isabella kept her head up, holding back from looking down like Sylvia had told her, and gasped, terrified and mesmerized at the same time.

The view was unbelievable.

From up there, she could see the exact point where the horizon curved, where the sky ended and land began - where dreams came into the world and where reality resided.

Sunrays cut through the few clouds scattered around them and never Isabella had seen a sky so colored and bright. It was a slate of several blues and oranges. A thin yellow line seemed to mark the horizon, the exact point where the two worlds collided.

I am in the sky. And I am dreaming, were the only thoughts going through Isabella's head then.

The world looked incredibly grand and magnificent from up there and all her worries and doubts felt suddenly tiny and pointless.

A memory crossed Isabella's mind and it all felt so familiar to her.

She recalled the day she had gone on the London Eye with Christopher, how incredibly free to be themselves they had felt, secured in that glass capsule, floating above the city landscape.

It felt similar this time. Isabella had the same feeling of awareness, her eyes were wide open, her chest felt lighter. Nothing down there mattered, what was important was that they were up there, together.

She caught sight of Sylvia's hand on the side of the plane.

They were in position.

"READY?" her instructor screamed to the top of her lungs, as the wind blew wild in Isabella's face.

"YES" Isabella screamed with all her breath.

She said yes, without giving it a meaning. She said yes, because it was the right thing to say. She said yes and felt like screaming no.

There was a strong push from behind and Isabella felt her legs go loose.

They leaped out of the plane and into the immensity of the blue sky- into wide nothingness.

She gasped for air and dug the fingers in her suit, suppressing her first instinct to turn and stretch her arms up enough to grasp a ledge, a handle, anything that would help her not fall down that vortices of thin air.

Instead, Isabella stayed still, her chest paralyzed as if her heart had stopped beating the second her feet had left that airplane.

She let her body float into the void, like she had been told, and kept her arms crossed over her chest.

I am going to die, this is it. I am dying.

She gasped, searching for air. Air was everywhere, everywhere but in her lungs.

Suddenly, the sky was not blue anymore, it was white and cold, as they cut through a small cloud and Isabella felt water splash on her face.

Her cheeks were wet in a second.

Sylvia extended her arms in front of her. That was the signal, Isabella could open her arms like her instructor was doing and slow down their fall.

Are you okay? Sylvia asked with her hands.

Okay, Isabella turned both thumbs up.

She focused on the landscape below. It was breathtaking. Literally.

From up there, it was all brown and green and little spots of lighter colors.

Isabella smiled- the horizon, which had turned slightly orange, was so strangely close to her. She felt her stomach twist in a knot, the things she was seeing so intense she couldn't think but just feel.

How absurd, she thought to herself.

How odd it was to realize how intense emotions were, once she stopped thinking and concentrated on the emotion itself. Reasoning was just wrong sometimes, it destroyed the beauty of the feeling.

She felt the sky and how cold it was, she felt the colors, how incredibly vivid they were. Isabella felt the greatness of the world and the tininess of what she was. And she felt so strong. Alive.

Christopher was by her a few instants later. He put his thumb up and Isabella did too. They smiled at each other, as Christopher pushed his body slightly forward to grab her hand. He squeezed it tight and smiled, nodding as he patted her helmet with his other hand.

I got you, he seemed to want her to know, his fingers wrapped tight around hers.

I got you, she squeezed his hand too.

Christopher was right, she thought as she tried to smile, her cheeks too cold and paralyzed by the speed.

He was right. Her mind was clear, her chest felt lighter. They were nothing but air, thin cold air and everything that worried them or scared them had dissolved.

They had both left everything back in that airplane, back on the ground. They could see, really see things as they were. Both were free to feel, the purest of emotions. They were now free to feel, without limits, without consequences.

I feel you, she reached for his helmet and Christopher grabbed her other hand, their arms forming a circle as they dived through another cloud.

It lasted a moment, their closeness - as Sylvia did another one of her signals and Isabella knew her free fall was almost over- but Isabella realized the bond between her and Christopher was anything but over. They had never felt closer and irremediably into one another.

I trust you.

She closed her mouth and crossed her arms over her chest again, while Sylvia pulled the leaver and the parachute flew open. They were pulled with such energy, their legs flew up and their stomachs felt like had reached their throats.

"Legs up" Sylvia shouted.

They glided down slowly, the grass so close to them now.

"Up, up Isabella" she repeated and Isabella placed her hands under her knees and lifted her legs up, as much as she could.

A second later, she felt the grass snap against her suit and a thud, as Sylvia touched the ground first.

"Brilliant" Sylvia said and patted her shoulder. "Great job, Isabella" she added, as she started to unbuckle the first hook.

"Thank you so much" Isabella panted, her hand over her chest, and laughed out all the tension and the adrenaline rushing through her veins.

She waited impatiently to be untied, her legs shaky and strong, like she had all the energy necessary to run a marathon.

"It was incredible" she covered her face with both hands, as she stood.

Isabella turned to search the sky and spotted Christopher, just in time to watch him land. He touched the ground with the tip of his toes and ran a few meters before slowing down his pace, the yellow and blue parachute brushing against the grass.

"WOHOO" he screamed to the top of his lungs, as he laid down on the ground, arms and legs spread wide.

He laughed and breathed in and out fast, his heart beat loud in his ears. When he turned to look at Isabella- his face the perfect portrait of happiness- she couldn't stop herself from running towards him.

She ran fast the distance that separated them, while the rest of the group started to land all around, her heart beat humming loudly in her throat.

Christopher sat up with his helmet off, sexy crocked smile stamped on his lips, just as

Isabella jumped on him, sending him down on the grass again.

He laughed hard and grabbed on tight to her suit.

Her lips were on him immediately, hard and uncaring of anything and anyone around them. She heard people laugh but it was far away.

She noticed her mind, how carefree it so strangely was. Isabella listened to her chest and how light it felt.

She laughed to the world that was still spinning all around her, for how her legs were shaking, how her arms were aching- as all the tension was released from her body.

Adrenaline rush.

"How was it?" he grabbed her by her lower back and shook her a little, the excitement still pulsing in his veins.

"It was incredible" Isabella almost screamed and laughed, laughed so hard like she had never laughed before.

She tried to get up but Christopher pulled her back down, back on top of him and Isabella tilted her head back and laughed again, as her hair covered Christopher's face.

"Did you see her? Did you just see her, how good she is? My girl?" Christopher asked, turning to look at Sylvia and to the rest of the guys, that had landed immediately after him.

Some chuckled and some congratulated Isabella, for her first jump.

Christopher let her stand and took her hand, squeezing it tight like before, like when they had been flying down in the sky.

They kept eyeing each other, as they crossed the runway and headed back to the airport, smiling and giggling as the adrenaline started to wear off slowly.

"You were amazing" Christopher went on and kissed her hair, wrapping his arms around her neck. "Absolutely amazing" his voice so excited, Isabella couldn't help but giggle.

"And you are incredible" Isabella said and turned to kiss him again. "You live like there is no tomorrow and you make it all seem so easy. You make everything seem possible. Thank you. For making everything possible" she laughed a little as she spoke, her head tilted back. "I can't stop laughing"

Nor stop my legs from shaking.

"Then don't stop" Christopher kissed her again "Don't stop laughing, ever"

Chapter 9

That morning of all mornings, Isabella was on time.

She walked to the small coffee place near Bond Street Station, dodging people on Oxford street, holding on tight to her suitcase and laptop bag.

She was going home. After three fantastic days with Christopher, she was going back to her place.

And feeling like a stray cat again, dragging my stuff around.

She spotted Alfred Jenkins instantly.

In the light, brown wood décor of the coffee place, packed with people in suits, he stood out like a black sheep in a herd of whites, with his clean-shaven face and cold blue eyes.

He was sitting at a small table at the very end of the narrow room. There was already a coffee cup on his table, but it seemed to sit there, untouched.

He was deep in to reading a newspaper and he hadn't noticed Isabella walk in.

From afar, Alfred seemed relaxed, looking casual for the first time since Isabella had met him. She had never seen him wear anything but pants and button up shirt.

That morning, Alfred Jenkins was off the clock- she could tell by his polo shirt and jeans- and he looked younger for some reason.

Maybe work is what stresses him, what makes his face crinkle.

Isabella moved past the counter and smiled briefly at the members of staff behind it.

Mr. Jenkins looked up just a moment before she took a seat in front of him and his jaw tensed.

He glared at her in silence, as Isabella gracefully placed her suitcase against the wall, her bags on the floor and straightened her pink stripy t-shirt just before taking a seat.

"Hello" she said and watched his eyes travel from her suitcase back to her again. His lips sealed in a thin line.

He closed the newspaper and crossed his arms.

"I thought our conversation in Toronto had served its purpose" he said, ignoring her greeting.

"It did. I didn't say a word about what happened in Cannes" Isabella told him and held his stare.

His eyes, so hard on her, so severe, were difficult to face. Even the most innocent of innocents would have shaken a little.

It was the look of a man who wanted answers.

About me and Christopher.

"Don't play dumb with me" he sat up straight and moved a little closer "The conversation wasn't just about Cannes. It was about trust. Wasn't it?"

Isabella stood still, her face expressionless.

"You said you didn't trust me" Isabella reminded him.

"Exactly. And I was right" he snorted, a bitter smile appeared on his lips. "What is it that you want, Isabella?"

She shook her head, her eyes stayed on him.

"Cut the crap and make it quick. I don't have time for this. Let's hear it" he leaned on the chair again, like it was normal what he had just said, what he had just implied.

Isabella was after something, he was sure of it. Maybe money, maybe success, a little popularity.

It didn't matter. In situations like that one, the best thing was to know who you were dealing with straight away. And sort the issue as soon as possible.

"Excuse me?" Isabella shook her head a little.

"Money? Minute of fame? Or is there something else you want to tell me?" he glared at her, his glacial, blue eyes piercing hers, hoping to break her and hear the truth.

Alfred wanted her to say it, to admit it herself what he already knew.

"There is absolutely nothing I want to tell you. Because there is absolutely nothing I want from you, from anybody" Isabella's lips settled in a thin line with determination.

She had spoken her mind, for the first time she had told him exactly what she was thinking. No filters, no diplomacy, no kindness.

"Look, I don't know what's going on and what you are used to dealing with, but…" she began to say, but Alfred cut right in.

"I am used to people like YOU. Profiteers, leeches, gold diggers" he said every word slowly, his tone so pungent it dug a wound in Isabella's chest.

She sat there in silence, searching for the right words to make him see how wrong he was about her, failing to see a way out.

Whatever I say, he won't believe me. I've been sentenced already.

Alfred rubbed his chin and looked sideways, doing his best to keep his temper at bay.

"Don't give me that angel face. Just tell me what the hell you want. I know what you are doing, I know people like you"

"You are wrong about me" she informed him, her voice steady but Isabella could feel the veins in her neck tense.

She closed her hands into fists under the table, outraged for being treated the way Mr. Jenkins was treating her.

The way he has always treated me, really.

"I knew you weren't to be trusted, that innocent face, that humble look of yours. It might have worked with Christopher, but you never fooled me" then he leaned closer, his eyes menacing. "Tell me one thing, are you in this together?"

"What are you talking about?" she gaped at him, her eyes wide.

"If this is her doing, I want to know. I want you to stop working for MB from tomorrow and I'll give you anything reasonable you ask of" he kept his face straight "On condition you stop seeing Christopher this instant. Ask what you want and make it quick, I haven't got time to waste after people like you"

"I have no idea what the hell you are talking about" Isabella raised her voice a little, her face dark. "What is going on here?"

"You tell me. What do you two want? You have all you need, just leave Christopher alone. You parasites can run along and make money with someone else"

And she snapped.

Isabella stood up, just as the waiter was approaching them to take orders. Isabella waved him off, trying to be as polite as possible- anger and resentment pulsing in her veins- and then turned to look at Mr. Jenkins again.

"You know what?" she grabbed her bags with one hand and her suitcase with the other "I'm not going to sit here and listen to you be so disrespectful to me. But just so we are clear, I am not leaving MB, nor walking away from Christopher and I don't want anything"

Isabella turned but Alfred Jenkins stood up too and grabbed her arm. His hand on her skin made her even angrier for some reason. This man that had just insulted her was reaching out to her.

She turned, a look of death written all over her face.

"Remember this, I offered you the easy way out. You refused. I'll destroy you and that bitch. You tell her that" and he let go of her arm, a little rougher than he had meant to, but it was clear there were two people angry and upset in that coffee place.

For different reasons, for reasons that were irreconcilable.

Just when Isabella thought her day couldn't get any worse, it did. It actually did.

She walked towards her flat from the tube station, anxious to see if there were any photographers waiting for her outside.

Ridiculous it can't be, it's been three days and they know exactly where I have been, so why would they wait for me here?

She walked quickly, hoping it might do her good to let off some steam, after the unbelievable conversation with Mr. Jenkins.

Nothing, it didn't work. It kept coming back to her, every single word, every single detail and the anger was growing out of proportion.

Asshole, fucking asshole.

That was when she made a terrible mistake. Isabella tried to comfort herself with a very innocent, common thought.

It can't get any worse than this.

Of course it could have gotten worse than that. And it did.

Approximately ten photographers were waiting outside her building and three police officers were standing outside the door, one was going inside.

"Excuse me, sir" she walked to the door, through the journalists.

They recognized her instantly and suddenly it was just clicks and people calling her name for attention.

Isabella stumbled her way through, without saying a word, and walked up to the first police officer at the door.

"What's going on?"

"Who are you?" he asked.

"I'm Isabella Bresciani, I live on the first floor" she mumbled and looked in the stairwell, hoping to see Mrs. William somewhere.

"Please follow me, miss" he let her through the door and up the stairs "My colleague is questioning your neighbor"

"Why? What happened?"

A woman police officer stood in the corridor, next to a shaken Mrs. Williams, who smiled at the sight of Isabella and then started to weep.

"Mrs. Williams, what is going on?" Isabella reached out for her bony hand.

"I'm so sorry darling. I didn't notice, didn't hear them come in. They must have drugged me or something, I woke up with a headache…"

"What happened?" Isabella pressed on, nervous to find out what the commotion was all about.

"Somebody broke into your apartment" the female police officer said.

"What?" Isabella gaped, incredulous.

Then, she marched to her door and saw it was open, wide open, and her studio flat had been turned upside down.

Broken glass was all over the floor, curtains were down and the mattress had been tossed to the ground. It looked as if a tornado had gone by, leaving everything eerily out of place. And broken.

Oh, my God.

"Miss, would you like to sit down?" the police officer offered her a chair and Isabella nodded. She slumped on it and looked around, distressed.

"Please take your time to answer the question, but do you think there is anything missing?" he asked and offered some water.

Isabella took it and thanked the policeman.

How could she answer that? It was impossible to be sure if anything had been taken in that mess.

"I don't know. I have to tidy the room first" she mumbled, still in shock.

It wasn't about things going missing. She had no valuables in her flat.

It was more about her stuff being touched by strangers, foreign hands in her house, on her clothes.

Two pair of underwear hung on a chair, like they had been thrown from the drawer, in the eagerness to search it.

I have to wash everything, clean everything.

Isabella felt exposed and shocked, her intimacy violated.

"Is there anyone you want to call?" the female police officer asked.

Isabella nodded but really her mind was elsewhere. She was scanning the room for her things and asserting the damage.

I can't call Christopher. He's at the doctor running tests all morning.

Isabella dug into her bag and got hold of her phone, her hand shaky.

She dialed the number and heard it ring, while she scanned the room again still incredulous.

"Hi darling" Hillary's voice sounded in her ear.

She was the only person Isabella knew she could count on. Hillary would know how to help, what to do.

"Hi, Hillary. I know we were supposed to meet at the photo shoot in an hour, but something just happened and I might run a little late" and Isabella informed her of her morning surprise, of how her day had just gone from bad to worse.

"What's this called, again?" Isabella asked, holding her glass up.

"Switcher, it's a citrus beverage. It's typical from the Bahamas, where my family is originally from. But I added some Rum to yours. I think you need it today" Hillary said and poured her friend some more.

"Thanks. I sure do" Isabella nodded and took another sip.

The fresh, spicy liquid filled her mouth. It felt weird, how the icy bits in the drink became pungent like fire when they ran down her throat- the alcohol made her tongue a little numb.

Numbness, is what I am trying to achieve.

Isabella leaned her head on the wall behind her and closed her eyes for a second. Burglars in her house, she just couldn't believe it.

"I am sorry they stole your things. It's just horrible" Hillary shook her head slowly. "Bastards" she mumbled under her breath.

"I honestly don't care about the lenses, the camera and the cash I had in the closet. I can't believe they took my necklace. That's what I can't get over" Isabella kept her eyes closed a moment longer.

Money wise, the light blue pendant wasn't worth more than fifty pounds, but to Isabella it was invaluable. It was the necklace her grandmother had given her on her graduation- her nan's only piece of jewelry she had ever possessed in life. And now it was lost, it was in the hands of strangers and gone forever. The police had been very honest about it. Chances to find her things were down to zero.

When Isabella opened her eyes again, Hillary was still there staring at her, a sympathetic smile on her face.

She looked outside - from the small window near the sink- and hoped the situation at the front door had changed.

Nope.

"Why are they still here? What do they want?" Isabella shook her head and took another sip of her drink.

There were still a few photographers talking on the sidewalk, even though the police had left half an hour before.

"Some action. They are probably waiting for Christopher to come over"

"They'll be waiting a long time, I'm not going to tell him to come over"

"I have this uncontrollable desire to shout 'Nothing to see here' out the window" Hillary grinned "Why don't you stay with me a few days?" Hillary offered.

"That's really nice of you, but don't worry. You have done so much for me already, helping me with the police and getting my head around sorting my stuff"

"Stop thanking me, I told you already" Hillary smiled and took a sip of her drink. She was having sparkling water. "Have you called Christopher, yet?"

"No" Isabella admitted and stared at her manager. "I haven't told him yet, I haven't told him about the conversation with Mr. Jenkins either" Isabella added.

But she had told Hillary alright- unable to hold back the desperation, after the intimacy of her flat had been breached.

Isabella had spilled it out, all of it, even that she knew someone was playing with Christopher's head and Mr. Jenkins thought she was involved.

"You have to speak to him, darling" Hillary said.

"Yeah, I know. I will, tonight after the photo shoot" Isabella brushed her bangs out of her eyes. "It's not easy to talk to him. He's always so elusive, he tries not to overthink things too much. I mean we talk about silly things, we flirt, make fun of each other but I feel like there is still a wall between us. We are both trying to bring it down, slowly, cautious not to get our feelings hurt. But we are still stuck, alone, each one of us on one side of it"

"Wow. You are good with words, in describing your emotions" Hillary looked impressed. "That's why I hired you" she added and winked.

"It's your Switcher here. Keep filling my glass and I'll write a bestseller for you" Isabella raised her glass and watched her boss laugh and cheer with her very own glass. Of sparkling water.

"Why are you not drinking? I mean, fine I am the winner of the worst day contest but surely you could be a little more sympathetic and join my alcoholic nonsense" Isabella grinned at Hillary.

She would later remember that as her last grin of the day. The last grin as the winner of the worst day contest.

"I am pregnant" Hillary said as soft as she could, her lips a little shaky.

The words shot out of her like a bullet, nonetheless.

"What?" Isabella mouthed.

"I am pregnant" Hillary said again and looked down at her hands. "And scared as fuck"

"But" Isabella began to say, but the words didn't come out of her mouth.

"It's Alfred's of course" Hillary said quickly, in case Isabella had any doubt of the sort.

Of course, it was Alfred's, Isabella could see it written all over her face.

Maybe Hillary was scared, but it wasn't just that. There were other emotions there.

She looked worried like any soon to be mother, but she was also happy. It was the sort of worry that came with an incredible joy, the worry of failing or not being worthy of something beautiful, extraordinary like motherhood.

"What are you going to do?" Isabella almost mumbled the words, afraid she might hurt Hillary's feelings.

She looked at her friend from tip to toe and saw that she wasn't any different. As if being pregnant came with a big giant poster that said, *"Knocked up and fabulous"*.

Hillary was though, she was exactly that. Fabulous.

Fabulously radiant- her dark skin had never been so smooth.

Fabulously calm – when had she ever been so calm? Isabella couldn't remember her sitting still for that long.

"I know this isn't how things should go. I mean, I didn't know until we got back from Berlin the other day. I certainly didn't plan this. I probably got pregnant in Cannes. We have broken up since then" Hillary explained.

She told Isabella she had no intention of becoming a mother, ever. It was something she had never thought about, she had never found a man that would make her dream about getting married and start a family.

"I will tell Alfred. I will inform him, but I don't care what he thinks or what anyone thinks. I don't need anyone's approval. I am keeping this baby. Baby and I will be just fine"

"Good" Isabella smiled warmly. "And I like the name you chose. 'Baby'…good call"

Hillary laughed a little, but it didn't last- her joy.

Isabella's phone made a sound and she hold in her breath.

Christopher.

"Don't tell him, please" Hillary begged her in a haste "Not before I tell Alfred"

"I won't tell a living soul" Isabella reassured her.

She placed a hand on her manager's shoulder and smiled.

Despite what Mr. Jenkins thinks, I can be trusted.

Then Isabella's eyes were back on the screen.

"Hey baby, how are you?" the text said.

Baby, I should be used to him calling me baby by now, she bit her lip and smiled. *Nope, still loving it.*

"I am good" Isabella texted back.

Just got smacked around by your manager and burglars paid me a little visit but I am good! What a morning.

She shook her head a little and carried on *"What did the doctor say?"*

Isabella checked the time and looked back at her manager.

"Would you like anything to eat?" Isabella stood up but Hillary reached out for her arm, making a face.

"No, thanks. I am basically eating little snacks all day. I am in that stage were everything makes me sick. I don't think I can hide it for long. Fred is already looking at me funny" Hillary frowned and touched her stomach.

Another sound, another text from Christopher.

"Doctor said I am good to go. I can start training again. How about dinner tonight after the photo shoot?"

Isabella texted back quickly.

"I am so happy for you. Sounds great. In a meeting with Hillary. Talk to you later" and her attention was back on Hillary.

They spent the next half an hour talking about work, while Isabella's washing machine whistled in the background – all her clothes, with the exception of the stuff she had carried around in her suitcase from Christopher's house, needed to be cleaned. The idea of strangers touching it made her freak out all over again.

"Honey, I should get going or I'll be late for the photo shoot" Hillary announced and got up from the chair. "Don't worry about coming. It's fine. Go sign the deposition at the police station. It's just a photo shoot today, I can handle it"

She picked up her handbag and secured it over her shoulder, over the light blue sundress she was wearing. Hillary's hands moved down to her stomach again and she made a face.

"Do you feel sick?" Isabella asked, alarmed all of a sudden.

And terribly guilty for having her help me out, when she is pregnant.

"I'm so sorry I called you up. I didn't know that you were..." she added but Hillary held out a hand in front of her.

"That's exactly why I don't want to tell people about it. I am still me, I'm not sick. I think I'd go all nine months without saying a word about 'Baby', If I could. But I have a feeling I'll look like a blimp soon" she made a face again, this time though Hillary looked down at her tummy as she did.

She looked great and not the least bit overweight. And she was almost in her second trimester.

"Do you think I could get away with it, by saying I'm bloated because under meds? That way, nobody would have the guts to piss me off AND I could avoid the extra attention on me and Baby" her eyes were wide, as she nodded.

Isabella covered her face and laughed hard.

"Ha, but that way you'll miss out on all the extra favors you can ask people. Think about it, you in the boxes going 'Guys, I can't pick this up. Could you help me?' or better 'I'm so in the mood for ice cream, who can get some for me?'"

"You are right" Hillary nodded and headed to the door. Isabella followed, her hand firm on Hillary's wide shoulders. "I could use a little pampering from the boys"

"Do you want me to call you a cab?" Isabella asked, just as her boss walked outside her door. Hillary turned and smiled, the dark skin of her face so smooth and shiny from the heat that day. Maybe her cheeks looked a little rounder or was Isabella just imagining it?

"No thanks hun. I can do it"

Isabella nodded.

Yes, yes you can, Isabella thought. And she was going to do it. All on her own, if necessary.

Chapter 10

Before she could see the car, Isabella heard the sound as it pulled over on Queensway Road. She took a glimpse from the kitchen window and watched Christopher get out, his face serious, wearing sunglasses, his training gear still on.

The two photographers outside took a few shots, but Christopher walked ahead and crossed the street without even acknowledging them.

He ran up the stairs, four by four and took Isabella in his arms as soon as his hands took hold of her tiny shoulders.

He kept her close to his chest and kissed her hard, his lips burning like fire onto hers.

"Are you okay?" he asked, still holding her tight.

"I am fine, Chris" she managed a smile, as her stomach tied in a knot.

It feels so good to be so close.

"I am sorry this happened to you. Did the police have any clue who might have been?" he asked, as they walked inside the flat and Isabella closed the door shut behind her.

"No. They said they would check the security cameras on the street but they weren't very optimistic. I don't even care who was it. I am just really upset they stole my necklace"

"What necklace?" Christopher asked, taking a seat on the small dark couch.

"It was a silver necklace with a light blue pendant. I wore it a few times" she told him.

Even the night we first met, she thought and the memory made her heart sulk even more.

Isabella shook her head.

"Anyway, it was my grandmother's. She gave it to me when I graduated from Uni. I was the first person in our family to graduate. It was precious to me. And I usually always have it with me"

Isabella held her head with both hands and then brushed her hair back, struggling to come to terms with it all.

The necklace was lost, forever and she couldn't forgive herself for not taking it to Berlin with her.

Christopher took her hand and pulled her on the couch. Isabella slumped on top of him and he took her legs in his lap.

"Why didn't you call me immediately?" he asked, his hands rubbing her back.

"You were busy. You had a busy morning. I thought it was best to tell you once you were done with the photoshoot"

"I would have come over to help you"

"I wanted you to run all the tests. I don't want to be a distraction"

"Fuck the tests, you are not a distraction. You are important to me. I would have come to you immediately" he cupped her face and Isabella leaned in it, her heart warming up to his words.

"Whatever. Pack your bags, signorina. You are coming with me"

"What? Where?" Isabella asked, her eyes wide now.

"You are not staying here. This place isn't safe" Christopher held her stare.

"Chris, this is my house. The police said they were probably junkies and they won't be back, since they hardly made five hundred pounds in here" she looked around and added "I am not letting a burglar scare me out of my own house. I'll change the locks"

Christopher shook his head, as she spoke.

"I am not letting you stay here. I could never sleep, thinking someone might come in at night"

"How about you stay here with me tonight and make me feel safe?" Isabella smiled to the side and ran a hand over his strong arm.

"How about you move in with me and I'll make you feel safe every day, in my house, where there are actual doors, with actual locks"

"Don't mock the shoebox, Christopher" Isabella tilted her head to the side and made a funny face. Then she looked at him and caressed his shoulder. "Look, I loved being with you these past few days but I think it's a little early for us to move in together. We just started seeing each other"

"And exactly when is the right moment to move in together, Isabella? Who makes the rules?" he said and smirked, enjoying the series of funny expressions going on Isabella's face, as she thought of what to say next.

"I have a lot of stuff" she pointed around the small apartment.

"I have a lot of space" Christopher retorted.

"I don't know. What if you get tired of me?" she tilted her head to the side.

Christopher's hand slipped under her top and snaked up behind her back, sending shivers of pleasure across her entire body.

"I can't get enough of you" he mumbled and moved in a little closer, running a hand through her hair. "Let's break the rules, signorina"

The rest of the week went by so fast, Isabella hadn't even noticed it was already Saturday when she had a chance to speak to her friend Cristina and tell her about living with Christopher.

Skimming through cereals and walking down the cookie aisle, Isabella took out her phone and dialed her friend's number.

"Are you sitting down?" was the first thing Isabella asked when Cristina had answered the call.

"I hate when people say that. It gets me all nervous. I can say 'yes I am sitting down' and maybe I am not, you can't see me so what's the point..."

"Jesus, Cristina. You are in a good mood today" Isabella's eyes went wide. She pursed her lips and examined a packet of chocolate cookies. "What's going on?"

"Nothing, nothing I am just very tired. I keep going back and forth from Milan to Rome. I am just so happy it's Saturday today. I can relax... but then you call and say that..." Cristina said, her voice playful now.

"Sorry, you know me. The drama queen" Isabella giggled and went on. "I'm just going to say it. Wait. I should have called you up and just blurted out the news, plain and simple. Can I hang up and do it again?" Isabella played along.

"Just say it, Isabella for the love of God"

"I am living with Christopher" she told her friend.

Plain and simple and so incredibly fantastic, she thought her stomach jittery.

When had she ever lived with a man? Never. She had always lived on her own, Isabella had always been put off the idea of sharing her house with someone.

Salvo had been living in her hometown, while she had been in Rome living with a friend.

"It's easier for me to live in the city, for work" Isabella had always told her boyfriends.

And even when one of her exes was living in Rome, they had never taken the big step to move in somewhere together and leave their friends' apartments.

"Oh, wow. Isabella, it's a big step… huge for you" Cristina pointed out, her voice so surprised, the news had been unexpected.

She knows me too well.

"It really isn't" Isabella shrugged it off.

It really wasn't. It didn't feel like a big thing. It didn't feel weird or annoying or unnatural to share her things with Christopher. It was absolutely fantastic to live with him, so amazing Isabella couldn't stop smiling.

She explained to her what had brought her there- in Christopher's house in Maida Vale- and she told Cristina their days together, how Christopher worked out and went out to the MB facility to run on the simulator, while she was out with Hillary most of the times, working on the blog and preparing the next race in Rome. They would only see each other in the evenings.

"Is he okay now?" Cristina asked, wondering if Christopher's physical conditions had improved since he was back on his schedule.

"He's doing great" Isabella said and moved down to the wine section, to pick a good bottle of red.

Her eyes scanned her little food basket and nodded. She had everything she needed to make dinner that night, time to head to the check out.

"How's the sex? Still hot?"

"Always hot" Isabella bit her lip and welcomed the fire in her gut, rethinking about last night.

"What's that sigh about? You can tell me, I am sitting down" Cristina mocked.

"Brace yourself, Cristina. It was hot and messy last night" Isabella lowered her voice and set her things on the self-check-out station.

She beeped the first item and began to tell her about their steamy encounter the night before.

It had all started in the kitchen. First, they had glanced at each other from the living room to the kitchen counter, where Isabella was working. She had looked up from the pizza dough she had had her hands in- her hair pulled up behind her head, just a stray stand brushed to the side over her right eye- and Christopher's stare had made her stomach clench.

He had crossed the room, only to sit opposite her on a stool and he had asked if it was okay for him to watch.

"Sure thing" Isabella had moved back the strand of hair with her arm and she had then walked around the kitchen, looking for some tools to spread the dough.

"Do you always make pizza in your underwear and t-shirt?" Christopher had asked, studying her back and perfectly toned legs.

"Only when you behave" Isabella had given him a sly smile and had turned around, her back to him, bending forward, as she went through a drawer of utensils.

Her shirt went up a little on her back, revealing her full round bottom and Christopher stood, his hands aching to touch her.

He had come up to her in his calm, cool stride, only to stop behind Isabella and help her look through a wide drawer under the kitchen sink.

"Found what you were looking for?" Christopher had whispered in her ear, as they had both bent a little forward, his hands slipping in between her thighs.

His touch had sent Isabella in ecstasy. She had closed her eyes, taking in a breath and had leaned back, her head against his broad shoulder.

"I think so. Did you find what you were looking for?" she teased, as her eyes opened again and looked into his, burning with desire.

His mouth was down to hers in a second, his lips a little hard on her, his hand pulling her hair a little roughly, making Isabella moan against his passionate kiss.

Christopher's other hand had stayed in between his legs, it had dug in her underwear, making her arch her back instantly, as she had moaned his name.

"Chris" she had breathed out in a small cry.

"Spread your legs for me, baby" he had groaned against her lips, as his hand had guided her body forward on the kitchen counter, only to slid under her shirt, while the other had pulled down her panties.

"Okay, now I need to sit down" Cristina mumbled from the other side. "That is so hot. Kitchen sex, so hot"

"You talk like you and Carlo don't have it anymore" Isabella pointed out, her cheeks a little flushed, while she made her way out of the supermarket, bags in one hand.

"We do but we have the kids around all the time. It's not as easy as before"

"How are the twins? I miss them so much" Isabella made a little sweet voice, thinking about Cristina's kids. "I bought them loads of chocolate for when I come to Italy next week.

"Only if you pay for the dentist, too" Cristina teased and Isabella laughed a little, as she made her way up the high street, Christopher's house already in sight.

The small gate made a loud sound while pushing it open and Isabella announced she was home.

"I am about to walk in" Isabella said, her keys turning in the lock "Will I see you in Rome next week?"

"I am not sure when but I will come down as soon as I can, okay?" Cristina said and Isabella was about to say something back, when the door sprung open and her eyes set on Christopher and Mr. Jenkins in the living room, talking – maybe discussing animatedly was more what they were doing.

"I got to go now. Speak to you later" Isabella told her friend and hung up.

Her handbag slipped down from her shoulder to her arm, as she looked from one man to the other, their lips sealed now, both staring at her.

"Hi" Isabella said to Mr. Jenkins, who grunted something that sounded vaguely like a greeting.

"Hey, baby" Christopher said and Isabella took a few steps towards him, as the door closed shut behind her.

She walked over and they kissed quickly, Mr. Jenkins' curious eyes burning behind her back.

Christopher held her by the shoulder and smiled.

"Making more pizza tonight?" he smirked and almost laughed, seeing Isabella's freckled cheeks turn red.

"Is everything okay?" she asked him, her eyes going to the side, to where Mr. Jenkins was sitting.

"Everything is okay. You need help with that?" Christopher took hold of the bag, but Isabella pulled it back a little, shaking her head.

"I got it" and she gave him a small smile, making her way to the kitchen.

Slowly, Isabella placed all the things on the counter and started putting them in the shelves, while the two men eyed each other in silence.

It was only, when she was almost finished that Christopher started talking again.

"Really, what is the point in discussing this? We shouldn't even be talking about it anymore" he shook his head and placed his hands in his trouser pockets.

"The more we let this go, the more it's going to get worse" Mr. Jenkins said and looked at Isabella as he spoke, her eyes looking up from the brown paper bag on the counter.

She saw him squint and Isabella walked out of the kitchen, ignoring his cold stare.

"I am going upstairs" she announced and passed by Christopher, touching his arm briefly.

"Why don't you go get ready?" he smiled. "We are going to a friend's club opening tonight, if that's okay with you"

"Oh…Sure" Isabella nodded and resumed her walk to the staircase. "Mr. Jenkins"

"Isabella" he grunted and sighed loudly once she was out of the room.

Isabella had made it to the top of the stairs, when Alfred's voice was back full on.

"You are fucking mad"

"You are out of order" Christopher raised his voice too this time.

"You are making the same mistakes over and over again. Why the hell is she living here with you? Christ, you have to fuck every single woman that crosses your path" Alfred's spat as he spoke and even though Isabella couldn't see his face, she knew exactly what it looked like. It was probably red and the veins stretched out all over his neck.

"This has nothing to do with the mistakes I made in the past" Christopher pressed on, his voice harsh.

"Look at this" Alfred made a sound and Isabella realized they were footsteps.

He's walking towards Christopher, Isabella asserted.

"Here it is. Right in front of you. All your stupid mistakes, written here. Almost all of your 'mistakes, your women' is in this fucking piece of trash of a book. They've all agreed to talk. How you fucked them, when you fucked them, the presents you gave them. Your weaknesses, your nightmares. Your nights out, taking shit and drinking. Every detail. There's enough material here, you want to add another page or two with Isabella?" Mr. Jenkins questioned him, this time his voice was a notch lower.

Christopher walked around the room, away from Alfred in silence. He brushed his hair back and shook his head.

"We are not just fucking here. I am serious about her" Christopher said. He pointed a finger and his jaw tensed. "Don't you fucking talk about her like that again, do you hear me? I care for you, you know that. You are like a father to me. But don't ever talk about her like that. Ever. Again. Or you walk out of here and our work agreements are off. Clear?"

Isabella sucked in a breath, the sudden eerie silence in the room was deafening. She heard her heart beat hum in her ears, as Mr. Jenkins stood there before Christopher, motionless and stunned.

"Are we clear?" Christopher asked again.

"Yes" Alfred snapped back. "Yes, clear" he said again, this time his tone was normal. "Just tell me you'll think about it. This is our last chance. We can walk out of this with a biography, a new agreement if you sign the contract making the biography official. They'll trash all this crap. You'll have some control on the content"

"It's the 'some control' part that makes me laugh" Christopher said and he did.

He laughed, a little. It was a nervous, disgusted sort of laugh. The laugh of a person that doesn't believe a single word he's hearing.

"I'm not giving her what she wants. She's nothing to me, not anymore. She doesn't exist and I don't want to give her the satisfaction of making money with my name, my father's name"

"She'll make money with your name either way, Christopher. Even if you don't authorize the book, she's going to tell this story. It depends how you want her to tell it"

Christopher went quiet again, as Mr. Jenkins' deep voice bounced off the living room walls again.

"Just promise me you'll give it a thought. Don't be stupid, Christopher. Think about it"

"I'll think about it" he agreed and within a few minutes, Alfred let himself out, not turning back.

Walking to the club, Isabella had a déjà-vu.

Suddenly, she was dragged out of adulthood, back to high school and it was that terrible moment of the year again. The moment she dreaded all year long- picture time for the school yearbook.

I just hate having my picture taken.

True, she wasn't wearing braces this time. No weird looking clothes – that once were considered trendy and nowadays looked like something you'd pick up in the garbage.

This time Isabella was wearing a designer dress and she was pulling it off like a diva.

Divas don't trip over, Isabella. Divas don't count the seconds till they'll get their heels off. Isabella looked down at her black, silky sandals and smiled to herself.

No, she wasn't a diva. She wasn't someone to follow around like the hottest, jet setting top model and she didn't care.

Isabella caught Christopher looking at her as they approached the club – a long queue was already forming at the left-hand side of it- and acknowledged that that look, the one he was giving her, was what mattered to her and nothing else.

He couldn't keep his eyes off her. It wasn't just the way she looked that night, it wasn't just how Isabella strutted in that short, light pink dress she had chosen for the evening.

It was the worry and excitement of being in the spotlight, her body seemed to vibrate every time his hand moved on her body, on her hips and over her shoulder.

Isabella was an open book, her feelings so strong and so hard to cover up made Christopher smile content.

She kept her head down as much as she could, Christopher's arm firm around her waist, while the photographers followed them almost to the door.

The flashes went on and off over their faces and she couldn't help but nervously pull down at her dress a little. It suddenly seemed too short, too flashy, too revealing.

"You look absolutely fantastic" Christopher leaned into her and whispered in her ear.

His lips wandered around her lob for a few instants, brushing slightly against her skin.

Isabella smiled and pushed her hair back a little, tilting her head up.

She looked at Christopher and mouthed the words 'thank you', as someone shouted in the crowd, just when they were about to get through the door.

"Christopher, Isabella. Just one more"

They turned in the man's direction and Christopher waved.

"Ha, they are onto you. They got my name right this time" Isabella said and they turned to look at each other, smiling.

More flashes lit their skins in the dark side street.

"Maybe I should kiss you, give them something nice to put on those magazines of theirs"

"Don't you dare" Isabella giggled and pulled him towards the entrance.

He walked slowly, his usual cool stance, totally at ease with a photographer walking backwards, in front of him to get one last shot. *This is not just a club opening, this is a top event.* Isabella thought and lowered her head again, hoping to avoid that last picture.

"Wow this is really a grand opening. So many people and the press…" Isabella looked around, as they made their way in.

She had already spotted a few models – male and female- some TV producers and British actors.

"My friend is popular around here" Christopher told her and he smiled and waved to someone to the front of the queue.

"Who is your friend?"

"Harry Craven"

"Harry Craven???"

Christopher nodded and watched Isabella's face change, as she realized who they were talking about.

"You mean that Harry Craven, the most popular DJ and music producer in the last ten years?"

"The one and only"

Isabella turned ahead, registering the beauty of the club, as the music pounded in her chest.

"Now I get what the commotion is about" she murmured more to herself than to Christopher.

It was impossible to hear anything but the loud, funky house music in the room. Christopher slapped hands with a couple of people- who eyed Isabella and nudged her- as they passed by and went deeper inside the club.

"This way" Christopher said, leaning into Isabella and breathing in her scent.

It was light, sweet and flirty. She smelled of lavender and fruit. Christopher looked at her flushed cheeks from all the attention they had received outside a moment before, and went down to her neck, planting a slow but intense kiss on her shoulder.

He watched her body shake a little, as he raised his head and took her hand, locking eyes with Isabella.

She bit her lip then and smiled, Christopher's stomach tightened.

"What's the matter? Want to follow me to the bathroom for old times' sakes?" Isabella shouted over the music, leaning forward, her hand wrapped around his nape. She moved closer, her hip against his, her eyes not hiding the pulsing desire to be touched.

Those lips, he thought, as he rubbed his thumb over them.

"Did you do what I asked you before?"

No underwear, Isabella recalled his last words to her back home.

She nodded and bashed her eyelids a little, enjoying Christopher's aroused expression on his face.

"Not that I don't believe you, but I'd like to check that out" he said and planted a kiss on her lips, while his hand moved to her hips.

Isabella gasped against his mouth, as he smoothed down her skirt looking for the seam of her panties.

There wasn't any.

He kept his eyes on her, the unaware crowd of people dancing around them, as Christopher's hand went down to her thigh.

"Chris" she sucked in a breath and took hold of his wrist.

He smiled then, his crooked sexy smile and placed his hand around her waist again.

"Good girl" he said. "Let's go" and guided her to the back of the room, where his friends were sitting. They had a table and they had already spotted him and Isabella.

"Chris, over here" a tall man with blonde hair and bright blue eyes shouted. He waved at them and Christopher waved back.

Harry Craven.

Isabella did her best to dodge the people on the dance floor, while she eyed the table they were directed to.

Four men and two women, she registered.

They were all smiling and talking amongst themselves. A brunette was dancing a little with a short man that had his back to Isabella.

"Hey, it's good to see you mate" Christopher grasped Harry Craven's hand and shook it hard.

He patted his friend's shoulder and then placed his hand behind Isabella's back.

"Harry, this is my girlfriend Isabella"

"Nice to meet you" Isabella said and smiled, as Christopher's words sparked a fire in her chest.

Girlfriend.

"My pleasure, Isabella. And welcome to my club" he took her hand and kissed it gently, his piercing blue eyes smiling more than his lips.

Chapter 11

Harry Craven stared at her from across the table, like Isabella was some sort of a rare animal that risked extinction.

While Isabella had indulged in small talk with his girlfriend Cecilia, she had noticed him staring and it had made her cheeks flush red.

Damn cheeks.

And Harry was still staring, even after Christopher had gotten up to get them a drink.

"I am sorry" he shouted over the music.

Isabella shook her head and leaned forward.

"I said I am sorry"

"About what?" Isabella shouted and shrugged.

"I am staring at you and it's making you uncomfortable"

Yeah, it is. Now stop.

"It's okay" she lied and thanked the loud music for once, for not giving her voice away.

Harry moved closer and looked around before going on.

"It's just that I have never seen him on a date before" he said, referring to Christopher.

Isabella's eyes widened for a moment but then she shrugged.

"Surely, Christopher has had dates before" she grinned, as Harry chuckled and sipped his drink before pressing on. "Quite a few, actually"

"True. But it's the first time I hear him introduce anyone as his girlfriend. Christopher is very reserved about his personal life, so it's a pleasant surprise meeting you" he smiled warmly, before handing her another glass of Long Island Ice Tea.

"Oh, not for me thanks. I've had one too many already" Isabella politely declined the offer and smiled back. "But thanks for your kind words. And congratulations this place is amazing"

Isabella looked around the room, the club packed with people, the music so good she couldn't refrain herself from swaying to the music a little, even if sitting on the small couch.

Her eyes wandered on the dancefloor a moment longer, until she spotted Christopher at the bar, waiting to place their orders, speaking to a couple of women, phone in hand.

Maybe the phone was ringing, Isabella couldn't know for sure, but she could tell he wasn't listening to the two gorgeous women that had come up to speak to him.

Christopher eyes kept going down to the screen, his face tense like he was contemplating answering or not.

"Thank you. It's a pleasure to have you here tonight. It's a pleasure meeting the charming woman that stole my friend's heart" Harry said and shook her hand.

Isabella turned to face him again and smiled, this time though it didn't reach her eyes.

Harry's words echoed in her mind, as her eyes took another glimpse at Christopher standing at the bar.

Maybe I've earned his heart, but what about his trust? Isabella thought and her mind went back to the conversation she had overheard between him and Mr. Jenkins again.

She was still in the dark, she still had no idea what was really going on, who was blackmailing him and what was worrying Christopher so much.

"I'll be doing a DJ set soon, it's better if I get going. Drinks are on me at this table. Order anything you like" and just like that Harry stood.

He towered the small table and couches, shaking hands with everyone there and taking his girlfriend Cecilia with him through the VIP area.

Isabella stared at them, as they made their way through the tables, thanking people for being there and making sure they were all having a blast.

Her attention was back on the bar a moment later, only Christopher was gone.

He wasn't there, nor walking back to the table with drinks. He was nowhere to be seen and it was getting harder to recognize anyone in the room, as people kept walking in the club.

As Harry stepped on the DJ control station, the lights dimmed and the crowd cheered. He welcomed everyone and someone in the room shouted his name.

Everyone was standing up now, as they clapped their hands and screamed, waiting for Harry's first track.

Isabella joined in the cheering at the table and nodded to Chloe, who was telling her what an incredible DJ Harry was- always in the first top ten with his hits, always keeping up with the trends.

It wasn't until they had sat down again, more Long Island Ice Tea going around at the table, that Isabella noticed someone was standing near her.

"May I?" Giselle shouted over the music to Chloe, who simply shrugged and nodded, too surprised to say anything.

Even if the lights were dim, Isabella recognized her perfect, slender silhouette instantly.

And for the first time Giselle recognized her too.

This is what it means to be in the spotlight, on those damn magazines. Isabella thought as Giselle stared at her in silence for a moment.

This time Isabella wasn't invisible, not like that night in Berlin when she had stood behind Giselle, as she had made her move on Christopher.

"So, it's you" Giselle said the words, like they needed to be spoken out loud, for how absurd it all was. She looked at Isabella from top to toe and smiled, the fakest of smiles.

"Isabella. My name is Isabella" Isabella shouted back over the music, keeping her face neutral, while her heart thumped in her throat.

"I know your name and you know mine" Giselle said and took a seat on a small stool near her. "He is always on the phone, isn't he?" she added, an understanding expression perfectly plastered on her beautiful face.

She knew what that was like, hearing Christopher's phone ring- messages from girls, phone calls from lovers picked up here and there, all hoping to see him.

"Why are you here exactly?" Isabella asked, shaking her head.

Get to the point if you want to say something, so I can just walk away.

"I can stand the other women. I've played this game for a long time with Christopher. It's always like that. He goes from one interest to another. He just can't sit still. But I can stand that. I can stand the other women" Giselle paused and tilted her head to the side, pursing her lips. "Can you?"

Isabella shook her head.

"It's not like that between us, not that it's any of your business"

"Of course it is. You just need someone to open your eyes a little. Enjoy your little moment of fame. Enjoy the wonderful view from his studio flat, until it lasts. I'll be here, waiting for him to get tired and come back to me" a ray of white light shone on her face then, as the music changed in the background and Isabella leaned forward, making sure Giselle could hear every single word she was going to say next.

"That's just the difference between you and me. I don't wait around for him and he knows. He knows I would never take him back" Isabella shook her head, seeing Giselle laugh a little, but pressed on ever the same. "I don't settle for a quick fuck, for a great view in his studio and for pretty presents. I want it all, I want all of him. Everything or nothing. Now if you'll excuse me..." Isabella stood, her clutch tight in her shaky hand and moved to the side of the table.

Giselle stood too, her eyes cold on Isabella, the fake smile nowhere to be seen this time.

"He always comes back to me" she told her. "We fight, we fuck other people but then we get tired and go back to being us. It's been like this for over a year" her voice trailed off, like only she knew what she was talking about.

As if Giselle knew the real Christopher, what he really wanted and what he really needed- no intimacy, no strings. He needed to come and go as he pleased, no stress, no distractions from the races. He had told Giselle so many times, she knew it by heart.

"We are not just fucking. I am going home with him" Isabella's eyes dug into Giselle's light blue ones.

And to that Isabella moved away from the table, down the stairs, back into the multitude of bodies, swaying to the music.

She crossed the room, heading to the bar where Christopher was last seen, hoping to spot him again. She was heading outside anyway, Christopher or no Christopher. And maybe she was just going to leave the club.

She swallowed hard, realizing he was nowhere to be seen.

"Shit", she cursed under her breath.

What the hell am I doing here? What the hell am I doing with him?
She thought, feeling like a fool, standing there alone, in the room not knowing where he was, who was calling him all the time and what was going on behind the wall he kept up between them.

I'm such a fool, her last thought was, before she felt a hand touch her shoulder and she turned.

Christopher smiled down at her, his perfect crooked smile, but it lasted only an instant.

"What's wrong?" he leaned forward, both hands on her bare shoulders.

"What the hell am I doing here, Chris?" Isabella shouted over the music. "I must be out of my mind"

She shook her head and breathed in deep.

"What happened?" he looked at her clueless.

"What am I doing here with you? I have no idea what is going on in your life. You keep me away from it. Your manager thinks he can jerk me around and treat me like shit" she said and watched him cringe a little, mentioning Mr. Jenkins.

"I told him I won't tolerate him being disrespectful towards you again"

"You are always on the phone, someone is blackmailing you and you won't trust me enough to tell me what's going on. Your ex just told me how much time we have left together, before you go running back to her…"

"What did she say?" Christopher turned towards the table where they had been sitting and saw Giselle staring down at them.

Isabella searched his face, her head shaking slowly.

"It's not what she said, Chris. It's what you are not telling me. It's what you are not saying, what you don't trust me to know"

"I do trust you" he cut in, his hands tightened around her shoulders.

"No, you don't. I am not going to stand here, not knowing what's happening with you. I am not. I am sorry, I am not the kind of woman to settle for anything but the whole deal" Isabella shook her head and looked down at her hands.

Her stomach tensed, just as she was going to tell him it was now or never. That was the moment, the only moment left for him to show her if he trusted her or not.

"You are right" he nodded, his deep green eyes on her the whole time. "Let's go" and Christopher cautiously wrapped an arm around her shoulder.

"Where?" Isabella let him guide her through the dancefloor, to the cloakroom.

"Home. We need to talk"

They crossed the living room hand in hand and in silence, until they faced the soft beige couches.

"Take a seat" he said and gently guided her on one of the pillows.

Isabella swallowed hard, Christopher's voice so serious just then, she suddenly felt cold.

He turned and walked to a drawer on the far back of the room, near one of the large bay windows and returned to the couch, carrying a dark brown envelope under his arm.

"This book is coming out in September" he said and slowly took out a manuscript from the bag. It was a first print, a mockup, with no hardcover but Isabella's eyes caught Christopher's picture on the front page immediately.

Christopher and James, Isabella stared at it speechless, as she rubbed her fingers on their closeups, her hands holding on tight to the manuscript.

"A biography?" she looked up, searching Christopher's face.

He was standing in front of her, at some distance now, hands tucked in his pockets.

"It was meant to be a biography, yes. About me and my father, from my point of view" he told her, registering confusion on Isabella's face.

She looked at the cover again, at how James' and Christopher's pictures were strategically placed side by side to stress their resemblance.

Like father like son. Memoirs of legend race driver James Taylor and the ultimate 'son of'

"Why meant to be? What is it then?" Isabella glanced at Christopher again.

My private life, Christopher thought. *Tell her, just tell her.*

Christopher ran a hand through his hair and looked down, searching for an easy way to say it and found out there wasn't one. No easy way, just the truth.

And he told her everything. He told Isabella how he had agreed to having a biography written about him and his dad. How he wanted to talk about their relationship, how it felt to be his son, to bare his surname, his legacy.

What a great way to honor him, Christopher had thought.

Maybe talking about it, agreeing to some sort of interview about my father, would have finally stopped the press from asking the same questions over and over again.

"Here is it is, I thought. The whole truth was going to be in here. Journalist would talk about the book and get over it. I guess that plan blew up in my face" Christopher paused, his eyes dark. "I trusted the wrong people with my story"

"Why? What's inside this book that's torturing you, Christopher?" Isabella stood and walked over to him, her hand wrapping around his wrist, covering his tattoo.

He looked down at her, his hands clenched into fists in his pocket as he pondered the words.

"Every stupid thing I've done in my life, is in here and it is being used to make me look like a unworthy son of a champion"

"But" Isabella shook her head, confusion written all over her face "How did they manage to…"

"Get the information?" Christopher finished her sentence. "They paid off almost every person that knows me- every school friend, every woman I went out with- to have a piece of me, a piece of information, a story to tell, a scandalous episode to write about. Do you know what it feels like to know that some of the people you thought were your friends, accepted money to be featured in a book, this book about you? For money, Isabella. For fame, for vanity. Call it whatever you want. They sold me off, to the highest bidder right here"

Isabella looked down then, her eyes stinging, her heart beating wildly in her chest.

So many emotions were stemming from her heart – confusion, stupor, anger, sadness.

"That is terrible" she said, looking into his eyes again and saw the scariest of emotions written all over Christopher's face.

Disappointment, the delusion of having his trust betrayed by those closer to him.

That's why he doesn't trust people, he doesn't usually welcome people in his life.

"I'm sorry I didn't tell you about this before, but I didn't want to ruin everything. I wanted our relationship to be trouble free. Because Isabella, I am in love with you and what I am about to say will change the way you see me. I wasn't always like this, Isabella. Calm, confident, in control. It took me a while to get here"

He is in love with me, Isabella took in a breath.

He took her chin in his hand gently and made sure she was looking at him again, straight into his eyes. She needed to hear what he had to say.

"Almost every woman I fucked, fucked me right back. It's all in there. What we did together, how I like to do it, how I partied hard, the things I said, how I kept at a distance, my mind on one thing and one thing only. Beating my father's performances, arriving a second before him, a second faster than him"

"Chris" Isabella murmured and watched his face harden.

"Read it" he said pointing to the book.

Isabella shook her head.

"I don't want to"

"It's better if you do. That way you'll be prepared for when it comes out"

"I don't care what's inside that book" she shook her head again, her voice hard.

She truly didn't. Whatever was written in there, had been taken from Christopher through betrayal.

Christopher's private life, his memories of his father had been taken from him. He had been misled and Isabella didn't want to have anything to do with it.

"I am not going to read about your private life. If you want to tell me something, I'll listen but I won't read about it from others"

"Read it Isabella. This is me in here. The press is going to be all over you when this comes out. They'll ask you questions"

"I won't answer them" Isabella cut in. "I'll ignore every single one of them"

Christopher looked at her and shook his head, a hint of a smile on his lips.

"I've taken drugs, partied hard. I was a shit head in my teens and thought that I owned it all. The attention I received, the interest in me for being a Taylor, I let it get to my head. I've had more than one woman in my bed at once. I splurged money here and there. I once destroyed a hotel room because I was out of my fucking mind" he paused and took in a deep breath. "My relationship with my father wasn't an easy one. He loved me and I adored him, but it wasn't perfect by far. He was a perfectionist, cold hearted when it came to racing. He wanted more from me, every single time he came with me on track. More, more. He pushed me to the limit, he demanded my attention. He wanted me to be like him. And I have become like him. I am cold blooded in that car, just like he was. You have no idea how many times he made me cry, because I was too slow, too disconnected from the track. He was hard on me, but I owe him everything. He started training me to become like him, better than him. I've achieved so much thanks to him and now this book will make him look like an ogre. His private life is in it, too"

"Oh, Chris" Isabella mumbled, as Christopher's words echoed in her ears.

"That's not all, Isabella. I want you to listen very carefully to everything I have to say. Cause I want you to know everything" he ran a hand through her hair and then let it slide down his side.

No more secrets.

"When I found out that this book was coming out last year, I went out my mind. When I found out who had betrayed me, I lost it. I partied for days, with several girls, and took any shit I could find. Alfred saved my ass, like in so many other occasions. He helped me keep things a secret and he covered up for me, saying that I was ill. I had to sit out a whole month of races, because If they tested me I would have been positive to the drug screening"

"Oh my God" Isabella mumbled. She felt a shiver run down her back, like the room was suddenly so cold, like Christopher's honest words had just slapped her hard in the face.

She blinked at him, trying to imagine how someone so strong, so focused like Christopher could have lost his mind completely. And why.

I wanted to know, Isabella reminded herself, before asking Christopher to carry on.

"He tried to cover up everything, told Mr. Johnson that I was ill" he said and his eyes didn't leave Isabella's. "He paid off some girls I partied with"

She held his stare and swallowed hard, keeping her face as straight as possible, while she felt her stomach clenched tight.

Girls you fucked with.

"But It was useless. It ended up in here, in that book anyway. I guess everyone has a price, what I offered was not enough" he let out a bitter laugh.

"Now you know everything, what a fucking mess I am" Christopher said "The door is over there, Isabella. I don't blame you if you want out" Christopher said then, his jaw twitched as he studied her dark face.

Her honey brown eyes lit up instantly, as he said the words, her full red lips parted.

"I am not moving" she looked back up at him, while she grabbed on to his arm, tighter this time.

"If you think you can ignore this, you are wrong. We'll have three times the attention on us that we have now"

"We'll find a way to control the situation" Isabella told him, her mind taking over, quieting her heart.

"There is no way out of this" Christopher said. "The publishing house offered me a solution: authorize the biography and have some control on the content. To be defined" he laughed it off. "Some control. I don't want some control. I don't want any of it out"

"We can talk with them and find a solution"

"You can't find a solution with them. They'll print it like it is, If I say no anyway. It's their way or they'll print it. I am not going to authorize it, I am not going to compromise with them. I already tried to pay for their silence"

Oh Chris, Isabella thought.

"They can write all they want. I don't care what you did, what took you to become the man you are now. Because you are amazing, not just as a driver. What you are going to do with the academy, helping so many less fortunate young drivers live their dream, is fantastic. This is the Christopher I care about and whatever it is you did in the past, it helped you become who you are now"

He shook his head and mumbled something under his breath.

"I am going to humiliate my mother, my father and you too. If you stay, you'll be dragged into this, too"

"We've all done things we are not proud of" Isabella started to say but Christopher didn't let her finish.

"Things are a little different when they are in the spotlight"

"I don't care, I am not going. I am staying"

"They'll stalk you"

"Io ti amo" *"I love you"* the words just flew out of her mouth, without thinking twice.

They came out as soft as a whisper and it warmed Christopher's heart, like a hot summer breeze.

"I love you" she said again, in English this time, and saw Christopher smile, his hands up to her cheeks in an instant.

"And I am not walking away. We'll take the blow. Together. I'll help you every possible way I can. I am not leaving"

She stretched up on her toes and kissed him, her lips sealing the deal. She was staying, no matter how rough things would get in a few months' time. They had been through the 'other girl' moment – Giselle- the crash and all the doubts and fears of getting involved in a dead-end relationship.

I am involved now, there's no going back. I don't want to go back.

"I don't care what they say. Your words are the only thing I'll listen to. The hell with everyone"

"Once you are involved, your name will be connected to mine for a long time, even if you walk away at some point. I want you to understand this" he said, holding her close against his chest.

He wanted to be sure, sure that Isabella knew what she was getting into. He knew too well how things worked with the press. It took just one moment to be in the spotlight, but running away from it took longer. Sometimes it was impossible.

"It's going to get nasty" he warned her.

"I can be nasty, too. We are in this together"

He played with a strand of her hair, as he guided it behind her ear and smiled.

"What did I do to deserve you?"

Isabella's shoulders went up a little and she shrugged.

"You must have done something right, Mr. Taylor"

Chapter 12

I wish you could be here right now, Isabella texted Christopher and opened the car door.

The hot summer breeze hit her instantly and she breathed in the saltiness of the sea air.

Home, Isabella thought. She was home.

Only six days to the race in Rome and Isabella had left London two days early, before the MB team scheduled arrival on Thursday – before the whole First Category Racing circus arrived into town. Before Christopher.

She had anticipated her departure, hoping to have enough time to catch up with her family and friends. She knew that once the race weekend begun, she would be super busy with Hillary, organizing their work, the interviews and attending sponsor events with the drivers.

As she got out of her car and made her way through the parking lot- into the crowd that walked the small town's old streets- Isabella noticed how different it felt to be home this time.

She was back, she was in Italy but her mind was somewhere else.

Her eyes searched the clear sky and for the first time wished she was under the gray London sky, with Christopher.

Stop it. He'll be here soon, Isabella reminded herself.

It was just a matter of days and the whole MB team would be flying to Rome for the race. It was almost time for cars to line up on track again after Berlin.

As Isabella did her best to keep memories of the accident out of her mind, she thought of how different it would be this time, to walk the box lane beside Christopher, their first race weekend as a couple.

A couple, she played with the word in her head and smiled.

Her last trip to Italy had been before Toronto, before she and Christopher had started seeing each other again- after the pictures of him and Giselle kissing in Cannes.

That time, she had run off to Italy to stop from calling him, to stop Christopher from looking for her in London.

And look at us now, she smiled content.

In just a few weeks, their relationship had gone from secret to real, from occasional to living together.

And in just two days, they had moved all her stuff to his house in Maida Vale.

"You could get tired of me" she had made her point several times.

"Impossible. I want more of you every day" Christopher had whispered in her hair, his hand wrapped around her waist.

I am not going to argue with that, and Isabella had snuggled up in his tight embrace.

But the best part of it all was that there were no more secrets between them.

He told me about the book.

It was all out in the open, Christopher's past, his struggles to become the man that he was- the crazy night outs, his ache to be worthy of his surname and the reason why he had never wanted a girl by his side. The lack of trust. He didn't trust easily, not after his loved ones had betrayed him the way they did with the book. The truth was out and for once, Isabella wasn't scared of what was to come- what was going to happen when the book was out and the press got a hold of Christopher.

For some reason, she still believed that something could be done, that it wasn't over yet, that maybe she and Mr. Jenkins could work something together.

If we set our differences aside, Isabella reckoned but she knew she would, she would work with Alfred if necessary.

Anything to help Christopher out of this unpleasant situation.

"I am sorry this is happening to you" Isabella had wanted Christopher to know.

She wasn't holding him responsible for anything. What was done, was done and there was nothing he could do to change that. It was all in the past now and what truly mattered at that point, was that Christopher had learnt from his mistakes. They would move on from there. Together.

We are closer, Isabella smiled as she walked onto a bigger street.

Not too far away, Maria was waiting for Isabella, for a night out on the town, as the annual summer festival took place.

Isabella breathed in the aroma of sweet cotton candy and smiled, her eyes a little closed, as if she could see it all over again- her childhood, her summers spent on fare rides and listening to live music around town.

She stopped, just as she rounded a corner onto the main town square, and placed a hand on a wall, to adjust the straps on her sandals. She could feel the music hum through the walls of the old town hall and she could hear children giggling, running around with sweet nuts and candies.

Those were happy days, Isabella recalled, when she was still a little girl and all the family would venture out on hot summer nights, to celebrate the Saint patron of the town.

Those were the few times she would have the freedom and light heartedness of a child, when her parents were there, present and watching out for her brother and sister, and Isabella would feel like a child too for once.

Her phone vibrated and she took it out, just as she spotted Maria, waiting for her near the big town clock.

She waved and Maria started to walk towards her, moving fast through the crowd.

Me too baby. I am in bed all alone, with a sore neck from all the weight lifting. I need your massage... Christopher texted back and Isabella bit her lip, picturing his perfect, fit body lying on the hard-wooden bed.

She thought about the headboard, how she had grasped the edge of it, while Christopher had made his way down to kiss her body, her whole body, the night before she left.

"I want you to think of this when you are in Italy" he had told her in between kisses, his lips brushing against the inside of her thighs.

I'll do more than that for you, once you get here. Hurry up, come to Italy. She texted back quickly.

A shiver ran down her spine, down her legs as Isabella looked up and smiled at Maria.

"Hey, you" her friend hugged her tight and sighed "It's so good to have you around here again"

"Aww sweetie, I am really happy we get to spend some time together" Isabella said, holding on to her friend a moment longer.

"So" Maria grinned excited. "When will I get to meet him? What's he like? I mean besides being man candy material. Is he reserved? Outgoing?"

"You sound like one of the journalists" Isabella teased and then went on "He'll be in Rome on Thursday. And he is very outgoing, laidback, attentive…" Isabella was saying, when her phone vibrated again. "Sorry"

She took it out and checked the screen.

Can't wait to kiss those red lips. I miss having you by my side. She read the text quickly and couldn't hold back a smile.

Christopher Taylor, the famous 'relationship allergic' race driver misses me, misses me hanging around him. Isabella could not suppress the happiness, the excitement.

"When I met you, I knew you were different. You weren't just another beautiful woman I met at a dinner. Your eyes, your wit… I wanted to know every little thing about you. I wanted to possess every single part of you. I knew I could trust you, that you weren't after something. You are not just a pretty face. You are real. And I want the real thing. I want you, all of you" Christopher had told her one night, while lying half naked in bed, entangled in a tight embrace.

"We will probably do something together with the team, after the race on Sunday. You and Giacomo could join us, if you are free" Isabella put the phone back in her bag and looked up at Maria again. She was staring, her brows up.

"We will be free. I want to meet him. And I think Giacomo wants an autograph" Maria grinned and Isabella wrapped an arm around her friend, while they discussed what to try out first: food or rides?

"Aren't we too old for rides?" Isabella expressed her doubts, seeing only kids in their teens and a few twenty-year old's in the queue.

"Honey, you were born old. Hence, you were never really allowed on the rides" Maria giggled to Isabella's crossed face. "Of course we can. Who cares, people are going to stare at you anyway, you are Christopher Taylor's new hot girlfriend. You are famous"

Wait till the book comes out, the thought crossed Isabella's mind for a second, but she firmly pushed it away.

She didn't care. She told Christopher it didn't matter and it truly didn't. It was a storm, they would walk through it and end up where it was sunny again, maybe with a few scars, but side by side nevertheless.

"Thanks for the 'hot' girlfriend but I am hardly the hottest girl he has had his hands on" Isabella made a face and followed Maria in the queue.

Rides first, food later.

"You my friend are blind" Maria eyed her from top to bottom and made her point, for how beautiful Isabella looked that night in her light blue summer dress.

"You my friend are too kind" Isabella said and watched Maria grin.

"Wait until we start this game and I'll kick your ass. Not so kind anymore, am I?" Maria pointed to the target shooting trial they were queueing up for and laughed, Isabella's glare too funny to resist.

It always ended in a pout and a look from top to toe.

"I'll kick yours and you know it. You've never won once since we started hanging out together, since like forever"

"I won that summer we were into heavy metal, remember our matching shirts?" Maria's eyes went wide, as the memory came back to her.

Her rebellious era- black lipstick, purple hair and heavy black eyeliner.

"I remember you cheated" Isabella's brow went up.

"You 'think' I might have cheated" Maria corrected her and they continued to tease each other, waiting for their turn.

They were half way through the queue, Salvo and Angela came out of nowhere- laughing hard, Angela leaning into her boyfriend's shoulder.

My ex-boyfriend, Isabella reminded herself. *And my ex best friend.*

She looked away when it was too late, Salvo and Angela had already seen her and Maria standing there by the ride.

As if they had belonged to another life, Isabella had forgotten all about them, her thoughts only for Christopher.

Isabella, Salvo and Angela stared at each other for a few moments- guest star Maria and her best of squints- but there was no smile, no wave. They were frozen in place.

How many times had they been in that situation, the same situation- the three of them together? Several, only now the roles had been rearranged and they were frozen in time, trying to figure out how to move on from there.

Inevitably, Isabella's face softened. There was no reason to make this more uncomfortable than it already was.

Time to move on.

"Hi" he said and eyed Maria to the side. "Maria"

"Salvo" she said and then stared ahead, nudging Isabella to take a step forward in the queue. "Hi" Isabella said back, giving them her best smile.

"How are you?" he asked.

Angela's blue eyes appeared behind his shoulder and maybe Isabella might have imagined it, but she saw the glimpse of a smile on her thin glossy lips.

Either that or a nervous twitch.

"I'm good" Isabella kept her voice cool, even though the formality of their conversation was making things worse. Uncomfortable. "And you?"

"Good. Can we talk?" he asked and tilted his head to the side, suggesting they took their conversation somewhere less public, like the parking lot nearby.

"I… I don't…" Isabella indicated Maria, like she was about to say no, but then something in Salvo's eyes changed her mind. "Okay" she answered and told Maria she was going to be back in time for the ride.

"I promise, five minutes" Isabella squeezed Maria's hand and walked down the cobble road, to a quieter corner- far enough from curious eyes- but she was still able to see Maria from there.

Then, her stare was on Angela again.

Her friend, or so she had been for as long as she could remember, looked down as soon as she met Isabella's eyes.

That counts for something, at least she's ashamed for sneaking behind my back with my boyfriend, Isabella thought.

"I don't want to make a scene" Salvo spoke again and eyed Angela.

"Nobody is going to make a scene, Salvo" Isabella shook her head and almost rolled her eyes "I'm not that kind of person and you know that" and of course she meant every word and more.

There was absolutely no reason to make a scene because first of all, she had found out about her best friend and his ex-boyfriend hooking up a while ago already. So all the anger, all the sadness was gone. It had left Isabella with a void, not necessarily painful in the end, as that experience had taught her a thing or two.

Nothing was what it looked like, not even the best of friendships, not even the best of men. Salvo had always been perceived as the boy next door, sweet and trustworthy and look what had happened.

And then there was Christopher in Isabella's life. The boat had rocked a few times already and It was going to rock some more soon, Isabella knew that but she was aware of what they had.

We are in love, she had realized a while ago and somehow nothing else seemed to matter. Their differences, the odds against them, the tensions. It was all worth it, it was all temporary, but their connection lasted. Their bond had grown. Their feelings for each other had found a name.

I am in love for the first time, the time it matters, Isabella realized, looking at Salvo and Angela just then and it didn't hurt.

It didn't hurt seeing them together, hugging and laughing.

It was something Isabella couldn't have given Salvo, it was something Salvo couldn't have given her – the feelings she and Christopher had for each other.

"I'm sorry I didn't tell you, about us" he looked over to Angela again and as on cue, she moved to the side and finally made her way out behind his shoulder, behind his shadow.

She stood there next to Isabella, in a short red summer dress, blonde hair down her back, no smile on her face.

So many times, Isabella had thought what it would have been like, to see them together, as a couple.

She had thought about it, the first few days after she had found out about them. She had thought of the words to say- how to hurt her, how to make her feel bad- but now Isabella's mind couldn't recall a thing.

"I didn't know how to tell you" Salvo went on.

"How about Angela and I are dating?" Isabella raised an eyebrow at him "I had to find out from other people, Salvo. We promised we would always be honest with each other" she added, her face reeked with disappointment.

"I know" he said and shook his head "that's why I want to talk to you about it. It's not true Angela and I were already seeing each other, when you and I were still together"

Isabella tilted her head to the side and smiled, finding it hard to believe.

"It's the truth" Angela spoke for the first time.

Isabella stared at her for a moment, speechless.

"Over the past three months you never picked up your phone, not even once. And now you are talking to me and I am supposed to listen to you? I am supposed to believe you?" Isabella retorted, her eyes a little sad, as she spoke.

It's not sadness what I am feeling. It's disappointment.

She realized it wasn't about Salvo at all. Deep down she was hurt, but it wasn't love that had hurt her. Not the end of her relationship with Salvo, but the end of her friendship with Angela.

"I was avoiding you" Angela said, her voice low.

"Why?" Isabella pressed on, her heart in her throat, realizing her sixth sense had suggested her the right thing.

Her best friend had been in fact avoiding her, but it was one thing to assume it was so, and completely another to know it was true.

"Because I cared for Salvo" Angela said, eyeing her boyfriend to the side. "I've liked him since the day we met him in that club. And I hated myself so much for the feelings I had for him. You guys started dating and you and I were friends, more like sisters. I couldn't back stab you and hurt you like that. But I couldn't stay near you either, near both of you, without hurting. I didn't want to make the mistake of choosing love over friendship" Angela paused. "So, I decided I was going to give up both. Salvo and you"

Isabella stared into her friend's blue eyes, as the truth settled in, as all the puzzle pieces finally fit together.

The vague conversations, the missed phone calls, the excuses every time Isabella had tried to set up a night out with Angela. She had been avoiding her because she wanted to stay away from Salvo and not risk making the mistake of hurting Isabella, of damaging their friendship.

Isabella gaped, her eyes wide.

Never, during the whole time she had been with Salvo, had she even suspected such a thing. It never crossed her mind, she never had any clues. Nothing. It was brand new information for her and like any new form of information, it shocked her completely. She was silent for a few instants.

"You never told me this" Isabella shook her head, incredulous.

"I know" Angela nodded.

"Why didn't you tell me?" Isabella kept looking at her with wide eyes.

"What was I going to say? You guys were together and you were great. I couldn't" Angela shook her head, her shoulders up. "But then you decided to leave and Salvo didn't want to be with you away all the time. I couldn't stand to see him suffer like that. When you left" Angela winced a little, as she said the words. "I got closer to him but nothing happened before you two were over"

They had accidently bumped into each other the night Isabella had told Salvo about getting the job in London. Angela explained how Salvo had been in a terrible state- sad for Isabella leaving. She had attempted to lift his spirits, trying to convince him that the long-distance relationship could work, it was just for a year anyway. But Salvo had told her his doubts, how he was sure it wouldn't work, how it didn't feel right to keep strings attached with Isabella away all the time.

"I know what the town is saying, that our relationship started before you and I broke up" Salvo said. "It's not true"

Isabella stared at them both, motionless while Maria took a small step forward in the queue.

"Salvo and I could never do that to you" Angela added looking from Salvo to Isabella again. "I am sorry" she mumbled then "For not telling you before"

Isabella let out a deep breath and shook her head a little.

"What do you want me to say? I don't know what to say" she told Angela.

And I don't know what to believe, Isabella kept her thoughts to herself and caught sight of Maria, waving at her as she had almost reached the head of the line.

"Don't say anything" Angela shook her head a little.

I don't want to say anything I'll regret, Isabella thought, feeling confused.

Salvo turned to Angela and whispered something, but Isabella wasn't quite sure she had heard right. It was only when Angela had waved briefly and walked back to the ride, that Isabella understood Salvo wanted to tell her something, something private.

"I really did love you" he said, turning to Isabella.

She breathed in deep before she spoke.

"I loved you, too"

"Not like I loved you" he shook his head, smiling softly as he did.

There was no bitterness, no resentment in his voice. It was something Salvo had become aware of, a while ago now, and he had come to terms with it. Isabella had never loved him like he had loved her. She had never really been in love, to the point she couldn't even imagine her life without him.

She had cared for him, but being in love was something else- Salvo knew it was something completely different.

"It's okay" he went on, nodding. "I know that now. We could never have worked. Not even if you stayed. I think you did the right thing, going away"

Isabella listened to his every word and pursed her lips, fighting a tear from rolling down her cheeks.

"I never wanted to hurt you" she said, reaching out for his arm.

Salvo placed a hand over hers and smiled.

"I know. I never wanted to hurt you too"

But we did, we did hurt each other.

Sometimes, intentions were meaningless. Sometimes, events led you in a direction instead of another. Some things were just meant to be, while some others were meant to cease.

"I watch you every weekend" Salvo smirked and told Isabella how he hoped to take a glimpse at her during the interviews. "Is it true? About you and Christopher Taylor?"

"Yes" she nodded, a little self-conscious now.

"I am really happy for you" he said.

"Thank you. I am happy for you too. I am" she smiled to that.

"I'll let you go now" Salvo said, glancing over to Maria "It was nice to see you"

"Yeah, you too" Isabella mumbled and her eyes followed him, as he joined Angela and they went through the crowd of people.

Isabella looked down at her hands while walking up to Maria, puzzled and lost in thought.

Do we ever truly know the people we live with? Do we ever really share our most intimate thoughts with our friends?

Isabella wasn't sure anymore. She had once liked to think that she and Angela could talk and confess just about anything to each other.

That's before a man got in our way.

The thought saddened her, the way they had lost each other and their relationship over a man.

"Are you okay?" Maria asked, her arm wrapping around Isabella's shoulder.

"Yeah, I am good" Isabella smiled warmly at her friend and filled in on her conversation with Salvo and Angela. "Just surprised. How could she keep it to herself for so long? You wouldn't do that would you? Keep something so important from me"

"Of course not. I can't keep things to myself, period. Especially from you" Maria smiled back. "By the way, your mascara is a little smudged" she pointed to her friend's left eye, right at the outside corner.

Isabella laughed.

"I was being serious"

"I know you were, too serious, in fact I wanted to see you laugh" Maria winked. "I would never lie to you. You know that"

"I do" Isabella nodded.

They took another step forward and finally reached the head of the queue.

The man sitting behind the ticket booth, handed them a plastic gun and told them to wait for their turn in front of a narrow door. Soon it would have been their turn to walk through the route and shoot at as many targets as possible, trying to beat the other player.

"So, do we believe them? Salvo and Angela?" Maria eyed her to the side, as she adjusted the safety goggle on her eyes.

"I am not sure what to believe. Does it matter at this point? I lost them both" Isabella glanced her way and saw Maria shrug.

"You have me and Cristina. Aren't we enough?" Maria smiled wide.

"More than enough, I'd say" Isabella giggled, as they took a step forward towards the door.

"Nice, very nice. I shall remember that once we are in there" Maria pointed to the shooting route.

They laughed and slowly the conversation went back to normal. They teased each other, as they stepped inside the shooting route and the game begun.

Every now and then, while shooting at the targets, Salvo and Angela's words would inevitably come back to Isabella. It felt as though their conversation had been long overdue, like she had waited for so long to hear the truth. Angela, her best friend for as long as she could remember, had been avoiding her, because of Salvo.

Keeping things inside, not being open about them with the people you love, could ruin everything.

It had ruined her relationships with Salvo, when they hadn't been upfront with each other about her job. It had ruined Angela's and

Isabella's friendship, when Angela hadn't told her the reason behind her weird, distant behavior.

One thought haunted her that evening: would things have been different, if they had been more honest, more upfront about their feelings with each other? Would Isabella have saved her friendship-with both Salvo and Angela?

Chapter 13

It was so hot, the tarmac was boiling. Isabella could feel the heat coming from the ground and it hit her face every time she walked, head down, from the starting line -where she and Hillary had stood before the race, to take pictures of the cars- to the box.

"I love this weather" Hillary said, face up towards the sun. A wide smile spread under her black shades.

"Hillary, I'd like to introduce you to 'summer', 'summer' this is Hillary. She hardly knows you exist, because she is British" Isabella grinned and did the same. She looked up at the sunny sky and closed her eyes, Hillary's giggling covered by the sound of the cars going by.

The sun felt so good.

Just two days home and Isabella had already tanned a little, spending most of her free time on the beach with her family and friends, just before her other 'family'- the MB family- had landed in Rome.

"Are you staying here for the summer break?" Hillary asked, as five military planes flew above their heads and let out colored smoke, while doing acrobatics in the sky.

The colors of the Italian flag.

The crowd clapped and cheered and Hillary joined in.

"Yeah, I am staying for a while. You?" Isabella shouted over the roar of the engines and clapped, too.

"I think I am going back to London for a few days but then I'm off to the Greek islands. I so need a holiday, far, far away from Mr. you know who" she looked at Isabella.

"How are things going?" Isabella dared to ask.

"Not well. He is being nervous and unreasonable" Hillary said but didn't add anything about her pregnancy. She eyed Fred and John who were standing next to them, coordinating the mechanical team.

Who, Mr. accusative and insulting? Nothing new there. Isabella kept her thoughts to herself and simply nodded.

"I'm having trouble working with him. He wants to get back together, especially now" Hillary shook her head "He has the nerve to say it like he is free, like he is not married. I don't understand him. Anyway, I am over him"

"You could stay here with me for a while, it would do you good and you could eat, eat, eat and tan on the beach" Isabella suggested.

"That is so sweet, thank you but I need some alone time right now. I will visit you though, some over time" Hillary smiled at Isabella. "Can you believe the season is nearly over?"

"No, I can't" Isabella shook her head. Where had the time gone?

She eyed Christopher then, sitting in his car, helmet on, looking determined and concentrated- second in line behind driver Simoncini. Noah had qualified sixth on Saturday and had broken his engine- his team of mechanics had spent all night fixing his car.

Almost six months had gone by, since Isabella had started working for MB, and it felt like it had all gone by so quickly. In just six months, she had changed houses, changed her life style, changed job, met new friends and Christopher.

She kept staring at him, still unable to explain how it had been possible for them to become what they were.

As if It served as a reminder, the girls on track that normally stood next to the drivers, walked off the tarmac just then- in miniskirts and with tops two size smaller than normal- and Isabella tried to shrug off any negative thought.

Yes, not too long ago, Christopher had dated models – more like slept with models. And now he was with her, a normal girl with a normal figure.

"And the prettiest ass… I mean freckles, I've ever seen" Christopher had told her some time ago, with the sliest of smiles on his face.

He looks great, Isabella reckoned, seeing him back in the car and adjusting his gloves. Christopher was back, physically and mentally back into shape.

The nervous Christopher of a few weeks ago had disappeared. Now that everything was out in the open, now that he and Isabella had been honest with each other about their feelings and past, Christopher was back to being himself- at ease, concentrated and determined.

"I don't want to be a distraction" Isabella had told him on a number of occasion, while he was training at home.

"Don't ever think that. You are not a distraction. Having you here, by my side, makes me focus even more" he had assured her, leaning forward to plant a passionate kiss on her full red lips.

And Isabella could see that now, checking the screen with the times on the grid. Christopher's qualifying lap had been almost perfect and

Isabella could tell by the soft smile on his lips that Christopher was satisfied for how fast his body had recovered.

"I feel hungry, hungry for a victory" he had confessed to her after the Friday free practice, while walking over to an autograph session. Isabella felt her stomach tighten, as she saw him glance her way, thinking of how it had felt to walk around track with Christopher- hand in hand at times, walking him to the interviews surrounded by photographers and camera men.

His hand had tightened around hers and a killer smile – his killer smile- had made an appearance under his black shades.

"Ignore them, signorina. Or do you want me to trip them over?" he grinned then and Isabella giggled, slowly relaxing under his touch.

Ten minutes to the recognition lap. Isabella read on the screen to the left-hand side of the track.

"I better head back. My brother is sitting at my work station" Isabella told Hillary.

He better not be touching anything, Isabella thought.

Racing was all about rituals, Isabella had come to discover in her almost five months with MB Racing.

True, the sport was mostly skill and ability- it was about being fast, efficient and ready to react in case of setbacks. What almost nobody saw was the preparation and the rituals behind the scenes.

It wasn't just about drivers training and preparation. There was so much more going on in the boxes.

When the race was about to begin, Isabella didn't need a clock to remind her how little time there was left until the traffic lights would go off. All she needed to do, was look around her.

Mechanics of both Noah and Christopher's team checked their tools and all the spare parts in a systematic and maniacal manner, until everything was double checked and in its exact place- every drawer corresponded to a specific spare part of the car and it included the tools necessary to screw the piece on the vehicle.

Tires were kept warm with special thermal covers on the side of the car.

When the beginning of the race was only minutes away, Mr. Johnson would take a seat at his control station, to coordinate and double check that everything was running smoothly with the cars and within the team.

Hillary would be standing up at that point, too busy checking her schedule, talking to the engineers, to Isabella and Phil, to everyone basically, expect for the drivers.

It wasn't a written rule, but everyone knew that drivers were not to be addressed minutes before the race, if not for very important issues, strictly related to the race.

Usually, Noah would sit in his chair, listening to music, his eyes closed like he was meditating and trying desperately to relax, while Christopher would always walk back and forth – his usual ritual- headphones on, suit halfway down his body, until a few minutes before the beginning of a race.

But Isabella would be sure that the race was truly about to begin, when Christopher would pick up his phone to say hi to his mother- like he had promised her so many years before, when he had started racing.

"I have to be realistic" he had said to Isabella once *"You never know what will happen."* That was the sign.

Lights on, drivers start your engines.

Only this time, there was a new ritual.

Just before Christopher had walked to his car, he had adjusted his suit, carefully zipping it all the way up, and grabbed his gloves. He had then locked eyes with Isabella and had walked the opposite direction to the car – towards her work station.

"Can I get a good luck kiss?" Christopher had asked, once he had walked around the counter, over to the stool where she was sitting. His hands had slipped down her back and Isabella's cheeks had turned bright red, the freckles so visible now that she was tanned, they made her face even prettier.

She had simply nodded, ignoring all the men working in a frenzy around them and had tilted her head up, to welcome Christopher lips- her arms wrapping tight around his neck.

"Well" she had said, clearing her throat and looking around the box.

"I am not sure that was a good luck kiss, but it sure was a pretty, hot one" Isabella had bitten her lower lip and had enjoyed every second of Christopher's sexy, crooked smile.

"You are a pretty hot one, signorina" he had smirked.

In another moment, the two of them alone, he would have lifted her up from the stool and teared apart that sexy uniform she had on, in an instant.

What was she wearing that day? A skirt.
Even better, he had thought checking out her legs.
"Stay focused" Isabella had told him, her eyes serious this time.
She had closed the button on the collar of his tracksuit and had ran her hands on his chest, to smoothen down the front, her hand resting on his heart for a moment longer. *"Keep your eyes on the track, your head in that car"* she had pressed on and watched him nod, while he had slipped on his grey and blue gloves and the balaclava over his face- his deep green eyes the only thing visible now under the white, fireproof protection.
"I will. Keep your radio on" he had winked at her and left.
Isabella had watched him walk away, helmet already on, his pace steady and in control.
This was his race. He was ready to get back in the car and determined to win.
Interesting new ritual Christopher, Isabella thought to herself, as her eyes never left him until Christopher had driven out of the box, ready for his warm up lap.
That was the moment when people in uniforms would start running back to the boxes, darting to their positions. The race was about to begin.
From deep down in the box where she was sitting, Isabella could see everything, hear everything and take in the excitement of the race. The smell of the fuel being burned, as the cars were set to life, the sound of the tires being screwed on the car.
It had grown on her, the frenzy and the adrenaline of it all.
Christopher had been right about adrenaline. It was addictive.
Yes, Isabella realized there were certain rituals to the sport, signals of war that was about to begin between teams and a promise that every single driver would do everything in his power, to show how strong he was, to show the whole world who was number one.
I'll use this for my blog post today, Isabella thought as she typed in her considerations.
She checked what she had just written and felt pleased with it. Hopefully fans would appreciate the insight from the MB box and feel even more part of the show.
"What are you up to?" Marco's voice sounded from behind her shoulder.

"I just finished writing something" Isabella pressed post and then closed her laptop.

A couple of photos were already up, the race had begun half an hour ago, Christopher was leading and the first blog post was up. *Everything's running smoothly.*

She was good for half an hour or so. "Did you go get something to eat?" she asked her brother.

"Yeah, I was starving. It's so cool, I bumped into Ben Kingsley"

"Who?" Isabella asked, with no idea who the man was.

"Oh my God. You don't know him? He was a driver in the Third Category Racing a few years ago. Now he is a sports journalist" Marco looked at her in shock.

"Sorry, I never heard of him" she raised her hands up and laughed.

"I'll pretend you didn't just say that. I should be doing your job" Marco grunted and shook his head.

"You are a terrible writer" Isabella raised an eyebrow at him.

"Whatever, listen I saw this woman in the café. She saw my MB badge and asked me If I could tell you she was there. Her name is Camilla, I think" Marco scratched his head.

"Oh, really?" Isabella sat up a little.

"Yeah, she told me to ask you, if you want to grab a coffee with her. She's there now" Marco took a seat in front of the screen again and put his hands in his hair. "Oh man" he mumbled, seeing Noah do a half spin at the fifth curb. Within seconds, Noah managed to straighten the car and drive back on the tarmac.

"I don't know If I can go now" Isabella looked for Hillary. She needed to ask her boss first.

"Shhh, I don't care. Go tell her yourself, I am watching the race" Marco kept his eyes glued to the screen and grinned, knowing her sister would be mad at him for snapping back at her like that.

"Watch it, kid. I got you the pass, I can take it away" Isabella pointed at him and then winked.

Then, Isabella went looking for Hillary.

"Yes, go ahead darling. See you soon" Hillary reassured her.

The coffee place was just a two-minute walk from the MB box. Isabella showed her badge a few times at the security checks and then made her way to the entrance of the place.

It was busy as usual, being the only facility accessible from the boxes. Isabella looked around and saw a parade of colored uniforms.

At the far end of the counter stood Camilla, leaning on the surface with her arms and elbows, holding a cup of long coffee. She was talking to the guy behind the counter, a wicked smile on her lips and she was nodding to his words. Her blonde thin hair was falling out from her small bun, her hair too short to hold it all in place.

"Ciao" she straightened up at the sight of Isabella.

"Ciao Camilla" they shook hands and decided to take a seat at one of the tables in the café.

Once Isabella had ordered a fresh pineapple juice and they had run out of pleasantries, Camilla started asking her questions about her job.

"So, how are things going? Is Mr. Jenkins still on your back?" Camilla wondered, suppressing a smile.

"Things are going well. He's still very controlling but I am learning how to let it wash over me" Isabella muttered the words, hoping Camilla would believe her.

She really was trying to ignore the pressure Mr. Jenkins was putting on her and Hillary all the time, but everything had changed since that private conversation they had had in London, at that cafe in Bond Street. It had gone way beyond work, it had become personal.

"Good, good for you" Camilla nodded. "I've asked you because I haven't had a chance to speak to you lately or even bump in to you. I haven't been present at every race weekend"

"Oh, is everything okay with you?" Isabella asked and then checked her clock. She had been gone for ten minutes, she had to head back soon.

"Yes, everything is fine but I am just so tired of this life. I've been doing it for too long. I am going to stop this year, there is already someone doing my job now, I just supervise so that everything runs smoothly. I'm looking for another job" she smiled confidently "And I think I've found something but it's nothing certain yet"

"Well, all the best of luck. I am sure you won't have any problems" Isabella reassured her.

"Thank you" Camilla checked her watch too. "How's Christopher? Did he really recover from the accident in Berlin?"

Isabella nodded and lowered her eyes for a moment.

Every time someone mentioned the accident, the images of him hitting the barriers- parts of the car tearing off- would play in her head and make her heart stop for an instant.

"He's doing great"

"Are you guys seriously dating?" Camilla smirked and Isabella let out a nervous laugh.

"So it would seem"

"Well, congratulations. He's a nice man" Camilla smiled again

"Listen, the reason I wanted to speak to you privately is that I have a preposition for you"

Isabella sat up and listened very carefully.

"This new career I am after, I can't talk about it until it's real, you know. But if It does become real, I need someone like you by my side, someone who knows her stuff, knows how to write and has a good impact on social networks and blogs. I am going freelance now, as a journalist and photographer, so I need someone I can trust. I need somebody that can proof read stuff and support my work. Are you under contract for next year?"

"Well" Isabella shook her head "my contract ends in November, as soon as the championship is over and I still don't know if it will be renewed or not. I am really honored that you, a person who is considered a legend in the field, has thought of me as assistant. Thank you so much, but I still don't know what I will be doing next year" Isabella shrugged a little surprised by Camilla's offer.

I actually don't know what she is offering, Isabella admitted to herself, but it surely did feel an honor to be considered for a position by a veteran in Communication and Marketing like Camilla.

Over the years, she had done the impossible. Camilla had worked her way up, she had been part of the sport, witnessed the evolution of First Category Racing and been an excellent photographer and press agent.

It truly is an honor.

"That's all I needed to know for now. We can talk about it again, maybe once we get back to London. I'll make you a business preposition, that you can valuate before signing up with MB for another year." Camilla stood up and shook her hand.

Chapter 14

It was so hot in the car, Christopher felt like his face was on fire.
"Last two laps, Christopher. You are doing excellent mate" Robert
reassured him on radio.
The car slid on the tarmac, just as Christopher drove out of the
second curb and he cursed under his breath.
"Damn it. How are the brakes doing?" he asked and Robert was
quick to answer.
From his control station, both brakes and tires were a little
overheated, Robert admitted but it was normal. The temperature was
going up as the race ended, it had been sunny all day.
"Just keep the car on the trajectory and easy on the brakes. You are
good"
"Okay" Christopher said, driving into a set of fast curbs.
On a city track like the one in Rome, where the city streets
themselves were the circuit, there were no escape routes, no grass,
nowhere to safely drive on, If the car lost control. It was only
barriers and it was hard to overtake, with little space to drive
through.
The car feels amazing, he thought to himself, seeing how it
responded perfectly under his touch.
Curb number five, straight. Curb number six, Christopher repeated
in his head and then he leaped out of the curb, on to a straight, so fast
the car drove so close to one of the barriers he heard Robert's voice
immediately after.
"Christopher, that was close. Keep the car in the trajectory"
"I got it under control. I was going so fast, I didn't want to change
the trajectory" he smiled under his helmet and pushed hard, harder
now, giving the car all it had.
"There is a wide gap between you and Harold. You can slow down.
You just started the last lap, he won't overtake you" Robert
reassured him.
Christopher smiled again, holding tighter to the wheel as he sped
past the stands, past the boxes and saw his fans hold up his flag.
"I know" he said. "I want the fastest lap record. Now let me drive. I
know what I am doing" he laughed a little and heard Robert chuckle.
"Roger that"

And just like that he was alone in the car again, alone with his thoughts, his heavy breathing the only sound in his ears.

Straight, curb, curb, straight, curb, his mind kept reminding him, as he was half way through the last lap of the race.

His stomach tightened, as he pictured the finish line.

He was alone in the car and yet he felt guided, every single step, every single moment. He wasn't, alone. Not anymore. There was someone in his life, by his side and he could feel her presence every step of the race.

Fastest lap, he ached to hear that on the radio. *Fastest lap, come on. Come on.*

With all the energy he had left, Christopher drove into the last curb, breaking as late as possible and picked up speed quickly on its way out.

The finish line was there, he could see it now. It was there, right in front of him.

Fastest lap, for you dad.

He closed his eyes a moment and then crossed the line, race marshals waving the checkered flag as he sped by.

"Fantastic! Great job, mate! You won the race and you just gave the track a new record. Fastest lap, Christopher well done. Well done" Robert told him.

"WOHOOO" he screamed to the top of his lungs. He raised his hand up and waved at the screaming fans on the stands.

Who is the fucking son of? He thought and continued his lap, slowing down the car and waving to everyone.

"I AM BACK!" he screamed and raised his hand up again, as he sped by another stand of fans. "Christopher is back! Thank you, guys. The car felt like it was flying today. Amazing job, you did with it. Isabella" he said and paused. He knew she was listening, he had told her to.

Isabella's heart stopped, the smile on her face grew wider now, after hearing him call out her name.

All eyes were on her in the boxes.

"This is for you. It's all for you, luv. It's all because of you"

Christopher held the trophy high above his head and enjoyed every little second of the crowd's screams.

Standing on the highest step of the podium, was still one of the best feelings he had ever experienced in his life, despite having been up there so many times. Hearing so many people shout out his name, was the best reward after two hours of racing. It wiped away every single drop of sweat, any issue and tension he might have had in the car.

He was never tired of it and never would be.

He looked down, as the British national anthem played in his honor and saw Isabella leaning on the railing, taking pictures of him and Noah up there and smiling wide. He knew she could feel it too now, the pride, the satisfaction of being part of the team.

We race together, it said on the wall behind Isabella's work station and it was the truth, they weren't just words. The team was what made him- the driver- so confident in the car and gave him a chance to be there on the podium.

He winked, pointing down at her and smiled wide, seeing her cheeks blush behind her camera. Isabella was quick to take a picture of him then.

It was perfect, that image of Christopher at the top where he belonged, pointing down, telling Isabella it was for her, it was also thanks to her that he felt so strong and confident.

"Congratulations" Noah held out his hand, after they had drunk and sprayed the champagne everywhere.

Christopher took it and shook it slowly, studying Noah for a few instants. They heard photographers take pictures as they stood there, both trying to make something out from their looks.

Before speaking, Christopher thought about it twice.

"Thanks" Christopher nodded "What are you going to say this time? My surname helped me win the race?"

Noah held on to his hand, as a smug smile spread across his face.

"I am not going to apologize for defending myself to the press. This isn't the end. We are still close in the championship" Noah said, referring to the points they both earned.

The championship was still open, their gap wasn't that wide especially after Christopher's crash in Berlin. "I am faster than you"

"Show me" Christopher smiled and let go of his hand to wave at the crowd, as if he and Noah hadn't just argued about the results, about the race and their friendship.

"Show me what you can do"

Then, Christopher took his champagne bottle and hopped off the podium. There wasn't anything left to say.

It was time to celebrate.

"I get it, stop repeating the same things over and over" Marco rolled his eyes and gently hit his head in a dramatic manner on the table, as if Isabella was nagging him to death.

His sister slammed her hand on the surface and the sound made Marco snap back up again.

"I am serious, no stalking, control your blabbing and don't embarrass me" Isabella pointed a finger at him.

"I promise. Now can I meet them?" Marco rolled his eyes again and waited anxiously for his sister's approval.

Christopher and Noah were walking around the box, drinking with their mechanics and engineers, after the conference, after the interviews. They were relaxing and posing for photographers and TV camera men, every now and then.

Summer holidays had officially begun.

"Noah this is Marco, my brother" Isabella introduced them briefly.

Marco shook his hand tight and grinned.

"Nice to meet you" Noah said with his usual, nonexistent enthusiasm.

"It's such an honor. Congratulations for the result. Loved the way you overtook Simoncini at the very end. The guy hardly saw you. Epic" Marco shook his hand again.

"Thank you" Noah smiled and the rarity of it caught Isabella off guard.

Damn, stop smiling Noah or we can kiss our summer goodbye, Isabella thought while checking out the sky for any clouds.

Nope. The sky was still a clear, light blue.

"And this is Christopher. Christopher this is my brother Marco" Isabella put her hair behind her ears and watched Christopher reach for her brother's hand.

He smiled big and welcomed Marco in the boxes.

"Thank you" she heard Christopher say to Marco's praises.

"It's incredible to be here, in the box with you guys" a tray of champagne glasses went by then and Marco reached over for one. Isabella snapped his hand away.

"You can't drink, you are underage" Isabella said through gritted teeth.

"I got carried away" his shoulders went up, defenselessly.

Christopher watched Isabella and Marco do their thing, amused at their jokes and exchange of funny remarks.

It was so interesting, seeing Isabella move around in her own environment, in her country, in the city she worked in for so long, around her brother. She was exactly herself, only two times sassier and full of life, around a person she knew so well like Marco.

"Do you want to sit in the car?" Christopher asked.

"Sure" Marco nodded. "Can I?" he turned to look at Isabella.

"Yeah, sure if that's okay with Christopher" Isabella said.

"Of course, come this way" he led Marco to his car and helped him in.

It was tight for a man his built but Marco, a lanky, skinny teenager, fit in beautifully. He explained the buttons on his wheel, how they worked and when to use them and Marco listened to every word without ever interrupting.

One of his idols was explaining to him how a race car worked, it would be considered blasphemy to even speak while Christopher did.

They were so concentrated on the car that they hardly noticed Isabella standing there talking pictures at them.

The box went quiet to the sound of a single, high pitched voice, demanding silence.

"Be quiet, people!" Hillary shouted over the music.

She stood on a chair, as people drank and celebrated Christopher's victory and the overall success of MB that weekend.

She pointed at the stereo and someone turned down the volume.

"Listen up, it's summer break and we won't be seeing each other for a while. And thank God for that, I am sick of you men around me all the time with your burping and testosterone" she made a face and everyone laughed at her joke.

"We've done the racing and the briefing, the debriefing, the chit chatter. Now it's time to PARTY!" she raised her arm up and everyone cheered.

"So, since this year we have an Italian lady in our group, it's her task to take us around the city's night life. Who wants to join us tonight? We are going clubbing in a cool place by the beach near Rome"

The chit chatter was back, as people tried to figure out where they would be going and at what time.

"Eleven pm" Hillary told everyone.

As Hillary kept answering questions and making jokes with the guys, Christopher sneaked behind Isabella, placed a hand on her hip and startled her.

"Sorry" he smiled cheekily, his face telling her he was anything but sorry.

"Liar" she smiled back.

"Can I talk to you, for a sec?"

"Sure" Isabella said and excused herself from the guys.

They walked over to the back of the room and, as they did, Isabella spotted her brother standing with Fred, listening to Hillary speak to the group. They reached the wall, just as the music was turned back full on.

It was the perfect excuse for Christopher to move closer to Isabella, so that she could hear him speak and he could touch her. Not that he needed an excuse to touch her now that their relationship was out in the open.

"What are you doing tonight?" he asked and his fingers brushed against hers.

His touch sent prickles up Isabella's wrist and all the way up her arm.

"We are all going out, aren't we? Except for my brother Marco of course, who is so excited about it but has no idea he isn't coming. I'll break it to him and I'll make it quick" Isabella eyed her brother, who was listening to Fred and Mark's conversation and laughing like he was having the time of his life.

"You are cruel" Christopher chuckled.

"I am the eldest sister, I have to be cruel. They stole all the attention from me" she kept her face serious as she spoke but then couldn't fight back a smile.

"Nobody could steal attention from you" Christopher said and then grabbed her lower back and made Isabella jump a little. He held her tight and kissed her.

Christopher's lips were warm and a little rough from wearing the helmet for so long, but his hands on her body felt amazing. Isabella opened her eyes unwillingly, secretly wishing the kiss would have lasted longer.

"Anyway, I meant after the clubbing. You are not going back home at that time in the morning, right? You are staying with me at the hotel" he nodded.

After all Christopher wasn't exactly asking a question, he was more like suggesting she'd stay with him since Isabella had declined a hotel room in Rome. She was staying home with her family, since it was so close to the city.

"What's in it for me?" she looked at him and bashed her eye lids at him.

Christopher smiled to the side and reached down to kiss her again, only this time the kiss was deeper and slower. It was a promise, a promise for a night together, a night to remember.

"You convinced me" she mumbled.

The sand was wet and cool at that time of night.

Or is it morning?

Isabella looked up to the sky and saw it was dark blue still but there was a thin yellow/orange line at the horizon. The sun was going to be up soon and she could tell from how the wind on the coast had started blowing - slightly warmer than before, since they had walked out of the club- that it was going to be a fantastic summer day.

Someone laughed at the front of the group and Isabella caught sight of Hillary, looking happy and joyful next to Fred and Mark. It was nice to see her smile, despite the last few weeks of anguish for having broken things up with Mr. Jenkins.

Everyone seemed to be enjoying the walk on the beach, after all the dancing and the drinking. Isabella had been so happy to see Maria, Giacomo and Cristina at the club, too. It had been the perfect opportunity for them to meet her coworkers all at once.

And to meet Christopher without making it such a big thing, Isabella thought and congratulated herself on how natural it had all seemed.

She recalled Cristina's words after Maria, Giacomo and herself had spoken to Christopher for a good ten, fifteen minutes alone. Her friend had crossed the VIP room to join Isabella at the bar and had told her exactly how she felt about Christopher.

"We knew he was handsome. What we didn't know was how mesmerizing he is when he speaks"

"Oh, stop it" Isabella had laughed and almost choked on her drink.

"I'm serious. How do you concentrate when he's talking with that sexy, posh, British accent of his, I don't understand" she had grinned and clanged glasses with Isabella. *"No, I'm serious he's a nice guy. Really outgoing and not stuck up at all. What's with him?"* she then had pointed to Noah, who had been sitting on one of the couches in the room, drinking and avoiding conversations.

What was wrong with Noah? Who knew, Isabella had simply shrugged and then they had gone on and on, talking about Christopher and how according to Cristina he was so crazy about Isabella.

It wasn't so much what he said when he spoke to her, it was how he looked at her, how his eyes never left hers. Even if he was busy talking to someone else, Christopher would always glance her way.

"It's not just that" Cristina had squinted her eyes a little *"Something's changed. You are different. You are different around him and I mean it in a good way. He's done something to you, I can't put my finger on it"*

"I feel different" Isabella had easily agreed with her friend, but wasn't quite sure what had changed in her.

It was like Christopher had opened her eyes to so many things. Everything seemed possible around him. There were no limits, no obstacles, no boundaries. When with him, Isabella felt free and overwhelmed by the passion.

He is teaching me how to let go, she had come to believe, just like she was showing him how to overcome the ghosts of his past.

Cristina's last words before she had gone home – her train for Milan left early the next morning- echoed in Isabella's head.

"Does he talk to you in English or in Spanish in bed?" Isabella giggled then and looked down, at her feet deep into the sand, holding onto her white, heeled sandals.

"Hey" Christopher had stopped walking and was waiting for Isabella to catch up with him. She hadn't noticed how slow she had been walking then, the rest of the group was a little ahead singing and doing a little dancing.

Isabella smiled wide, her hair over one shoulder to the side.

"I'm coming"

"Are you tired?" he wrapped an arm around her and at the same time he waved to Robert, who was telling the others to wait up for Isabella and Christopher.

"No, I'm alright I was just thinking about my foot prints in the sand" her voice trailed off.

"What about your foot prints?" Christopher looked at her and smiled amused.

"I was thinking of how we all leave our prints here and there. Then something bigger than us, like the waves, comes and washes them away" she pointed at the small waves that brushed against the shore. "But people like you, so great at what you do, will leave their marks forever"

"I vote you stop drinking when we go out" he grinned and watched Isabella's face change color.

She was blushing and giving him a dirty look. Her face softened, as he kissed her head and they laughed it off together.

"For what it's worth, you are leaving a big print in many people's lives. You are leaving a big one in mine" he looked ahead and let his arm run down her back, as he moved away from her and listened to something Robert was saying to him.

His words made Isabella smile again and she felt a burning feeling in her stomach, the same that Christopher left her with, every time they were so close to one another.

I'm madly in love with him, Isabella admitted to herself.

She had come to realize that what they had, was more than sharing the things they had in common. It wasn't like that at all. What did they have in common?

Their connection was all about being their true self with each other and feeling proud of the person they were with.

Love, she tried on the word in her head.

To love meant to trust. To love meant to have faith in someone, to put one's happiness in someone else's hands.

Standing next to Christopher, Isabella felt bare, free to give in to their passion, free to be herself and it didn't scare her one bit. She felt strong, like never before.

"You are one hell of a host" Hillary wrapped her arm around Isabella and hugged her gently. "What a night! Rome is beautiful. And your friends are so cool. Cristina has a smart mouth"

"She's a lawyer" Isabella laughed a little and Hillary grinned.

"I liked them all" her boss told her again and then they heard a small chorus rising among the group. Some guys from Noah's team had started singing with Christopher, Fred, Mark and – surprisingly enough- Noah himself.

The guys were doing a little dance too, their arms on each other's shoulders and they were moving towards Hillary and Isabella, the only two girls of the group - as usual.

When they were close enough, Isabella was able to make out some of the words of the song.

She covered her mouth and stiffened a laugh.

It was an Italian song- or it was meant to be in Italian anyway- and they were getting one word every five but they were so cute, Isabella couldn't stop laughing and smiling.

The song was a classic, one of those tunes that everyone knew was typically Italian and it was of a man talking about how beautiful his girlfriend was.

Fred, Christopher and Mark were singing, more like shouting the words and pointing at Hillary and Isabella as they did.

"Awww you guys" Hillary clasped her hands together and looked at Isabella with sweet eyes. "You are so cute. But stop seriously, stop. Don't quit your day job"

To that, Isabella laughed hard, so hard that she stumbled on what felt like a small hole in the sand and fell to the ground.

Hillary sat down next to her, laughing hard at the guys' funny faces until Fred bent down to grab a now screaming Hillary and walked towards the water.

"Help" she said, as her foot dipped into the sea.

"Fred!" Isabella shouted, panicking a little as Fred wasn't aware he was holding a pregnant woman in his arms.

Fred turned her way and winked, mouthing the words "I know" and didn't drop Hillary in the water but looked back at Christopher, who had started talking.

"Let's dive in" he said and looked around.

Some of the guys didn't even say anything back. They simply looked at each other and started stripping.

In a few seconds, the sand was covered with shirts and pants and twelve of them were already jumping in the water in their underwear.

Gently, Fred placed Hillary back on the sand and started stripping, too.

"Come on" he said to both Isabella and Hillary and started running towards the water.

Noah jumped in too, his muscular back disappeared in the dark, blue water.

"I told Fred" Hillary mumbled to Isabella. "We are close, I've known him for years and he is the only one I am really friends with"

"Did you tell him who is the father?" Isabella had lowered her voice.

Hillary shook her head and without saying anything else, she pushed her short, black dress down and walked to the water in her black underwear.

Isabella could hear the guys laugh and dive in the sea and having the time of their lives.

She looked at Christopher and noticed he was pulling down his pants, his shirt was already on the ground. He flexed his arms and despite the darkness of the night, Isabella's eyes captured the perfect lines of his toned body.

"Come on" he told her and walked over to Isabella.

He wanted to help her out of her clothes but he stopped midway, seeing Isabella had already started to push down the tank top she was wearing.

Isabella kept her eyes on his- a soft cheeky smile playing on her lips- as she removed her top and then her tight skirt. She watched with a certain pleasure how Christopher was enjoying her stripping.

He walked over to Isabela and lifted her up on his back, guiding her into the water.

The water was warm and black as oil.

When was the last time I did something like this? Isabella wondered as the water reached her hips and Christopher let her go.

It had been ages, maybe she had been twenty or something, the last time she had dived into the sea with her friends at night.

She had forgotten how exciting it was to walk into a sea of darkness, how good it felt to be cuddled by the waves, under the moonlit sky.

Someone sent Robert flipping on his back into the water and the games begun.

For a while, it was all about splashing and laughing, until John asked for everyone's attention and pointed at the sky.

"Look, guys" the thin yellow/orange line at the horizon had become thicker, brighter.

"It's sunrise" Hillary smiled and Isabella closed her eyes, welcoming the shy, thin, sunrays on her wet face.

This is how I want to feel, always.

Not a thought going through her head, just the pleasure of spending time with people she cared for and being one with the sea.

She opened her eyes again and looked for Christopher. He turned her way too and smiled.

"Let's go, people. Time to get some sleep" Hillary said to the guys and started walking back to the shore again.

Someone said he had once been told that jellyfish usually come to shore at sunrise and everyone started running out of the water.

"Why the hell didn't you say that before I got butt naked?" Hillary ran ahead.

Christopher laughed hard and was still laughing when he grabbed Isabella by her thighs and lifted her up, on his back again, and started making his way out of the water.

"I can walk you know" she kissed his neck and then placed her face next to his, on his wide, tattooed shoulder.

"I know you can. I just don't like the guys checking out your naked bottom" he grinned and placed his hands on her lower back, cupping her buttocks.

"Are you jealous of my bottom?" Isabella's mouth went wide and she giggled.

"It's mine" he said and squeezed it a little more, making Isabella giggle again.

"I know it's yours, they know it's yours, the whole world apparently knows it's yours. You can stop squeezing it now"

"Never" he squeezed it again.

Isabella closed her eyes and enjoyed the feeling of his wet, naked body against hers.

Just say it, now, tell him you love him.

"Stay here with me" she said against his ear instead.

"Stay here with you, where?" he asked as the water started going down and it now reached Isabella's ankles.

"Here, in Italy. Stay with me for a while" she bit her lip "I mean, I know you have sponsor duties and you are going to Spain next week before London, but you could maybe stay a couple of more days here. You could come home with me… if you want to that is. I mean" Isabella paused and shook her head a little, as her inner debate took place "We don't have to say that we are together, not necessarily, not if you don't want to. Or we could just not visit my parents and just…"

"Is Isabella done talking to Isabella?" he looked sideways at her.

"Yes, Isabella is done" she made a face.

"I would like to stay with you a few days. That would be nice" he held on tight to her, his arms felt so big around her small body. "Meeting your father scares me, but I'll wear a bullet-proof vest, just in case" he chuckled as the waves swayed against their bodies.

"What? Why?" Isabella shook her head a little, surprised.

"Italian father… meeting his daughters' boyfriend. Don't they all have guns where you come from?" he chuckled again, the sound coming from deep down his chest.

"He's not in the Mafia, you know" Isabella giggled a little and kissed his cheek.

They were almost out of the water, the shore only a few steps away.

"Besides, my father is nothing like that" Isabella told him and shrugged.

He's actually the opposite, she thought.

He had always been a man of few words. He had always kept to himself, communication with his children had been exclusively formal – how was school, did you study, did you get good grades, did you behave?

"I'm sure he is jealous of his signorina bella" Christopher teased.

"I don't know" Isabella said and looked ahead, at the rest of the group laughing and running out of the water.

"Let me just call Alfred later in the afternoon and reschedule a few things I have planned. I'll move an appointment I have at the drivers' academy"

The thought of Mr. Jenkins cast a dark shadow on Isabella. His name ripped the smile off her face and made her body tense.

I should tell him about Mr. Jenkins. I should tell him what he said to me in that café.

But Isabella couldn't. How could she have ruined a perfect moment like that one?

It had to wait, that conversation had to wait a little longer. She would tell him one of these days, they would spend in Italy together.

As her mind found another excuse to push back the conversation with Christopher, he placed her gently on the sand. They were out of the water and the sand felt even colder now.

Isabella was shivering all over.

"Here" Christopher handed Isabella her clothes and covered her up, as Isabella removed her wet underwear and bra from under her top and skirt.

"You can use this too" he gave her his jacket and then took off his wet boxers –with the nonchalance of a person who hadn't just stripped to the bone- and put on his pants.

Isabella's cheeks went red and she looked around, only to look down again, seeing everyone was doing the same.

Oh my god, I hope there aren't any police officers around, at this time in the morning.

Christopher closed the zipper on his pants and looked into her eyes again.

"Do you want to see something?"

"You mean besides what you just showed me?" she tilted her head back and looked up at him. His chest was still wet but Isabella didn't care, it didn't matter that her tank top was going to get soaked, she embraced him tight.

He moved down to kiss her lips and savored the salt on her mouth.

"You left a big print in my life. Right here" he raised his right arm a little and showed her the inside of his forearm.

There, just below a tribal was a word, written in cursive.

Isa.

She gaped at him, as she looked down at the tattoo again, stunned and speechless.

It was small, maybe six or seven centimeters, but it was there, it was real and It was beyond words overwhelming.

"When did you do this?" Isabella wondered. How could she not have noticed?

"A few days ago, when you left for Italy" he smiled and picked up his shirt from the ground. Christopher looked back and saw that the rest of the gang was almost done putting their clothes back on. "You are my right arm" he winked.

"This is… incredible" she kept her eyes on the tattoo, on how her name seemed to curl a little under his arm, little red spots still visible for how fresh the tattoo was.

Even though it was small- in comparison to his other tattoos, the word stood out, like it had been branded on his skin.

"I never wanted to keep anyone close to me, the way I want you" he told her, his eyes burning into hers.

How could she have even thought to keep away from him, that it would have actually worked- spending all that time together and pretend nothing happened, pretend they were nothing.

What was going on between them was impossible to hide, impossible to keep aside.

It was as if the fire they shared was burning them alive, consuming their skins and they were enjoying every single moment of it.

Burning never felt so good.

In that moment, Isabella could sense the countless unintended words among them, as she searched for his face and a wide smile spread on her lips.

"I never wanted to be anywhere else" she said and kissed the inside of his forearm, right on the letters of her name.

Chapter 15

The idea came to Isabella the following morning over breakfast.
It struck her like a lightning, making her all jittery and excited, as she stood in front of the room service breakfast trolley, pretending to be interested in the wonderful trays of food.
She wasn't.
All she could think of was this idea she had had, to get back at Christopher and to show him just how much she had changed, how much she trusted him.
I want to do something special for him, she eyed him to the side and turned to stare at the tray again, as she saw a picture of him in the sports' column of the morning newspaper.
Christopher looked up from his plate and gave her a weird look, his brow up.
Isabella grinned and busied herself with the food, finally taking some fresh fruit and toast with her to the table.
But it wasn't until lunchtime, when Christopher was busy taking an interview with the national Italian TV network in Rome, that Isabella could go through with the plan. Thanks to race driver Pietro Tommasini.
He had called her back by two pm and had confirmed their arrangement. Everything was set.
"Aren't we going to your parents' house for dinner?" Christopher asked, seeing they were heading north instead of south on the highway.
"Yes, but we have to be some place before that. It's an hour drive from here" Isabella said, keeping her eyes on the road.
"Some place?" Christopher looked at her funny.
"Some place" she repeated and couldn't fight back a smile.
"What game is this, signorina?" he turned to look at her.
"It's called 'you never tell me where we are going, so I am not going to tell you where we are going'. It's a fun game, I wanted YOU to try it for a change" and then she giggled as Christopher placed a hand over her bare thigh and squeezed it a little.
"Are you getting back at me?" Christopher dared her.
"Apparently so and I have to say, I am really enjoying it"
"I can see that" he smirked.
Isabella eyed him to the side and grinned.

"Just sit back and relax. It's – what did you call it the other time-showdown"

"Are you trying to scare me?" he teased.

"Does anything scare you?

He laughed hard.

They were ten minutes from their destination, when Christopher realized where they were headed.

"International Circuit of the Center of Italy. Why are we going to the Circuit of the center of Italy?" he smirked at her.

"Surprise" she grinned and didn't say anything else, until they had parked the car, stepped out on the gravel pathway and reached the entrance of the track.

"Isabella, what did you…?"

"Trust me, ok? Nothing is going to happen to you. You are safe with me, baby" she winked and laughed, biting her lip as she did and Christopher pulled her in for a quick kiss.

Then they walked to the entrance, Christopher's arm wrapped around her neck, shaking his head with a huge smile on his lips.

"Ciao" Isabella shook hands with the member of staff – driver instructor Massimo- that greeted them at the reception.

"It's an honor to have you" the man looked from Isabella to Christopher, while they shook hands.

He was a fan, of course and told Christopher how much he admired him – even though being Italian, the instructor quite rightly supported Chiellini racing team.

"It would be great to see you race in Chiellini someday" the man said, as they walked through the building.

"Maybe someday. It would be an honor" Christopher said and watched the man breath in with pride.

They pushed through a set of glass doors and Isabella's legs began to shake.

Right in the middle of the lane, shining like a diamond on the gray tarmac, was a white sport's car waiting for them to climb in.

"This is your car. Both helmets are inside" the man told them and ran a hand through his hair a little embarrassed. "I don't need to tell you how to fasten your safety belts or any recommendation, of course" he gave Isabella the keys and told them they could take all the time they needed. The track was closed to the public, as a big sports' car event would take place the following day, but they were allowed to drive thanks to their mutual friend.

"What friend helped you with this?" Christopher gave her a funny look and Isabella tilted her head back a little.

"One of my very, very powerful friends" *Pietro Tommasini, your friend.* She held back a laugh.

"Is there anything you would like to say to me now, Bresciani?" Christopher took her hand and placed a stray strand of curls behind her ear.

"Yes, I would" she tilted her head to the side and looked straight at him. "I never felt like this before. I've never felt so alive, before I met you. I realized, as I got to know you, that I was holding back all this time. You changed all that" Isabella smiled and looked down at his hands.

"I feel like I can finally breath out. I was holding my breath for so long, I forgot how liberating it is to breath out and just let go. I used to think that everything had to be perfect and safe to be happy. But I was wrong. I wasn't truly happy. I was missing out and keeping things, keeping people at arm's length. But with you…I am happy with you. It's perfect now, that I am not in control all the time, now that I let you take my hand, now that I trust you" Isabella opened his hand and placed the set of keys in his palm. She closed it into a fist and kissed it softly. "I trust you. Take me for a ride. Teach me how to race. Teach me not to be scared"

His hand ran down her shoulder, over her chest and lingered for a moment around her breasts before slipping in between her legs and the safety belt clicked.

Isabella closed her eyes, while Christopher's hand played with the belt on purpose, sending sparks across her body.

"Are you ready, signorina?" he asked and his lips dived for her mouth, kissing her with such passion Isabella's chest grew heavy.

He's excited, she could feel it, the excitement, the adrenaline pulsing in his body.

Christopher took his place behind the wheel and secured his body to the seat. Then he placed his helmet on and made sure Isabella's had tied hers correctly.

He turned the key in the ignition and the car roared to life, as Christopher's foot stepped on the gas, before inserting the gear.

"We'll do a warm up lap first" he said, as the car gently started moving ahead.

Christopher took the curves gently, studying every single one of them in silence, registering the ups and downs of the route. It took them a few minutes to complete the first lap.

"Okay" he said as he stopped the car on the starting line. "This is it Bresciani. I go when you say go"

Isabella nodded and held on tight to the side door.

"On your marks" she screamed over the sound of the car, rumbling under her seat.

Christopher pressed on the gas again and the engine roared louder, his crooked grin making a triumphant appearance.

"I am not going to slow down" he shouted over the sound.

"Get set" Isabella yelled and Christopher pressed on the gas again, making Isabella gasp.

"It's going to be full on, Isabella"

She nodded and took in a breath.

"I trust you" she shouted. "GO!" she screamed then and the car skidded forward, as Isabella was pushed back hard on the seat.

The tires spun and the car lunged forward, leaving a trail of smoke.

Second, third, fourth gear, Christopher changed gears quickly on the big straight road ahead, as he prepared himself for the first curb.

Turns were the fun thing about racing. Not straights. Anything could happen in a curb. Only when driving in a curb, you could tell if the driver was valid, if he had talent. It was all about how he approached it, how he prepared the car to make the best of it, take as much speed as possible using the right trajectory.

"Chris, Chris the curb" Isabella screamed, seeing he wasn't breaking at all.

He smiled and pressed hard on the brake, only a few instants before turning. The car was picking up speed again, it made Isabella's head jerk sideways.

They were out of the first curb and onto the next.

"It's almost a loop" Christopher shouted and took hold of the hand brake. He pulled it up a little and the car skidded sideways, into the curb and straight out of it within seconds.

"Chris!!!!" Isabella screamed and then laughed hard, with all the voice she could find inside her.

"Did you like that?" Christopher asked, eyeing her to the side and turned left, then right quickly as a set of fast turns followed ahead.

"Say it" Christopher shouted. "Say it, Isabella"

"I love it" she shouted back and he switched gears again, this time putting his foot down hard, all the way down on the straight road ahead. "I love you"

"What did you say?" he shouted, a beautiful, sexy smile on his thin lips.

"I love you" Isabella screamed to the top of her lungs, as her head moved sideways again approaching another turn.

Christopher smiled wide then, just as he eyed the finish line ahead.

"Boxes, Isabella" he shouted and turned the car, making loops on the ground.

The car skidded, it went round and round until Christopher turned the wheel again and pressed hard on the brake.

He laughed.

"How was that?" Christopher asked, his breathing heavy.

"Absolutely amazing" she panted out and covered her face.

Isabella's fingers were shaking. She laughed in her hands and then looked at Christopher.

"It's your turn now" he told her. "I want to teach you how to leave your marks on the tarmac. Let's run wild"

Timing was everything.

And I seem to be always a second too early or too late.

Somehow Isabella had never been truly a master at timing.

She knew there weren't any excuses left to keep putting off the conversation about Mr. Jenkins and their encounter in that café in London.

And with September around the corner, she knew it was about time to have a serious talk with Christopher about the book release.

Even though the situation was personal and Isabella knew it would have a strong impact on her life too, she couldn't refrain from thinking about the issue as a press agent.

They needed to prepare a strategy, statements and decide how to handle the situation. Ignore and give the 'no comment' reply or face it with press conferences and a plausible counter story.

But every time she had tried to bring up the conversation, something or another had interrupted them. The timing, in fact, was never right. *Why do I have to mess up the time we are spending together?* Isabella kept telling herself.

She had been on the verge of telling him on their way to her house the day after the night on the beach, but on the short ride to the town, Christopher had done nothing but tease Isabella and then he had been on the phone for a while, rescheduling his appointments.

Isabella saw a window before going to her grandmother's house for lunch but then her brother Marco had cut in their conversation and Isabella had just given up the idea. It would have to wait again.

Just as her mind kept thinking of the perfect moment to talk to Christopher, a strand of hair went down, over her forehead and Isabella blew at it, trying to push it out of the way. Her hands were deep into the dough, she couldn't possibly move it herself.

Christopher walked behind her and placed his hands on her hips.

"Are you okay here, Bresciani? Is that a new move you are doing there, to make better gnocchi?" he smiled to the side and then checked out what she was doing.

The wooden table was covered in flour and small little balls of heaven called gnocchi.

They were all lined up at the center of the surface, where Isabella's grandmother was busy giving them their unique, round shape.

"It's my secret move" Isabella grinned. "Is everything okay? Are the boys giving you a hard time in there?" Isabella nudged towards the living room, where her father, her brother, her uncle Franco and all her cousins were.

Isabella had heard them talk to Christopher, ask him the usual questions about his life, about racing, and what always surprised her was how Christopher was so nice and available to everyone.

It wasn't a problem for him, to answer the same questions. He enjoyed seeing people so interested in his life and liked to share as much as possible.

That's all going to change once the press gets hands on that book. Isabella cringed a little at the thought.

"Yeah, we are having fun, talking about men's stuff" he nodded.

"Cars" Isabella mumbled.

"Basically" Christopher scratched his head a little.

"And they are trying to get as much as possible out of you, aren't they?" Isabella's eyebrow went up.

She knew her family, quite well. If anything, they wanted Christopher to tell them everything about his life and his relationship with Isabella.

"Pretty much" he smiled to the side.

"Don't give in. Keep your mouth shut" she brought a finger to her mouth, as to advise him to be quiet and then laughed.

"Stop worrying" Christopher protested "They are being nice"

"And loud and nosy and petulant" she mumbled and moved her head from side to side, in that mocking tone of hers.

Christopher laughed "You are so bad. These however look so good" he pointed to the gnocchi and smiled at Isabella. "What is your secret?" he mocked.

"The secret is… to do everything my grandmother's orders me to do" Isabella looked up at her nan, who had been staring at them in silence.

Isabella watched a soft smile spread on her wrinkled, old face. It was the smile of a person who knew something, who had had some sort of revelation. The smile came with a few nods, like she was giving herself credit for something.

"He's a real stud" Isabella gaped at her grandmother and instantly thanked humanity for the existence of different languages.

Stud, my grandmother said stud.

Christopher looked puzzled and waited for Isabella to explain. After all, Isabella's grandmother had just spoken looking straight at him. It must have been about him.

"Nonna" Isabella's eyes went wide and her grandmother chuckled.

"Well, it's the truth and you know it" she said.

From the height of her almost ninety years of age, Isabella's grandmother made her point "He is really handsome and charming. There was no chance you could have resisted this one"

"What did she say?" Christopher asked Isabella, entertained by their vivid conversation.

To him Italian sounded like a relaxed version of Spanish. It was slower, the sound was so smooth and totally incomprehensible. Especially when Isabella's grandmother spoke.

It must be slang, he realized.

"Nothing" Isabella cut it short, giving no importance to her grandmother's words. "She's senile. She is saying you are nice and funny in Italian"

"Oh" Christopher said "Likewise, she's very sweet"

She just called you a stud, not exactly sweet, is she? Isabella stiffened a laugh, as her eyes met her grandmother's.

"You know" Christopher started saying, but he moved to the side – on the right-hand side, where nobody was standing and nobody could hear him- and began to whisper, "You look so sexy, with your hair up like that, the short dress, the apron… makes me want to try you out on this slate of wood, you are using for the gnocchi" his voice was low.

"Is that so?" she said through gritted teeth.

Isabella's cheeks went bright red, just as her mother walked from the stove to the table.

"What did he say, honey?" her mother asked and stopped whisking the tomato sauce for the gnocchi. She pointed to the sauce and then to the bread, welcoming Christopher to have a little nibble, if he was hungry.

"Nothing, nothing. He's foreign, doesn't translate" Isabella waved it off, like a real Oscar winning actress. She figured how to lie through her teeth.

Don't look at people in the eye.

"Christopher" her uncle Franco and her brother Marco waved in his direction and Christopher told them he was coming. His presence was needed back in the living room.

"Coming" he said. "I'll see you in a while" his hand touched her hip again and he disappeared through the door.

Stud, Isabella shook her head and gently threw a kitchen towel at her grandmother.

The kitchen filled with laughter.

Chapter 16

Isabella grinned at her reflection in the mirror.

Drops of water ran down her cheeks and forehead. She wiped them off quickly and then checked her reflection again.

I might as well wear a red, clown's nose or walk around with something in my teeth, she giggled at the thought and reckoned it would be the same, the same as walking next to Christopher.

Two days home with Christopher at her family house and everywhere they went they attracted attention. Most of the people in the town just stared. Only the brave ones – and the nosiest ones- would try to approach them and ask questions – at the café during breakfast, on the beach, in shops.

Walking beside Christopher is like walking around naked, Isabella acknowledged.

He was impossible to miss, tall, broad shoulders and killer smile, so handsome despite his attempts to cover his face with sunglasses and hats.

And then there was another thing: everyone in her hometown knew Isabella of course and the word had spread that she was there with a famous auto race driver.

Isabella slipped on a pink, ankle length summer dress and dried her hair, letting her curls dangle down gently. She loved what the sea air did to her hair in the summer- the curls were softer and perfectly shaped.

She touched her warm cheeks and noticed just how tanned two days of proper sunlight, she had become. A lazy day on the beach with Christopher had given a different light to her eyes.

"Christopher?" she walked down the stairs, into the living room and saw it was empty.

Isabella went to the kitchen and asked her mother if she had seen him, if she knew if he was done washing up.

"He waited for you for a good twenty minutes, then he headed outside. He's in the garden with your father" she pointed at the big window next to the sink.

With a heavy weight on her chest, Isabella looked outside and saw him, picking fresh figs off a tree and nodding.

Her father was telling him something and showing him the fruit on the branches.

He's telling him to pick the ones higher up, they are the sweetest, Isabella recalled her father's words.

That was exactly what he had taught her and her siblings many years before, what felt like another life.

Christopher reached up and took hold of another fruit. His fingers started peeling it but her father stopped him immediately.

They are much better with the skin on, Isabella interpreted their conversation and realized she was playing Christopher's game, the same one they had played in the airport vip waiting room once, making up conversations between people. And he had been right that time, just like she had been right in that moment.

Christopher stopped peeling the fruit and took a bite. She watched his jaw move up and down, side to side and then he closed his eyes for an instant, nodding as he did. Isabella's father was right, it tasted two times sweeter.

"Dinner is ready, why don't you go tell them to come back inside?" her mother asked and just as Isabella nodded, her father saw her at the window and informed Christopher.

He turned towards her with an incredible smile on his face –his dimples showing, his bruised cheek just a memory of the past- and he waved.

Isabella waved back and moved to the front door. Christopher was right behind it when she pulled it open.

"Hey, you" he said and quickly scanned the corridor for people.

Empty. He leaned down and kissed her.

"Hey, you" she said back and pulled him closer, gripping around the sides of his shirt. "Everything okay?"

"Yeah, I've been outside with your dad. He showed me all the trees you have. Unbelievable the size of the olive trees in the backyard" Christopher's eyes were wide.

"They are really old. My great, great grandfather planted those ones and they survived throughout the war and the depredation of this area" Isabella smiled at his amused face.

"I know, your father was telling me all about it. Amazing" Christopher said.

"Anyway, dinner is ready so wash your hands and get ready for yet another great experience at the house of Bresciani. Big, loud family moments" Isabella rolled her eyes and heard Christopher laugh at her.

"It's perfect, you have a great family"

A great family and a great, dirty secret, Isabella gasped a little for air, feeling oppressed all of a sudden.

"It's not perfect Christopher" she mumbled under her breath and shook her head.

"It's a family, a real family that's what's important" he smiled at her. Isabella looked at him for a moment and weighted out his words. Her heart was trying to explain to someone like Christopher- someone who hadn't had a normal upbringing, someone who hadn't had a proper family life since he was ten- that her family wasn't what it seemed.

She hadn't spoken to her father for so long, the disappointment of realizing he had cheated on her mother for most of his life too painful, too ugly to face.

How could she have explained that to someone like Christopher, who would have given anything to have his family back?

"I'm going to go call my dad" she told him, clearing her throat and turned for the door.

"I don't know why you don't talk to him" Christopher said, a hand resting on Isabella's bare shoulder. "And I don't want you to tell me, if you don't feel like it, but he misses you"

Isabella tilted her head and closed her eyes for a moment.

"Did he tell you that? That we are not talking?"

That he misses me? Her heart didn't dare ask.

That was just the problem with disappointment. She hated the idea of her father walking up to speak to her, but at the same time Isabella was hurt that he hadn't.

He had never tried, not even once. Whatever it was that she wanted from her father, it hurt deep inside, his inability to reach out for her, even in a delicate situation like this one.

"He didn't have to. You are all he talks about, but you never talk about him. Never talk to him" Christopher smiled a little and leaned closer, his lips brushing against hers.

He looked up into her eyes, as shivers ran down Isabella's back, and let go of her shoulder.

"I'll be inside" and Christopher walked away, leaving Isabella shaken and lost in thought.

She walked into the garden, her chest heavy, her throat suddenly dry.

The sun had started to set and already Isabella could see a few stars light up the blue sky. She moved through the grass, her feet naked, knowing by heart every little inch of that garden. It had been the battle field of many adventures with her friends, with her brother and sister. It didn't scare her, that place, that grass. She was on safe ground.

She looked up and saw that her father was picking some more figs and placing them in a basket, so they could serve as desert later on.

It's not perfect but It's real, that's what's important, she told herself, making Christopher's words about her family, her own personal little treasure.

"Dad" Isabella said and watched the surprise on her father's face, as he turned to look at her. The wrinkles around his mouth seemed deeper, as his lips parted to speak but no sound came out.

Yes, I just called out for you. Isabella cleared her throat.

"Dinner is ready" she looked at him again, like she hadn't seen him for so long, for years. Had his hair turned grayer? Had he lost weight? How much time had they lost?

"Isabella" he was quick to speak, afraid to miss out a chance, his chance to speak to his daughter after so long. "Thank you. I'll be right there"

Isabella nodded and turned to walk away. She clasped her hands together and walked quickly to the door, her chest heavy.

She had wanted to say more, maybe tell him exactly what she was feeling. Maybe it was thanks to Christopher, for how happy she was lately, maybe it was thanks to him that she had had the guts to walk up to her father, after so long and for the first time without anger. Somehow being with someone like Christopher- feeling his never-ending loss for his father- had set everything into proportion.

Isabella wanted to tell him she wasn't angry anymore, that she was starting to forgive, but her lips were sealed. She would have to find some other time.

But I will never forget, and she knew it was true. That was never going to change, it couldn't be undone.

Christopher switched gears and then leaned his elbow on the side window.

The traffic jam was slowing them down a bit, but neither he or Isabella seemed to mind.

Rome was like that, traffic was part of its beauty. It was the additional adornment to the city's ancient streets.

He looked sideways at her and took in a breath. Her hair was all on one side, on the other side and her shoulder was bare. Her skin had turned amber, it was tanned and so incredibly sexy. The summer dress, she was wearing over her bikini, was a little see-through and Christopher's eyes lingered around her fantastic curves, where her waist ended and her hips begun.

For the past ten minutes, Isabella had been tapping her fingers on the side of the car and singing to an Italian song on the radio.

He loved when she did that, sing in a low voice. Christopher had noticed she always did so when she was happy and at ease.

Isabella was completely lost in her own world, so lost in thought that Christopher didn't dare interrupt her.

He just watched her move a little, while she tapped to the rhythm, and felt bewitched by her beauty and the fire that burned inside her.

That was the pull she had on him. He liked her in every possible way. That was the difference, he realized, with all the other relationships he had had.

Usually, the women he had been out with had been attractive. Period. He had never felt involved, he had never really been interested in getting to know them.

But with Isabella, it felt as though he had been sucked into her vortex of beauty and wit from the very beginning.

"Why are you looking at me like that?" she caught him giving her a side look at some point.

"I was just thinking you should be terrorized by now, me driving a car with you sitting in the passenger seat…" he teased and then pressed on the gas a little without taking his foot off the brake, so she could hear the engine roar, just to prove his point.

"After driving on track with you, nothing scares me. And it's my car you are driving around Rome. How could I be scared? We are stuck in traffic and this car doesn't go more than 130 km per hour…downhill…maybe" she tilted her head to the side and smiled.

Christopher laughed and kept his eyes ahead, his foot pressing on the gas again to make the engine roar, trying to prove Isabella wrong.

Maybe the car isn't fast, but that doesn't mean I can't play with it and scare you a little, Christopher thought to himself and eyed her to the side.

Slowly, the cars ahead began to move and Christopher triumphantly made his way to their exit.

"It's been great, meeting your family, a real big Italian family" he smirked and looked at her briefly again.

"You asked for it and you got it. All the attention, the questions, the fighting…be careful what you wish for next time" she smiled jokingly at him.

Isabella moved a little closer and wrapped her arm around his, as if to hug it. She turned his forearm a little and brushed her lips against his tattoo.

Isa.

"Well, to me they all seemed nice. I liked spending some time with your friends too, seeing what you are like around them. Even if I understood maybe ten percent of what you guys were saying" he said and added how he enjoyed also helping Maria sort out some stuff for her nursery.

They had gone to see the place one day and had found her totally stressed out about the painting on the walls. The painters had cancelled last minute on her –some sort of emergency- and she was due to open the place in four weeks, with the furniture arriving in two days' time.

"Fear not my friend" Isabella had placed a hand on Maria's shoulder and asked her boyfriend Giacomo and Christopher for assistance. And just like that, they had helped Isabella's friends paint the entire nursery.

She gives herself to the people she loves, like it is no hassle whatsoever, Christopher thought as he watched her do her little show in the car. The witty jokes, the sassy remarks, they all just served as a cover up, to mask the kind heart she had.

He listened to her make fun of him, for not understanding what she and her friend had said in Italian and he couldn't help but laugh, too. The sound of her laughter filled the car and Christopher felt something in his chest grow wider, bigger, out of proportion. It was like a weight, something that made him feel uneasy. The smile was gone off his face.

"We have ten days of holidays left before we go back to London" he said then and saw her nod to the side of his eye. "Spend the summer with me"

"Isn't that what we are doing already?" Isabella smirked and tried to keep her voice cool.

"I'm flying to Spain in a couple of days before I head back home. Come with me"

"I can't come with you" she laughed it off, like it was the silliest thing she had ever heard.

"Why not?" he shrugged innocently. What was holding her from joining him on holiday?

"Well" she began to say but found she had nothing.

"Come with me" he said, "Come on, signorina. Say yes"

"Only if you promise me we won't be jumping off bridges, planes, racing" Isabella grinned.

"You know I can't promise you that" Christopher chuckled and then added "I'd like to take you to this charity gala I've been invited to in Tenerife. I have my boat there waiting for me"

"Your boat?" Isabella turned his way, stunned.

Wasn't it in Cannes?

"I always ask a crew to take it to Spain for the summer. We could tour the islands, tour Spain. Just you and me"

Christopher looked ahead and crossed an intersection with caution. You never knew what to expect in Rome.

Isabella went silent for a while, but he could see she was smiling and trying to find the right words to say.

Spending the summer together, just the thought made her jittery, her heart beat picked up.

"Okay, Mr. Taylor. I'll be your guest" she held on to his arm a little longer and curled up on the car seat, leaning her head against his shoulder and closed her eyes.

"Are you tired?" he asked, enjoying the feeling of her warm, suntanned skin on his.

Isabella nodded but didn't have the energy to speak. They had been in the sun all day and they had swum quite a lot, Christopher unable to sit still as usual.

"Sleep, Bresciani, sleep. It will be an adventure, you'll see" he mumbled and she let out a small laugh, her eyes still closed.

It already is an adventure Christopher, it already is.

Chapter 17

Twenty days of summer break felt like barely seven.
One moment Isabella and Christopher had been in Madrid, the next it was time to go back to London, before the second part of the First Category racing season begun.
Isabella stared outside the MB facility window and sighed. Summer was officially over and London was wet and cold again, even if it was just the end of August.
Twenty days, twenty very intense days with Christopher. She played with her pen, while Hillary spoke to one of the sponsors on the phone, and thought of all the things she and Christopher had done together.
They had visited her family in Italy, then toured the Spanish islands on his boat, ending up in Madrid just before they left for London, to spend some time with Christopher's mother.
She had gotten a chance to properly meet Carmen and it took Isabella the duration of a meal together, to confirm just how wonderful and kind Christopher's mother was.
Carmen had welcomed them to stay as long as they had wanted, her house such a wonderful little piece of heaven in a green residential area of the city.
Isabella had admired all her paintings, her art and the wonderful black and white pictures, hung in her white and beige modern living room.
One picture in particular, Isabella couldn't shake from her mind.
"This photo of you and James is wonderful" Isabella had wanted her to know one evening, while Christopher had left the table to take a phone call from Mr. Jenkins.
"Thank you, my dear. It was taken on our first date. Did you know James had a passion for photography?" Carmen had informed her.
"No, Christopher never told me that" Isabella had shaken her head.
"I said no five times before agreeing to go out to dinner with him. When I accepted, he said he had to take a picture of the 'event'" Carmen had laughed a little, as the memory wandered back into her mind. "He was so used to having girls say yes, he couldn't believe I had said no...five times. I was very focused on my dancing career. I had no time to waste on men. I actually told him that, to his face"

Isabella had smiled to that and her eyes had examined the photograph more carefully.

Carmen hair was tide back in a ponytail and it must have been summer, her top was lowered on her shoulders. They had been sitting at a dinner table, a hint of a smile on her lips, while James was smiling wide, the smile of someone who had finally achieved his goal. Take one of the prettiest ladies he had met out on a date.

He had the face of a player, of someone comfortable in his shoes, someone who might have had many problems, but women hadn't been one of them.

Just like Christopher, Isabella had asserted

"You remind me of myself when I was younger" Carmen had gone on *"You are very down to earth and sincere. Eyes don't lie"*

"Thank you, that is a really nice thing to say" Isabella had smiled, looking away for a moment. *"Of course, I have half the elegance you have, when it comes to dancing"*

Carmen had laughed a little, setting down her fork and placing her dessert to the side.

"Well, Christopher could teach you a few moves" she had smiled and told Isabella how much Christopher had loved to dance as a kid. He would start moving to the rhythm, every time she would play music for him. *"But I was referring to how different you are from the women that normally surround Christopher, that surround the racing environment in general"* Carmen had paused and the two stared at each other, as a private a conversation seemed to take place without speaking. *"I was like you. I wasn't after tabloids or money. I was happy as it was in my own world, good at what I did and I was only there, in those boxes for James. I only wanted to be with James. I was the main reason why James had calmed down a lot the years he had started winning all those championship in a row. Did Christopher tell you about..."* The book, was what Carmen was going to say, but Isabella nodded immediately, sensing it was a touchy subject for her.

"Yes, he has" she had quickly said.

"Stay close to Christopher. He's tough, he's a fighter, but I am afraid this will have a strong impact on him. He never wanted for any of this to come out. He never wanted to be compared to James, always dreaded questions about him. I worry for him inside and outside that car" Carmen had admitted.

"Everything is going to be okay" Isabella had reassured her. *"We'll find a solution, a way to keep things down to a minimum"* she had smiled, but her chest had felt heavy all of a sudden, as mentioning the book had cast a shadow over their heads.

September is around the corner, Isabella thought placing a hand on the glass window and kept her eyes on Christopher, as he sped by on the straight below her with his car.

The glass vibrated until he was out of sight, down at the first curbs.

He's pushing, she said to herself, seeing how fast he was driving.

He needed to, it was one of the last days of testing the new improvements on the car- the usual changes that every team applied to the cars, before the last part of the championship begun.

Down on the left side of the MB circuit and training center, Isabella spotted a serious, rather sad looking Noah. He was holding on to his helmet, looking distressed and possibly tired. He surely didn't have the face of someone who had just spent his summer holidays in the South of France.

Christopher drove by the window again and Isabella's stare followed the car.

He's pushing harder now, she looked back at Hillary, only to see she was still on the phone.

Isabella's phone beeped and she checked it immediately. She had time anyway, Hillary was still busy talking to one of Noah's sponsors.

"The opening is two weeks from now, Friday the fifteenth of September. Tell me you'll be there" Isabella read Maria's text and smiled.

"Of course, I am going to be there. I'll book a flight as soon as I am out of this meeting" then she added *"Everything okay with the furniture, then?"*

It took Maria one minute to reply. *"Everything is perfect, thanks to you and Christopher. You guys saved me and Giacomo from further delays with your painting skills. You are a fantastic friend"*

"No, you are a fantastic friend" Isabella replied.

"No, you are"

"No, you are" Isabella stopped herself from giggling and switched off her phone.

"Here we are" Hillary walked over, to kiss Isabella on the cheeks and gestured her to take a seat at the table.

"You look great" Isabella told her boss.

She looks fantastic, actually.

The week in Greece had really did wonders for those lines Hillary had lately developed on her forehead.

Worry lines, Isabella used to call them.

And Hillary was beginning to show. Under the pencil skirt and short sleeve polo shirt, Isabella could see how rounder Hillary's belly had become.

She had told everyone obviously, as she had entered her second trimester, but Hillary had been very secretive about the father and nobody had dared to ask.

As they talked briefly about their summer break, Hillary gave Isabella the presentation of the new components on the cars – they would be attending a press release later that week with the drivers and Mr. Johnson- and set all her things on the table.

"I know exactly what you did on your holidays" and she pulled out a tabloid from her bag.

Isabella frowned and glimpsed at the pictures of her and Christopher. They were in Tenerife at the charity event and she had her eyes closed in one of the pictures.

Of course.

"So, bad news first" Hillary shuffled her papers "Two sponsors are letting Noah go. Part of the problem was Noah not meeting his contract duties. His attitude doesn't help" she sighed.

Isabella made a face but didn't say anything to that. Noah's actions spoke for themselves.

"Good news. Christopher has been called to take part to a car TV show. This will be great publicity for us, for MB and for his Drivers' Academy that is due to open in a few months…" and Hillary went on about how to plan the following events for both drivers.

They worked at the table for a good hour or so. They checked the progress of the blog and social networks' profiles of both drivers and gathered the data to hand over to both Mr. Johnson and Mr. Jenkins.

"We should write a new post, a new blog entry too, about how the last part of the championship is about to begin and what are the new components the team will use on the car" Hillary said.

"Got it. I just went to take some pictures of the cars and the drivers this morning" Isabella downloaded the photos on her laptop and caught sight of one picture in particular of Christopher touching the front part of his car. She had taken it earlier, just moments before he had turned to look at her, wide smile on his face and looking gorgeous as ever, in his MB tracksuit.

"Hey, at what time are you done today?" he had asked.

"Around three in the afternoon" she had kept her face straight, but inside the butterflies had gone wild.

"Good. I'll see you home, I finish a little after that" Christopher had walked behind her, with his usual nonchalance, holding tight to his helmet. *"I can't wait to jump back into that shower with you tonight"* he had whispered in her ear.

Isabella had looked down and bit her lips to hold back a smile.

The shower, just thinking about it, had made her cheeks go red again.

And even now, sitting at the table with Hillary, she felt the heat spread on her skin.

"Excellent. Let me see" Hillary stood up and walked to the other side, to check the pictures she had taken.

Isabella and Hillary were still looking at the files on the screen, when the meeting room door opened and inside walked Mr. Johnson, Mr. Jenkins and Christopher.

All three of them were very quiet, a serious expression on their faces. They exchanged glances before Mr. Johnson started to speak.

"Hillary, Isabella can we have a word, please?"

"Of course" Hillary went back to her seat and they all sat at the table, Christopher choosing the chair exactly opposite from Isabella.

He was looking straight at her, his eyes piercing and distant, like he was focusing on something inside Isabella's eyes, something far and hard to make out.

She smiled at him and shook her head slightly, not sure what that look meant, what he was trying to tell her. But he didn't speak, he kept looking at her, his green eyes digging into her soul.

"The reason why we are all here is that Alfred has just informed me of something, something very serious. I want you to listen carefully" Mr. Johnson stare turned to Mr. Jenkins, who crossed his arms over his chest and grunted.

"I asked Mr. Johnson to fire Isabella this instant" he said, his tone harsh.

"What?" Isabella turned to look at him and then at Mr. Johnson.

Lastly, her eyes stopped on Christopher. He was still staring, his face hadn't changed.

He knows about it already.

"Alfred, what the hell…?" Hillary said.

"She has breached a part of the contract, by damaging Christopher's image and helping another person with the intent of blackmailing him" Mr. Jenkins blurted out and Hillary gaped.

"What are you talking about?" it was Isabella who spoke then.

She looked around the room again, in shock.

"Don't you dare deny this, I saw you speak to Camilla. You two were talking business I heard you"

"What does Camilla have to do with this?" Isabella demanded to know.

"Oh, for Christ sake" Mr. Jenkins slammed his hand on the table. "You know very well she has been blackmailing Christopher for the last year and you just helped her get what she wanted. Now thanks to you, she has more shit to write in that damn book of hers"

"Camilla is the person behind the book?" Isabella's eyes went wide. She stared at Christopher, waiting for him to say something but he didn't speak. He just let out a deep breath and kept looking at her, like he was waiting for Isabella to say something else.

Confess, you knew about it. His face became hard.

"What book?" Hillary asked, looking at Isabella now.

She was totally out of the loop and, from the expression on her face, she was hating every second of it.

"Stop with the act!" Mr. Jenkins shouted and it was Mr. Johnson who intervened, to calm everyone down.

"Camilla is blackmailing you? She is the one who is blackmailing you?" Isabella asked Christopher, her voice low.

He nodded, without saying a single word.

"See, she just admitted she knows about the blackmailing" Mr. Jenkins pointed at her and then looked around for confirmation.

"I know because I heard you and Christopher talk about it. I know because Christopher told me everything" she said but Mr. Jenkins burst out in a hysterical laugh.

Isabella looked down at the table and then up at Christopher again.

"You talked to her…" Mr. Jenkins went on.

"I took a break with her from work during a race and she asked me if I wanted to work with her. I assumed over at Chiellini"

"She has pictures of you and Christopher, private, intimate moments of you two together. She showed me and asked an extra three hundred thousand pounds If we don't want her to write an additional part of the book, of how Christopher likes to crap where he eats, fuck every person he works with…"

"Alfred" Christopher shouted.

The veins in his neck tensed and Isabella saw his jaw twitch.

"She will use your pictures and the story you told her about you two together"

"I didn't tell her a single thing" Isabella shook her head. She didn't understand how she had gotten involved in this, she didn't understand how Camilla had their pictures or how they could possibly damage Christopher in any way.

They had probably been taken while going out secretly during race weekends, when their relationship had still been a secret to everyone else. Maybe some shots were taken in bed, but they were never compromising in any possible way. They were just about happy moments, they had shared.

"Those pictures I don't even have them anymore. They stole the camera from me"

"Of course they did" Mr. Jenkins grunted and went on talking to Mr. Johnson, about how pathetic Isabella's story was.

"They robbed my house. I don't know what this is all about, Chris" despite the shouting in the background, Isabella ignored everything and everyone and looked straight at Christopher. Her heart was in his hands.

He stared at her for another moment and then something in his eyes changed. His voice came out sad, defeated.

"I don't know, Isabella"

"You don't know what?" Isabella asked.

Christopher didn't say anything back, but for the first time since he had stepped in the room he looked down for a moment.

He doesn't believe me, he doesn't trust me. He thinks I am behind all this.

There were so many things she didn't understand, so many events and details had been kept from her- why was Camilla behind all this? Why had she written a book about Christopher? Was she the person he had trusted?

It hurt to know someone was trying to damage Christopher, but that could be overcome. What killed her though, was to realize Christopher didn't believe in her innocence.

How could he even think that she could do something like that to him? Sell him off, agree to be on a book. How could he doubt her, after all that they had shared and been through?

Had it all been just a joke? The connection, the feelings, the intimacy?

Isabella stood up and closed her laptop. She shook her head, as she realized that she and Christopher could overcome everything – a meaningless kiss, the exes, the madness that came with popularity, the life style differences- but not this. Trust was essential and it was clear that there was none between them in that room.

That was it, the end. His doubt had just written the end of their story. She willed her eyes to take a last snapshot of him, his ruffled hair and his deep green eyes. She willed her eyes to trace the lines of his scars- the one on his upper lip and the fresher on the side of his mouth- one last time.

She looked away.

"It's okay, Christopher" she said, as she gathered her stuff.

Bag in hand, she walked over to Mr. Johnson and stretched out her hand. The man took it and held it tight, no smile, no angry stare.

"Thank you, for everything" Isabella said to him and then walked over to Hillary, who was sitting right beside Christopher.

Isabella placed a hand on her shoulder, sensing Mr. Jenkins hard eyes on her, and smiled weakly.

"I'll email you my resignation" and she took off her badge and placed it on the table.

"No" Hillary shook her head but Isabella gave her a weak smile.

"It's okay" Isabella said and eyed Christopher to the side. He looked her way too without speaking, hand over his mouth. His silence was killing every single breath of air that Isabella was trying to take in.

Handbag and laptop in hand, Isabella walked out of the room and closed the door behind her.

No tears, she closed her eyes shut tight and pushed them back. She let the disappointment run through her, she let it hit her where it hurt the most. Her chest, her heart was in pain.

"This is fucking crazy" Hillary's voice sounded from the other side of the door but it didn't matter. Isabella was already walking down the long blue and green corridor of the MB training facility for the last time.

The bedroom was dark and lifeless. Isabella didn't switch on the lights, but only a side lamp near the bed. It was better that way, so she didn't have the time to look around and see what she was really saying goodbye to.

She moved around the place like a robot, not feeling things the way she should have, like she was numb. She told herself to feel nothing, even though the part of her she was repressing was screaming to storm out.

She filled the suitcase with her stuff and didn't have the energy to look around for more.

Her fingers went to her ears, as she sat on the big double bed and she gently took the earrings off.

Christopher's earrings. She stood then and dragged the suitcase down the stairs.

On the small table near the entrance, she placed the earrings down and wrote a note.

'Thank you for letting me stay. These are yours, they can never be mine. I told you once I only wanted you and nothing else. So If I cannot have you, if I haven't owned your trust, I don't want anything.

Thank you, for making me feel so alive, for loving me like nobody ever has. For seeing things in me that I was scared to let out.

I love you.'

Isabella placed it down and wiped a tear from her eye.

I feel dead now. A sob echoed in the empty, dark house.

She pushed her hair back and kept inside the tears, her sobs, her emotions.

She knew she had to get out from the house now, before she would crumble and wait for him to get back.

No, I won't wait for him. She straightened up and walked to the front door. Isabella stepped on the porch and closed the door behind her, her set of keys spread next to the note on the table.

"I believe you" Hillary said and Isabella's heart warmed to the words.

They were exactly the words she had hoped to hear from her- from a person she had worked with for six long months, from the person who had trusted her from the very beginning.

If only Christopher felt the same way, the thought stabbed her in the chest, but Isabella didn't even wince. She held her face straight.

While they sat in Hillary's living room and talked, Isabella was informed of everything that regarded Camilla and Christopher.

The story was surreal and at times it made Isabella sick.

Camilla and Christopher had had an affair, before and during her time at MB racing team.

This is why everyone kept warning me, of what I was getting into. Isabella realized all of a sudden.

That was why from the very beginning, Mr. Jenkins had been hostile- and had never really trusted her. That was why, everyone had warned her, of what a flirt Christopher was. He had been in that situation before. He had been involved with someone he worked with before.

Camilla, Hillary informed her, had won Christopher's trust over the years, as she had known James quite well, too. They had become close, to the point she had comforted Christopher in a delicate moment of his career. He was feeling under pressure at times, not living up to the expectations, stressed for being under the spyglass of certain sports journalists.

Then the most shocking thing had happened. Last year Camilla had started asking for money. Money or she would publish this book she had been writing about James Taylor and his son Christopher.

"Why is she doing this? Why would she write a book about Christopher and his father? Why would she want to hurt Christopher, why write a story about James?" Isabella asked.

Not for money. She doesn't need money, one would think she is well off.

As Isabella reasoned with herself, Hillary took in a breath and went on.

"She has a great story in her hands, Isabella. She had a relationship with James, when he was at the beginning of his career. When they both were at the beginning of their careers. She had a relationship with both James and Christopher" she gave Isabella a worried look, as horror registered on her assistant's face.

She's been in a relationship with both. Father and son.

"Oh god" Isabella covered her mouth and felt sick.

Apparently, Camilla had pictures of her love affairs, she had documented many aspects of it and had wrote about her role in the book, as the woman behind the man. Or as Hillary put it, the woman behind the 'men'. Yes, Camilla had slept with both James and his son Christopher. At some point, she had been their lover, their friend. And she had written one hell of a romance novel on the two drivers.

"Christopher had no idea about her being his father's lover" Hillary cleared that point immediately, seeing how distraught Isabella looked. "He was unaware of it all. He just trusted the wrong person"

Then, Hillary went on. She told Isabella that Mr. Jenkins and Christopher's lawyers had tried their best to negotiate with Camilla and find a solution- the best way out of this unpleasant situation- but Christopher had put his foot down.

No. He wasn't going to authorize the biography, not even if that meant having some control on the content. He didn't want to give Camilla any authorization on his life, his father's life. He didn't want to give her his blessing. And he surely didn't want her to gain profit from her story.

"Poor Chrisotpher, he had to tell his mother about it too. He wanted to prepare her for the scandal" Hillary had said at some point.

"Thank you for telling me all this" Isabella looked down at her hands "And thank you for letting me stay, before I leave. I just gave the keys back to my landlord"

"You are very welcome. I am sad to see you go" Hillary gave her a glass of wine "So, what now?"

Isabella shrugged. "I guess I'll go back to my old job, try and talk myself back into it. Or maybe just go do something else. I'll go back to Rome and start from there"

Hillary nodded and went quiet.

"Just please, do one thing for me" Isabella looked at her wine. It was so dark and ruby red, she craved the soothing taste of it. "Help Christopher with the advertising of the academy. He needs a lot of help now, with the book coming out"

"Of course" Hillary nodded.

Isabella smiled and knew she would, she would really do her best to help Christopher sort that out.

"Take care of him" and her voice broke into sobs.

Her hand shook a little, but she steadied it before knocking on the door.

Breathe, Isabella. Breathe and don't you dare fidget or mess this up. Do it for him, do it for him.

Camilla opened the door immediately and looked at Isabella a little stunned.

"What a surpr…"

"You can stick your circumstantial lies up your ass" Isabella talked over her. "I know what you are doing to Christopher and wanted to tell you that you are a sick bitch"

"Well, I am sorry you feel so strong about it" Camilla kept her face neutral. "I was actually hoping we would get a chance to talk about it"

"About what?" Isabella asked, giving her a disgusted glare.

"About working together at the book, at my advertising campaign"

"You must be crazy. That book is filth, it is pure filth. You stole Christopher's memories. You used him. That book is just a bunch of lies, it's just gossip on Christopher and James"

"Is it? Is that why you are here? If it's just lies, what are you so worried about? Nobody will read it…"

Isabella laughed in her face.

"You know very well that people will read it, especially because it is filled with crap like every gossip magazine in the news stand. But it's anything but a biography. Don't you see?" Isabella said "You are going to write a book, that is just rubbish and it will be a big hit for sure at the beginning but then what? What is it going to be left of you? The whore that wrote silly fiction about two legends. Christopher and James will be remembered forever, you on the other hand, only until you keep sleeping around"

"You are so stupid. You don't understand how this could have come to your advantage. You could have made real money out of this" Camilla shook her head and moved as if to close the door.

Isabella put her foot through and clenched her teeth.

"Enjoy the money, you'll need it to buy all the antidepressant when you will be a nobody again"

"Take your foot out of the door or I'll call the police" Camilla threatened but Isabella didn't move an inch.

"You do that. Please, now. So I can tell the police the exciting story of how you got a hold of my pictures, the ones that were in my camera, the one taken by burglars from my apartment" Isabella tilted her head to the side and waited for Camilla to come up with an answer.

"I'll say you sold them to me" Camilla shrugged.

"Really? Where is the proof you gave me money?"

"Where is the proof I didn't give you money? I could have given you cash" Camilla said.

"Yes or maybe you paid the burglars to give you the pictures, which is even a better story. Imagine, how nice it would be to have the police search your place, sticking their nose in your business. I could also ring a few magazines myself, just to fill them in"

"Leave, now" Camilla threatened again, this time her face was tense.

"No, not yet. Give Christopher every single piece of trash or pictures you have, sign whichever agreement he has written for you or I swear if you publish this book the way it is now, I will do anything in my power to make your life hell. My lawyers and I will dump everything I can on you and I'll have the police look into your things. I promise you that" Isabella kept her eyes on Camilla for the entire time "Have a lovely evening" and she walked away for real this time.

Chapter 18

The weeks that followed Isabella's departure from London, were confusing and surreal.

Pulling up her driveway again, her suitcases spread in the trunk and her emotional baggage in turmoil, was liberating in a way. She was home, next to her loved ones and that was all that mattered for now. *It's all I need.*

She hadn't cried at all since she had left and Isabella was already back on her feet. She kept her head busy, anything not to think of him, of them.

When she walked back in her old work place on a Monday morning, her boss hugged her tight. They talked for a long time and she was offered a job, not her old job, but still Isabella had her own little space in the sports magazine again and that was all that mattered.

She was surviving.

"What was he like?" a girl, sitting at a desk beside her, had asked one day.

Isabella had smiled softly. It almost made her laugh how people referred to him in the past tense. Christopher was good, he had won two races in a row and even though there were still three races to go to the end of the Championship, he was technically the winning champion of the year.

"He is a great person. An incredible person" Isabella had replied, a lump forming in her throat as she spoke.

"It was too good to be true" the girl had said then and Isabella had simply nodded.

Yes, in the end their relationship had been just that. Too good to be true.

Isabella had stayed in her home town for a week or so, then she had started working in Rome again and Cristina had handed her the keys of her flat in the city.

"Take the keys and don't be silly. I live in Milan now and I'm only here once a week" her friend had said.

"Once a week? You are getting better at this. Are you liking Milan now?" Isabella's eyebrow had gone up.

"It's not so bad you know, you should come visit" Cristina had smiled.

And so Isabella had travelled up north, making funny comments and mocking her friend for warming up to the 'cold' north –as Cristina herself had once referred to it- and she had stayed with Cristina, Carlo and the twins for a weekend.

"Do you miss him?" one of the twins had asked her at some point.

Isabella had nodded.

"Every day"

Every moment.

Maybe it was because their relationship had been so intense. Maybe it was because they had shared so many moments together, that she missed Christopher's presence like one misses a breath of fresh air. You can live without it, but to do so it never feels quite the same.

That's why she hadn't cried. She was surviving and she knew Christopher was doing just fine.

He was okay. Christopher was winning every race and he looked happy. He was going out with his friends around London and across the world.

He was always surrounded by girls, at parties and galas – even though there was no new girlfriend in sight.

Christopher was fine and she was fine, there was no need to cry. The disappointment of not making it through the lack of trust, would always be there, but Isabella could only recall the beautiful things they had done together, the amazing sensations she had felt thanks to Christopher.

Nothing could change that. And during those first moments of her new life back home, she had held on tight to those memories, not sharing them with anyone, almost worried they would end up worn out and become insignificant.

One morning, Isabella was sitting at her desk, writing up her article for the next issue on a motorbike freestyle show to be held in Rome, and her eyes caught sight of Noah on the blog page of MB.

Driver Noah to be replaced next season by Robert Rowling, age twenty-two from Second Category Racing.

Isabella blinked a few times, registering the news. A younger driver was replacing Noah and from what the blog entry said, Noah was now without a seat for the next year. No team was offering him a new position in First Category Racing.

He knew this was going to happen, she realized at some point during that morning – her mind had kept going back to that article.

Now she could see it all clearly, his moodiness, his lack of interest, his anger with the press, how he had lashed out on Christopher and on the other drivers. Noah had known his career was over. He had been aware since the beginning of the season, that MB was letting him go.

Despite his attitude, Isabella couldn't help but feel sorry for him. First Category was a harsh sport, you could only do your best and hope it was enough, until you were too old to be considered for the next season.

Or hope for good sponsors.

After that, for a whole week Isabella didn't think of MB, of Christopher or Noah. She worked and then went back home one day for the opening of Maria's nursery.

It was a hit, the community responded with enthusiasm to the new child day care center and to the unique things Maria and Giacomo were offering- like an organic garden, where the kids could plant their fruit and vegetables.

"Christopher sent me an orchid and a note to congratulate Giacomo and I for the opening" Maria told her that evening. "It was very nice of him"

"Very" Isabella swallowed hard and the mentioning of his name, took her back to her limbo of unhappiness.

"Can you let me know when he opens the academy? I'd like to reciprocate" Maria asked.

"Of course" Isabella reassured her and then Maria asked her the usual question, how she was doing. "I'm good, thank you" she said.

By November, Christopher was all over the sports news for two reasons.

His academy had been open for a month or so and the courses of every age range were already fully booked. To Isabella's surprise, Noah had started working with Christopher at the facility as one of the instructors.

The other reason why Christopher was in the news, wasn't the book.

By the end of November, there was still no sign of James' and Christopher's biography anywhere in the press.

All the sports magazines talked about, was Christopher winning the First Category title. He had won the championship and his smiling face was all over the TV.

I am so happy for him.

She watched him celebrate with the team and ached. Isabella's chest felt heavy, she had to change channel at some point. How she longed to be there, too.

Text him, don't text him, text, don't text. And in the end, she hadn't. Isabella thought it was better that way, not to reconnect.

It's better this way, definitely.

She worked extra hours that week. She did all she could, to fill her day and go home tired enough to slouch on the bed and sleep.

Christopher was out of her head, until she stepped inside the Aquarium in Rome one day, during her lunch break and Isabella took the old habit again, of eating there most days.

It was a cold December afternoon, when Isabella took a seat on the wooden bench in front of the jelly fish tank – her favorite- and ate her salad slowly.

She laughed, as some of the kids stared at the jellyfish amazed. One of them, standing in front of the tank, knocked on the glass and the fish moved quicker. Some of them gasped, some of them jumped happily.

"Would you like some desert?" Francesco, her colleague asked.

"No, thank you" she smiled.

"I'll be right back" and he walked to the small cafeteria.

Isabella's eyes were back on the jellyfish. She sighed and put down her salad.

She couldn't stop thinking about Toronto, the night Christopher had taken her to the Aquarium for her birthday, with closed doors to the public.

Of all the nice things that he had done for her, that was her favorite one. She was so jealous of that memory, she hadn't shared it with anyone.

"Where are we going?" she had asked him that night.

"There is only one way to find out" he had smirked at her.

And where am I going now? Isabella thought. Nowhere was the answer. She was stuck, in between time and she couldn't move ahead. Not really. Her mind kept taking her back.

It will get better with time, she told herself every day.

She stood and walked to the tank in her black fitted jumpsuit and white button up shirt. Her hand went up to her neck, where the shirt tied in a bow around her throat, and played with it for a while, as she stared at one big jellyfish that danced before her eyes.

She smiled and let her mind imagine Christopher's hands behind her head, his fingers playing with her hair.

"I knew you would be stalking the jellyfish" his voice was a little low, like a whisper. Isabella smiled again and didn't turn.

Congratulations Isabella, you are now the craziest, crazy person in the madhouse.

"I missed that smile"

Her eyes darted to the left and saw Christopher, standing there.

He was real. His hands were in his jeans' pockets, his hair was styled back and he was wearing a black leather jacket.

He smiled and his lips drew a perfect line across his upper lip.

The scar, she thought. *It's really him.*

"You are here" she breathed out and swallowed hard.

Her eyes filled with tears but Isabella kept them safe, locked up in her eyes, forbidding them to flow down her cheeks.

"I am here" he nodded and kept smiling.

"Congratulations… for winning the championship" her voice almost a whisper.

"Thank you" he said and kept looking at her.

Her hair was longer, even though it was tied in a bun behind her head, he could tell it was. The tan was almost gone, her lips were so sensuous in that dark pink lipstick she had on. She was so beautiful, Christopher felt something he had never felt being next to Isabella before. Jealousy. He was jealous of every man that set eyes on her perfect, round hips, on her soft full lips.

"I saw that Hillary handled the publicity for your academy" she found the nerve to speak.

"You are all I think of"

"Well, she did a good job" Isabella looked down, ignoring his words, afraid all the work she had done on herself over the past months, would just disappear in one instant, looking into the deep sea that were his eyes.

"I'm sorry" he said and moved closer "I'm sorry, I didn't believe you"

"You don't have to say that. It's okay. I get it" she nodded.

"I did believe you" he said and Isabella went quiet. "Only I didn't trust myself. It wasn't you, it was me. I was scared I was making the same mistake again, of trusting someone and failing" he said.

Like I trusted Camilla and many others over the years.

"And I did fail. I failed you"

They both went quiet, as they studied each other closely. He looked tired and a little thinner, but his shoulders also looked broader.

He's been doing exactly what I've been doing, she thought seeing his body so muscular, noticing a hint of dark lines under his eyes.

Christopher had been focusing on work, concentrating on something else, pushing all the memories of them somewhere far away.

And he had failed.

He is here.

"She gave me everything, all the nasty things she was planning to put in the book. Even the pictures. We signed an agreement and she will publish a biography. She will have the merits but my story, the way I want it to be written. She told me you threatened her"

"I should have spat in her face, only I never learned to do that with my cousins" Isabella smiled a little and jumped, as Christopher started laughing.

Her chest vibrated to the sound of his laughter and it shook her deep down.

"Come back" he said. "Come back to me"

"Christopher, I really have to thank you for coming all the way here. It means so that you trust me. The thought of you believing I could hurt you so bad, was literally eating me up inside. But I can't come back. It will never work" she looked down at her shoes "It's always going to be like this between us. Our relationship will always be in the spotlight. And then there is the lack of trust, the past... You are the man that flies high and I am the woman with her feet on the ground. And they are back on the ground now, where they belong. It's better this way, we get to keep the good things we shared"

"I don't want memories of you, I want you" Christopher moved a little closer and Isabella took a step back.

An arm went around Isabella's shoulder then and she turned, realizing Francesco was back from the cafeteria.

"Is everything okay? What is he doing here?" he asked.

"Everything is okay" Isabella reassured him.

"What do you want from her?" Francesco asked, his eyes darted to Christopher.

"Francesco, can you please wait for me at the exit. I'll be right there"

After a moment of confusion, he nodded and walked away, but from time to time he turned to squint at Christopher.

"Listen, Isabella. I don't know who that man is but the doubts, the popularity is just a load of bullshit. I realize, I am a mess when it comes to relationships. I obviously don't have a clue, I trust the wrong people, I never get attached…but I know one thing. I kept looking at that note you left me and I think It hit me then, what it is all about, relationships I mean" Christopher ran a hand through his messy hair.

A total mess, but so perfect.

"Relationships aren't perfect. We are not perfect. But you and I, are what we are- perfect for each other. And I'm in love with you" he paused.

Christopher moved closer and took her hand into his. "All I know is that I love you. Tell me you want me to go, tell me you don't want me back in your life and I will leave now. I won't bother you anymore, if this is what you want, if he is what you want" Christopher stared ahead and his face hardened for a moment, as his eyes set on Francesco, who was looking over Isabella like a hawk. "But I know that If I walk away from you now, I will never feel the way I feel with you. The way I feel when I hold you in my arms. I will miss everything of you, your lips, your smile. I love every single thing about you, the way you sing when you are happy, how you give yourself with all your heart. If there is one thing, one thing I am sure of, is that I will never love someone the way I love you" his eyes were on her until he caught sight of someone moving in the background and his stare darted in that direction.

Francesco was checking them out from afar. Christopher gave him a serious glance.

In that moment, Isabella moved closer and let go of his hands. Her arms reached out for his, as Christopher's words seemed to echo in her ears.

Like every single time Christopher had been by her side, her mind had stopped thinking, her heart had taken in, his every word and all she could do was feel. Not think, but feel.

She felt not what was right, but what her heart needed. What she wanted. What her heart really wanted.

"Chris" she shook her head and closed her eyes for a moment, thinking of what to say.

"Tell me what I can do, to win your heart back. I am on my knees" Christopher pressed on kneeling to the floor, as Isabella's mouth dropped open.

"Chris, don't…" Isabella murmured and noticed people were staring at them from the benches.

"I will never make the mistake of letting you go, ever again." He said, holding onto her hands. He looked down, searching for the right thing to say "I have everything and yet nothing, If I don't have you"

"Oh, Chris" she sucked in a breath.

Isabella was on the floor, on her knees in an instant. Her hands reached out for his face immediately, her lips pressed hard onto his.

"I love you, too" she whispered against his mouth and smiled, as Christopher cupped her face. "All these months, I felt like I wasn't breathing"

"You don't realize how many times I wanted to come and see you" he rubbed his finger on her lips and brushed his mouth against hers.

Isabella's pulse quickened, as Christopher's hands got hold of her waist. He then ran them behind her back and all the way up to her neck.

"I thought I had lost you for good this time" he pressed on, as he moved down to kiss her, his lips craving for more, his heart thumping wild in his chest.

Then, he looked behind Isabella again, his eyes setting on Francesco.

"Stop looking at him like that" Isabella said, brushing her nose against his, unable to hold back a smile. "He is just a colleague. And he is gay. And totally mad at you for letting me go like that"

"He's absolutely fucking right. I am a wanker" Christopher smirked.

"Uno stronzo, ma sei il mio stronzo" "You are an asshole, but you are my asshole" Isabella corrected him and laughed.

They looked into each other's eyes again and smiled wide.

They were together. They had found each other again and they were lost, completely lost into each other's arms.

All walls were finally down. No secrets, no misunderstandings, no unspoken words.

They felt bare, exposed and they had never felt better.

"Kiss me now, quick" she looked into his deep green eyes. "Don't say later, baby. Later might be never" she teased, saying the exact same words Christopher had said to her when skydiving.

"Not my style" his lips pressed gently on hers and it was like they had never been apart.

Epilogue

Christopher waved to the crowd and waited for the national anthem to be over. He looked up to the sky and saw there were no clouds. For the very first time since the history of First Category Racing, it hadn't rained a single drop during the race in Berlin. Not one. There were no clouds in the sky, he could tell from where he was standing, high up on the podium, on the first position.

He tilted his head back and laughed. How great it felt to have finally achieved the goal of his life. Win the race in Berlin, win the race his father had never won in his career and take home the trophy that was legitimately his, legitimately his father's.

He raised the cup high, as high as he could and enjoyed the people cheering as he did.

As the anthem came to an end, he took a picture with the other two drivers on the podium and then took the Champagne bottle in his hands.

He looked down and smiled wide.

Christopher ran down the stairs, into the crowd of judges and journalists and went to the barriers were his mechanics, his team was all standing in his honor.

"Take it, it's for you guys. It's all for you" he gave them the bottle and hugged his engineer and the other guys.

Then he moved to the side of the barriers and pushed one open, ignoring the security guard's warning.

He took Isabella by the hand and let her step in, under the podium right beside him. They were surrounded by journalists and photographers, as the guys of MB started cheering.

Isabella laughed, covering her face a little as she did, and then let Christopher kiss her passionately.

She hugged him tight and whispered in his ear just how proud she was of him, how her heart was pounding hard in her chest, so happy to see him up there on that podium, where he belonged. He let her arms hold him tight and he leaned in to kiss her neck.

Then he got on his knees and kissed her baby bump, both hands wrapping around it.

He leaned his forehead on it and smiled, hearing Isabella giggle, her fingers playing with his hair as she did.

"It's going to be one hell of a ride James" he kissed it again "And you are going to love every second of it"

THE END

At this point I was in tears.

Dear reader, first of all I have you to thank. I never thought I would truly be on this side, on the side of the writer.

I can only hope that you enjoyed "the ride" and fell in love with my characters.

I have so many people to thank, because a book and an indie author's life is all about people. People you meet, people that help you and people that support you when you are high and when you are down.

So first, I would like to thank the first person that took me to the side and told me what it was all about. Thank you Johnna Seibert, for being so kind when I was a little lost and clueless. You are a great friend.

I have to thank Gem Louise Evans, for believing in me even when I didn't myself. For reading, supporting and editing the book and for everything she does on a daily basis.

Thank you to my girls, my lovely girls that support me on facebook: Stina Andersen, Vera Fowler, Angela, Carolann Evans, Talia Redhotink (thank you also for designing this awesome book cover).

I would also like to thank every single person in my Reading Group on Facebook, for being kind and being silly with me.

Thank you to Amy Halter and Tiffany Landers.

Thank you to every blogger, reviewer and group administrator that has showed me kindness.

Thank you to Helene Cuji, Michele Muns Dyson, Cindy Muns Wolken, Kristine Marie, Lori Cino, Samantha Marie and all The Book Hoarders.

Thank you to my friends Susanna Ceccacci, Eleni Papadopoulou, Saeid Ahmadi, Carlo Nalli, my fantastic brother Carlo Rossi, his girlfriend Ekaterina and my son Alessandro and my daughter Veronica- for understanding and supporting me along the way.

Thank you mom and dad, for teaching me that everything is possible, if you work hard enough.

Thank you to Luca Carducci, my life partner for being so amazing. I never imagined my soulmate would be the boy next door. It feels like we are old souls and we've known each other since forever- but we still laugh like the first day.

Lastly, thank you Isabella and Christopher ☐ I will surely miss you.

You can find me here, I love to interact and chit chat □ come and say hi

Facebook: https://www.facebook.com/laurarossiauthor/

Instagram: https://www.instagram.com/laurarossiauthor

Readers group: https://www.facebook.com/groups/1652427688131420/

Amazon: https://www.amazon.com/Laura-Rossi/e/B01M7O2JHZ

Goodreads: https://www.goodreads.com/author/show/2381552.Laura_Rossi

Cover art by Talia's book covers
https://www.facebook.com/Taliasbookcovers/

Blogs I fell in love with:
https://www.facebook.com/notenoughpagesbb/
https://www.facebook.com/hopelesslyaddictedtoromance/
https://www.facebook.com/ObsessiveBookWh0reBlog/
https://www.facebook.com/IamABookHoarder/
https://www.facebook.com/bookhavenbookblog/
https://www.facebook.com/dympnasbookblog/
https://www.facebook.com/bookramblings/

Printed in Great Britain
by Amazon

81350397R00120